An Undiscovered Country

An Undiscovered Country

M.A. Cumiskey

Copyright © 2012 by M.A. Cumiskey.

ISBN: Softcover   978-1-4797-6197-5
           Ebook   978-1-4797-6198-2

All rights reserved. No part of this book may be reproduced or transmitted in any form or by any means, electronic or mechanical, including photocopying, recording, or by any information storage and retrieval system, without permission in writing from the copyright owner.

This is a work of fiction. Names, characters, places and incidents either are the product of the author's imagination or are used fictitiously, and any resemblance to any actual persons, living or dead, events, or locales is entirely coincidental.

This book was printed in the United States of America.

To order additional copies of this book, contact:
Xlibris Corporation
0-800-644-6988
www.Xlibrispublishing.co.uk
Orders@Xlibrispublishing.co.uk
305291

CHAPTER ONE

1962

News: Northern Ireland: The IRA calls off its five year session of violence

Diary: Me Dad works so hard in his little shop. He worries that us being Catholic might cause a problem with his customers—mostly they are Protestant. Fortunately he seems to get on well with everyone. He doesn't believe in violence but he must be one of the few who doesn't. The area is always being upset by IRA setting off bombs or Loyalists forcing some family or other out of the Province. Thank God Dad gets on so well with our neighbours. He says that he's a butcher not a politician and that he keeps his nose out of trouble.

* * *

"You're a reasonable man Geraint Donnelly," said the first man, "so why won't you listen to reason?"

"I don't think he properly understands." The other one added unnecessarily.

The two strangers had entered Geraint's butcher's shop just before closing time and, after spending four pounds on a meat package that included steak, sausage, bacon and a pie, he'd thought it only polite if not prudent to pass the time of day with them. Although hardly a gregarious person by nature, Geraint was nevertheless prepared to adopt the pose as such when it was good for business, and the addition of four pounds to his takings was appreciated as just that. Unfortunately, after opinions had been exchanged about the usual subjects, the weather, sport and the politics of Local Government, the conversation took a different turn.

They had been discussing money and the need for real investment in the Province when Geraint commented how hard it was to make his shop turn a worthwhile profit. At first the taller of the two men had sympathised, commiserating with the butcher about the location of his business.

"Being on the cusp—as it were—between the two communities must be a trial at the best of times." He said with apparent sincerity. His eyes were as cold as the marble slab that served as a counter top.

"D 'you have any trouble through that?" the other one said, echoing the thought.

"I try to keep politics out of the shop altogether. I don't take sides and I keep my nose clean," Geraint told them, "I'm a butcher and all I'm here for is to sell my meat. If it's fighting or arguing they want, I tell them to go to the border."

This seemed to satisfy his customers but then the suggestion was put to him by the last speaker, that he might make himself a little extra cash by occasionally telling them about local IRA activities.

"And sure—what the hell would I know about the Republican Army. Like I told you I'm just a butcher."

His claim was ignored and the tall man argued that as many of his friends and neighbours were active members of the IRA, he must hear bits of gossip that included names and dates. Geraint was annoyed. He had tried to keep his family apart from the internecine disputes, so far successfully. Given the ferocity of the possible consequences for being an informer, it was in his opinion a wise course of action. He was not about to be tempted therefore into a situation that might jeopardize the security of his future.

"I don't know who y 'are or who you might represent gentlemen, but you've come to the wrong man. Now without meaning to give offence, I'd like you both t 'leave."

They thanked him and left without further comment. However, they came back exactly one week later and their visit this time followed the same pattern as before. They spent four or five pounds and then tried to persuade Geraint into making an arrangement with them.

He had opened his shop just before Christmas the previous year. It was his first venture as a self-employed businessman but being a Catholic in largely Protestant Ulster was inevitably a huge gamble. Fortunately in his case, it was a gamble that had proved well worth taking. He had lived and worked close to the boundary that separated the two communities all his life and had enjoyed the friendship of a number of non-Catholic acquaintances. Sometimes he even went for a drink at the 'Billy-Boy' a predominantly Loyalist pub and there had never been the slightest suggestion of trouble there. Indeed, his confidence in his business venture was based as much on his reputation as someone who ignored religious and political bias, as it was on his butchering skills.

"We know all their names alright," Terry told him—by now they had introduced themselves as Terry and Martin, "it's just that we'd like to know what they might be up to."

"But hasn't the IRA declared a cease-fire?" he asked, knowing full well that this was now common knowledge.

Both men laughed cynically, and then Martin said, "True enough—for the time being that is until it suits them not to have a cease-fire. If you see what I mean."

"I see what you mean," Geraint muttered reluctantly, "but I want no part in sectarian disputes. I'm a butcher—I sell meat to those who want it and I don't care a fig what their political or religious beliefs might be. Meat is ecumenical." Terry smiled at this but the smile remained only on his lips, "So you want the Protestant money from your customers—but you don't want anything to do with Protestant causes. I think there's some who could take offence at that. It might even cost you business." He paused but the menace was explicit, "Show the man your badge Martin."

As instructed Martin produced a wallet, he flicked it open to reveal a Police ID. "Y 'see it isn't quite as simple as you might have imagined." Terry continued, "We're not Loyalist soldiers fighting the Union cause. We're Law officers—trying to bring a halt to all the violence. Now—as a law abiding citizen we expect you to co-operate, because you don't want all the bombings and shootings to continue. Do You?"

Geraint found himself nodding, he couldn't argue with that but he knew full well that any degree of acquiescence would be misinterpreted—and it was.

"So you'll help us then?" Martin concluded still grinning.

"I never said that." Geraint responded quickly.

"I suppose we should alert you to the fact that sometimes, if selected members of the public are resistant to our requests, we drop a word in the ear of one of the rogue punishment squads . . ."

Terry made the threat explicit and in a strange way Geraint felt relieved. At least now it was out in the open. His anger was therefore allowed to surface, "I'd heard tell how you play dirty—you British—now I know it's true. Well you can both go to hell for me—and don't show your faces in my shop ever again. Next time you'll . . ."

He wasn't allowed to finish his threat. As he spoke Martin pulled an automatic pistol from beneath his coat and laid it on the counter top. In itself an innocuous act but given the context, it was charged with meaning.

"We hoped it wouldn't come to this Mister Donnelly," Terry said quietly without the trace of a smile, "but if you're not with us, then you're against us—and as you can see, we come prepared. Don't even think of making threats."

Martin returned the gun to its hidden holster and addressed himself to Terry as he did so, "And they say he has a family. Several kids . . . who'd want to gamble with the security of his family—takes a brave man."

"Or a complete fool." Terry added.

* * *

On his way home that night Geraint clutched two English ten pound notes in his trouser-pocket—the down payment for betrayal. Twenty pounds was a lot of money to the butcher but it felt more like thirty pieces of silver to him. Given the dangers implicit in his actions, he was therefore determined that no one, not even Rita his wife, would ever know about the contract he had made. The deciding factor had been the threat to his family. He could allow himself to be brave—for himself, but to endanger his wife and children, that was unacceptable To help alleviate the guilt; secretly he had made a compact with himself that he would only tell the Englishmen the most pedestrian tit-bits of local gossip. His information would comprise exclusively of things they could pick-up themselves in any local pub.

Nevertheless, the pressures exerted on him by Martin and Terry had struck through his tough exterior, making him feel nervous and more stressed than usual. Now he had something else to worry about. The business was just beginning to show a profit but there were always things the kids needed, they grew out of their shoes and clothing at a phenomenal rate. And Rita was pregnant again with her fourth child.

By the time Geraint arrived home that night his children were already in bed. Rita sat with him as usual as he ate his dinner. She had kept it warm for him in the oven but made fresh gravy on his arrival. Her day was circumscribed by the children's' needs and other than occasional visits from their near neighbours, she seldom therefore had an opportunity to enjoy adult company. Accordingly, it was her practice to sit with her husband each evening and listen to him recount the detail of his day. She was not to know it, but this was often the most trying period of the day for Geraint.

His time at work was spent normally, talking, joking and generally trying to entertain his customers. The last thing he wanted when he arrived home late in the evening, was to relive the minutia of his day—or even, for that matter, to engage in much conversation. By nature he was a quiet man, temperate as much in his views as he was in his mode of behaviour. He seldom lost his temper and was not given to passionate outbursts, whatever the provocation. Rita's personality was quite different. Consequently she would sometimes complain to Molly from next door that Geraint was a difficult man to have an argument with. She often accused him of sulking or brooding on things rather than bringing them out in the open. Given his own background however, his behaviour was not surprising.

Geraint had been one of twelve children and, being the second eldest, he had been obliged to forget about schooling as soon as he was able to read and write. His father, a sometime farm labourer, wife-beater and child-abuser had disappeared when Geraint was approaching his ninth birthday, leaving the two oldest boys as the only breadwinners. They worked at whatever employment they could find and in an economy at that time, with access to an almost unlimited labour force, times were hard. Fortunately, those seeking to employ unskilled labour, preferred to use the two boys due to that fact that their expectation of wages was governed by their ages. They were cheap labour.

Geraint therefore, had to be prepared to do anything and he grew used to working long hours for little recompense. He mixed cement on building sites; toted Hods full of bricks; he painted fences, some of which he had helped to erect; he ran errands for neighbours and delivered goods for shop-keepers. For a while he even worked for a demolition company, helping them to knock down buildings. But surprisingly, it was when he had a job picking potatoes that he found the trade from which he would eventually earn his living. The farmer he worked for owned two butcher's shops and he was so impressed with Geraint's effort that he offered him full-time employment. Geraint therefore learned to sweep sawdust, to scrub and scrape chopping blocks and to wash and clean the trays and the knives. It was some time before he was eventually allowed to learn the intricacies of sausage-making and pie production.

In the Ireland of the 1930s and 1940s, his was not an unusual story. Many children were obliged to sell their labour in order to supplement a family income. Had he been a little older he might have taken the King's shilling and joined the Armed Forces as the war in Europe seemed insatiable for Irish troops as fodder for the front line. Indeed, as soon as he was old enough, his brother Michael gratefully took this path, only to meet his Maker on a French beach during the Normandy landings. During that conflict the Donnelly family also lost two daughters to diphtheria and an infant son to measles. Geraint's mother never remarried, although in the short time left to her, she enjoyed the attentions of a succession of 'uncles', some of whom were generous to her children and some notably brutal. Not surprisingly, Geraint learned to keep his opinions to himself, to mind his manners around strangers and to live a private life inside his head.

And even years later, as a grown man with his own family, Geraint Donnelly maintained some of the same characteristics. He could tolerate the necessarily gregarious nature of the retail trade during the day but in the evening he needed time to accommodate the day's events. He loved his wife dearly but her incessant questions, particularly after that day, turned his mood completely. As he ate his dinner, he became irritable and more uncommunicative than ever. Eventually, Rita went to bed leaving him alone to ruminate before the kitchen fire. And whilst her early departure to bed was not an unusual event in the Donnelly household, that night she went with a greater sense of isolation than ever.

In his turn, Geraint also felt badly done to. Didn't he have the constant worry of the business on his mind, meat prices fluctuated ever upwards in the Province, and now he had Martin and Terry on his back. He never slept easily at the best of times and was often found wandering the house in the hours of darkness long after the rest of his family had fallen asleep. That night was exceptional only in that he felt lonely. His normal preoccupation was making plans. That night he was depressed considering money making schemes that had so often failed to satisfy their potential. He spent his time commiserating with what he saw as his bad luck. Just when it seemed that the shop had reached a reasonably profitable state, he had been forced into adopting the position of an informer. Naming the situation frightened him even more and he had to dwell on the financial gain to take his mind off the inherent dangers.

It was his practice usually at some stage to discuss his latest schemes with Rita; she was his sounding-board for new ideas. However on this occasion that was impossible. He knew what her reaction would be and did not want to concern her. Unfortunately the absence of someone with which to share his new situation left him feeling very much alone.

He stood looking out of the parlour window into the dark street outside and began to wonder if he should move his family across the water to mainland England. It was a prospect that excited him as well as filling him with doubt. At least in England, the proximity of the punishment squads would be distanced—and the interference of the British Secret Service in his life would be removed. He decided it would be worth making inquiries about such a move and concluded that if he planned it for twelve months in advance; he could save a considerable sum of money from that paid to him by Terry and Martin.

The big question was—could he keep the matter secret. Did he have the self-control to maintain his silence? Self control—that much vaunted bulwark demanded by his religion; the mainstay against temptation, especially in matters of the flesh. How many times had the priest, hidden behind his confessional curtain, whispered the need for self-control? But he had never been able to determine how one was supposed to prohibit impure thoughts. Didn't they just spring into one's mind unbidden often without any kind of provocation? For example, a sexy magazine cover, a cinema poster or a glimpse of a pretty face—however accidental—immediately prompted images and ideas qualifying as sinful. And could such innocent preoccupations actually offend God? It wasn't like masturbation, that was a conscious act, in which one deliberately dwelt on salacious images—but he didn't do much of that recently any more.

The notion of self-control made him think about his recent sexual relationship with his wife. Since she had fallen pregnant there had been little contact of that sort. Indeed there had been little enough since the birth of their last child. It was almost as though the act of love-making was now somehow degrading in her eyes and even the intimate asides they had once shared were now a thing of the past. Now, Rita regarded them as rude and unnecessary.

He found himself wandering silently along the upstairs landing, peeking in at his children. Lorna was fast developing and even at six years of age, she was a sexy little madam, always flaunting herself when she came out of the bath. He found himself excited at the memory. It would not be long before they would have to make her bathe separately from her brothers. The thought disturbed him. He projected the idea of Lorna's sexuality into her future—her teens—then the trouble would start. Spotty youths trying to get their hands on his lovely daughter; back-street scenarios; visions of her in the back seat of old cars ; disgusting fumbling with her as a curious—God forbid, even a willing participant. The images were repugnant.

CHAPTER TWO

The man calling himself Terry came back to see him again the following week and as before, he called on Friday night. Old Mrs. O'Callaghan had just paid for leg of lamb when the man arrived. He held the door for the old woman and she muttered something about good manners and the English as she left.

"Are you English then?" Geraint asked.

"Does it matter?"

"Huh y 'must be. Only an Englishman would ask that."

Terry pulled a face, "Well do you have anything for me?" he asked.

"They're all talking about the cease-fire—some of them are furious about it. One or two are even saying they might form a splinter group and carry on with the campaign."

Terry paled, "Are you sure about that?" he asked.

"I'm only telling you what I heard."

"You'd better be sure Donnelly. If I take this back and it proves to be gossip . . ." He drew a finger across his throat making his meaning explicit.

"It's what I heard," Geraint said defensively, "but you can't blame me if it's wrong."

This seemed to satisfy Terry and he slipped another twenty pounds across the counter to Geraint's palm.

"See," The Englishman said, "we told you it would be easy money, didn't we. Mind it's just my luck that they have a cease-fire when I get to the Northern Ireland desk."

His statement confirmed Geraint's suspicion that his employers were in fact the British Secret Service—probably MI6 and his betrayal felt all the worse.

"Tell you what Donnelly," Terry said staring into the window display, "those lamb chops look good, how about giving me a couple of pound for my supper?"

Geraint couldn't resist, "Fuck off back to England and buy your supper," he said bitterly, "I may have to deal with you but I don't have to serve you favours in my shop."

He was home earlier that night, time enough to spend with the kids before they went to bed. Rita had a good fire going in the kitchen and he sat before it with Lorna on his knee, Patrick stood next to him and little Peter was in his pram. The older two were full of children's talk—the story their mother had read to them, the drawing Lorna had brought home from her nursery school and the dog that had barked at them on their way home. Rita watched them, smiling as she put her husband's dinner on the table. It was good to see Geraint enjoying the company of his children and they quite obviously adored him.

"There you are Geraint, steak and onions—just as you like it." She said. "Come on you two; let your Da have his dinner. Anyway it's bed-time."

A little while later they lined up to kiss their father goodnight, a ritual they observed whenever it was bedtime—whenever he was home. Lorna clung to him a second longer than the rest, insisting on long sloppy kisses.

Later on that evening Molly came in from next door to baby-sit whilst Rita and Geraint went to St. Joseph's church to make their weekly confession. There were two priests on duty that night, so for a change the benches were not crowded with penitents. Consequently it took only a few minutes before Geraint was kneeling in the darkened cubicle.

"Bless me Father for I have sinned . . . ." He said quietly, "It is one week since my last confession and I accuse myself of . . ."

The priest eventually gave him absolution and asked him to say three decades of the rosary as his penance.

He left the confessional and knelt next to Rita his head bowed. Whilst he had been confessing his sins, the nearby pews had filled and one or two people stared at him when he reappeared.

"Where have you been?" Rita whispered from behind her hands.

He turned and frowned giving her a questioning look.

"It's just that you've been in there for twenty minutes." She explained, "I thought you must have done a murder."

He smiled weakly knowing that he would be damned by the other penitents in the nearby pews even if he was forgiven by God.

* * *

Some months later a representative of the local IRA visited Geraint at his home. He was to deliver the first of several warnings concerning Geraint's association with MI6. Jerome Casey was the commander of a wing of the Republican Army and he called at the house late one evening. He was welcomed and offered a drink and whilst he accepted the single malt whisky, he chose not to accept the offer of a seat in the parlour. Instead he stood by the bay window, glass in hand and told his host that he had heard Geraint was leaking information to the British. A small man with a thin frame, Casey was nevertheless a charismatic presence. His voice was soft with a Cork accent, but no amount of softness could disguise the menace in his warning.

"Should y 'choose t 'ignore us Mister Donnelly—I can't speak for the consequences." He said, "If y 'see what I mean."

Initially Geraint assumed an angry posture and declared his fealty in a loud voice, declaring that his family had already given martyrs to the Cause. Casey listened to him in silence but when the tirade finished, he drained his glass and left without further comment. The warning had been delivered. It was to be repeated on four more occasions and successively, the consequences were made clearer each time. On one of these occasions a slightly more sympathetic Casey explained that, if had not been for Geraint's family history, he might have been punished already.

"You're right in thinking y 'belong to a good family Geraint Donnelly—and y 'have a wonderful gang of kids y 'self, so don't throw it all away for the sake of a few English pounds" he paused and then added quietly, "We'll kill you f 'sure if we have to."

It was rumoured in the pubs nearby that Geraint survived the warnings simply because he was not privy to any information worth protecting. All that he could offer the English agents was unsubstantiated gossip, guesswork derived from bar-room theorists. And generally these were people, too full of Guinness and their own importance ever to be trusted by the hierarchy of the IRA with anything of any real value. However, he could—and did—describe the names and status of the Republicans responsible for organising the local group. This was information that was not new to Whitehall but, in their eyes, signified his willingness—it also justified the payments of twenty pounds per week to the butcher. Not surprisingly, Geraint was excluded from any Republican meetings at which important decisions were made, leaving him to glean only snippets from conversations in bar-rooms. It was nevertheless a situation that promised tragic consequences.

Geraint came to regard his isolation as a compromise worth making. On the one hand he knew full well that he could not pass on any information worth having and on the other, he benefited financially to such an extent that moving his family to England became a real possibility. He discerned also that the threats made against him were based on unsubstantiated evidence and as such, were made probably more as an example to the community, than to chastise him. This situation persisted until 1967.

The demonstration inspired that year by the IRA and due to take place in Londonderry on October 8th was not kept secret. The unrest that provoked the march was caused by the sectarian bias in housing and employment that was seen to discriminate against the Catholic community. However, it was on account of the two days of rioting that preceded the march, that prompted the Home Affairs Minister William Craig to impose a ban—or so the Authorities argued. Over one hundred Catholics demonstrators were injured when the Police brought the march to a halt and the violence was widespread. A number of the organisers were arrested and the speed and efficiency of the arrests caused the commanders of the Republican side to suspect that the Police had inside information. Geraint became the prime suspect and, after examining the evidence of his previous warnings, and listening to opinions about his moral standing a decision to eliminate him was taken that night. Casey announced that when a suitable opportunity presented itself Mr. Donnelly should pay the ultimate price for his apparent treachery.

CHAPTER THREE

November 1967

News: Riot police broke up a demonstration by 800 Catholics and sympathizers last night after two days of bloody street battles in Londonderry. Some 100 demonstrators and several police constables were taken to hospital. The Catholics, their student supporters and trade unionists were protesting against sectarian discrimination in housing and employment.

Diary: December 1967

Dad and Mam still want us to go to England. They talk about it all the time and it makes me cry. The way they go on about it will spoil Christmas for sure. I hope something happens and they have to wait till I'm a bit older, then I can stay here where I belong—with all my friends.

* * *

It was towards the end of 1967 when the family began to talk more seriously about moving to England. Often Lorna's Dad and Mam sat up late into the night discussing the details and planning the move. Lorna, being the eldest, regularly sat at the top of the stairs to listen, whereas Patrick, Theresa and Peter had to content themselves by pressing their ears to the bedroom floor. She always gave them an edited version when she came to bed but continued nevertheless to claim her limited prerogative. She was able therefore to gather far more first-hand information than them and, as a consequence, she knew that despite some hesitation on her Mother's part, the migration was almost certain to go ahead. This left her in a state of real agitation . . .

Having reached her eleventh birthday that April, Lorna had only just started at St. Mary's Secondary school. And, now that she had settled, in the company of all her friends she felt that she could not face another start at another school. Furthermore, she could see no good reason why she should have to do so. She had heard her Father argue his case: the job market, the level of earnings and the housing prospects, but she did not believe things could be so different across the water. She listened to him describe the increasing danger of violence on the streets from the Proddy-dogs and the likelihood of one of them being hurt but she had been an eye witness, to at least some of the violence and she had never felt in any danger at any time.

Wasn't it common knowledge that the IRA would defend them and didn't Sean O'Malley's older brother Gerald and his Dad both fight for the Republican Army on behalf of the Catholics. There was no way that any Proddy could stand up to the O'Malleys, not for long. Gerry O'Malley had beaten that feller outside the pub good and proper. She'd seen him do it.

Unfortunately, her parents did not share her confidence in the IRA nor did they seek her opinion about the move and it seemed to her that within weeks of the matter first being discussed seriously, it was settled.

The night it was finally decided, Fergal and Molly from next door came in for a drink and even after the bedroom-floor listeners had long since crawled back to their beds, Lorna sat shivering at her usual station trying to glean the minutia of her parents intentions.

Originally the date set for the move was in January'69 but, for some reason to do with money, her Dad postponed it to the following March. The delay was announced in mid October and to Lorna's reckoning, the March prospect made it look like a reprieve. She was so convinced of this that she even told her brothers and sister (quoting her Mothers repeated accusation) that maybe this was 'just another of their Dad's wild schemes', like when he was going to be a chicken farmer, or move to Dublin and, maybe therefore, it wouldn't happen. Wasn't her Mother always saying how he was full of good ideas but that he never followed them through to completion?

To Lorna's eleven year old mind, this was an occasion when she would be glad if he didn't, 'follow through'. She liked to think that for years, she and her Dad had had a special relationship but now she smarted at the fact he had not sought her opinion about the migration. It was a betrayal.

The first heavy fall of snow came on November 10th that year and, despite the initial adventure of snowballing in the street, the daily walk to school regularly left all four children shivering with frozen toes and red noses. The seasonal adventure lasted only for one week, and then it quickly turned into a trial. The slush froze into furrows then more snow fell and walking became a serious hazard. To make matters worse, a virulent flu bug adopted the local community as its breeding ground. Patrick, the next eldest, was the first to succumb; Peter, the youngest, followed suite within days and when Theresa was infected, Lorna was left to make the long walk every day to St. Mary's on her own.

"Now don't dawdle," her Mother told her each morning. "I don't want t 'be worrying about you if you're late home. And you don't want your Dad to be out looking for you—do you—so?"

Agreement was mandatory. However, as with children everywhere, no matter how sincere the promises, the temptation to gossip with friends, to hang about the boys' entrance after school and to share illicit copies of less reputable magazines inevitably took precedence when the time came and Lorna was no exception.

That Friday evening she found herself flirting with Sean at the school gates. A performance as much for the benefit of her two closest friends who stood by as giggling witnesses, as it was for herself. She knew Sean liked her and, although she thought he was a bit scruffy, the power she was able to exercise over him was good for her image. To be able to tease an older boy was an achievement much admired by all her friends. However, it was only when he tried unexpectedly to kiss her that she realized the limit of her control and she did not like it.

He grabbed her suddenly without warning and held her arms tight to her sides, forcing his face into hers. She screamed but it had no effect and his cold, damp mouth searched her face whilst he made animal noises in the back of his throat. It was a nightmare, making her rigid with fear. Eventually, her friends managed to pull Sean off but not before he had succeeded in planting several sloppy kisses on her cheek near her mouth. She was almost hysterical. To make matters worse, throughout the attack, his mate Steven Donovan stood by cheering him on and making obscene suggestions. Afterwards the boys went off together laughing.

It took half an hour before Lorna was fully recovered. Thirty minutes spent in a shop doorway with sympathetic friends offering their support and paper hankies.

"Y 'should have kicked him in the privates." Mary McGuire said bravely.

"Or scratched his nasty face." echoed Bessie Devlin, miming the action with her fingers hooked.

The belated advice was little comfort and provided more of a therapy for their own trauma than for the badly shocked and still tearful girl herself. The mood of violent reaction they suggested however, proved infectious and Lorna found herself considering the various ways she might get her own back. And, as the contemplation of revenge proved sweet, her strategy for achieving it became ever more exaggerated.

Being the eldest child at home, Lorna had always enjoyed a position of authority inevitably at school therefore, on account of her self-confidence; she was treated with respect, her views being seen as a model for her peer group. Sean had shattered that confidence by reducing her to tears and in the process had undoubtedly left her public position challenged, her status impaired. Her only respite was in thoughts of revenge and for the first time in her life her anger consumed her. She was determined to see him punished.

They set off to walk down the high street and it began to sleet.

On the way, having regained her composure and in order to communicate the level of her determination, Lorna swore and cursed Sean and every member of his family. Warming to the task, she dredged every obscenity from the depths of her limited acquaintance with gutter-vocabulary. Every morsel of lewd coarseness she had ever heard, she applied venomously to the O'Malley clan. She questioned their cleanliness and scorned their honesty; she claimed that the children were illegitimate and that they lived like pigs; she poked fun at their appearance and at the crudeness of their manners and finally, when there was nothing left to ridicule, she told the others, in the strictest confidence of course, that she had heard they were traitors to the Cause.

In Northern Ireland, even to children, this was the most serious accusation that could be imagined.

"My God Lorna are y' sure?" Bessie asked in a shocked whisper.

"Didn't I hear my own Da say so?" Lorna lied without hesitation.

Now she was beginning to enjoy herself. The barbs of her vengeance were clearly beginning to bite. Conscious however, of the possible need at some stage to change her story, she took the precaution of keeping her fingers crossed behind her back when she replied, "I heard tell that one night soon, the Army r 'going t 'send a punishment squad round to the O'Malley's house."

Mary McGuire's face paled at the thought.

It made a change for Lorna to claim inside information about the Troubles. The war was more usually Mary's province. It was no secret among the small group of friends that Mary's family belonged to the upper echelons of the Republican Movement and that her father was a senior member of the ruling council of the IRA. Mary seldom talked about it. She had imbibed the culture of secrecy from early childhood but, just occasionally, usually after some spectacular explosion or the like, she would let drop a tit-bit of information that would liven the tabloid images. Now, it was she who was surprised.

By the time the trio reached the corner, the place where they normally parted company, the icy rain that swept down the high street had soaked through Lorna's thin coat and her friends had fallen silent. It was clear that her statement had struck home more successfully than she could have ever imagined. Indeed the effect was so pronounced that Lorna began to fear that she may have gone too far. She could not decide if her shivers were caused by the damp cold of the weather or by her growing feeling of guilt.

They had just parted to go their separate ways when Lorna's Father appeared. A tall thin man in his long mackintosh and, on this occasion, his height was accentuated by the big umbrella he carried if not by the severity of his frown. When he saw Lorna he hurried in her direction and she realized suddenly how late it was. The look in his eye confirmed her worst fears about his mood.

"So y 'can't be trusted girl," he muttered down at her, "and with the heathens taking over the city y 'know that no-one's safe. Yer mothers in a state and you're standin there like it's a Bank Holiday. God forgive Yer."

In fact both Lorna's parents were predictably furious that night but, long before they had opportunity to fully express their anger, it became obvious to them that their eldest daughter was ill. It came on suddenly, taking them all by surprise. On the way home, it seemed to Lorna that the cold damp of the fog had penetrated her lungs making breathing difficult. And, by the time she and her Father reached the corner of their street, the tickle in her throat had become a rasping cough making her feel hot and weak. As soon as she laid eyes on the girl, her Mother realized the state she was in.

"Look at her Joseph," she exclaimed accusingly, "she's burning up. Get the kettle on for pity's sake."

In no time at all Lorna was stripped down to her knickers and coddled in thick blankets before a blazing fire in the parlour. A hot water bottle was pressed to her chest, cough linctus was poured down her throat and a bowl of thick soup was produced as if by magic from the kitchen. Unfortunately, by then she was in no condition to enjoy all the attention. Her rising temperature left her semi-conscious; her chest burned; her nose streamed and fits of shivering shook her from head to toe, painful spasms that left her breathless and exhausted.

Although it took the doctor about an hour to arrive at the house, he was able to diagnose pneumonia within minutes. Arguments about the need for hospitalization followed and, albeit reluctantly on Doctor Tomlin's part, it was eventually agreed that she could stay at home and be looked after by her Mother. She was given an injection, a prescription for pills and strong linctus and Doctor Tomlin promised he would call to see her each day himself. He warned that she still may need to be taken in to hospital to be x-rayed. "She'd be better off in a hospital bed." he said for the third time disapprovingly, "But if you insist on keeping her at home, she must be closely monitored. God knows how you'll find the time for that, with three other children in the house."

"Leave that t 'me, I'll find the time." Her Mother replied.

Lorna was only dimly aware of these discussions, by then she had drifted off into a deep, if somewhat troubled, sleep. She woke several times during the night only to find herself in a nightmare of confusion about her location. Unbeknown to her, a bed had been erected for her in the corner of her parents' bedroom where a fire had been lit. Fortunately therefore, each time she stirred, one or the other of them was always on hand to administer medicines, to sponge her forehead and to keep the blankets pulled tightly around her quaking shoulders. She remained in a similar state for the next twenty-four hours and for twenty-four more, she was so weak that she could hardly feed herself.

Due to the strength of a new medicine called an antibiotic, prescribed by Dr. Tomlin, by the end of that same week the infection in her chest had begun to subside. She was occasionally able to sit up and take notice but she still slept most of the time. Although the medicine was having an effect, a side effect left her without an appetite. She picked at her food and seldom finished a whole meal. And in a household where food had always been seen as a panacea for most illnesses, this was particularly disturbing for her parents. As he was a butcher by trade, each evening her Father was able to bring home a variety of tasty cuts to tempt her palette. Tenderloin pork was grilled to perfection, fillet steak and tiny lamb chops were fried in best butter and choice shin beef was cooked to make the most delicious broth. Unfortunately none of this had the desired effect and Rastus the dog became the beneficiary, the best fed mongrel in the Province.

Once on the road to recovery however, Lorna began to enjoy all the special care lavished on her by her parents. She had always loved to be the centre of attention. As a small child she had experienced an unusual lack of confidence and, during that period when she had first started to attend school, concern had been expressed by her teachers that she may be suffering some form of psychological deficiency. Conscious that such a condition could prove a stigma for the whole family, her mother had reluctantly attended a series of consultations with the school management and, on the advice of the Head teacher, Mrs. Mahon, the problem was referred to their GP. Consequently, Doctor Tomlin had given Lorna a thorough physical examination and had spent half an hour talking to her on her own about her worries, her ambitions and, surprisingly (as it seemed to her family) about her dreams. And, although after the examination he had no clear explanation, to offer he was particularly interested in why the young girl should sometimes scratch herself. Her arms bore the scars of this obsessive, self-hurt preoccupation. Her Mother told him that Lorna had formed this habit in early childhood, for no apparent reason.

"It's not so bad now." she said," but when she was very little, she used to tear chunks out of herself all the time. Sometimes I've even caught her banging her head against the furniture. Her dad reckons it was just attention-seeking. "Doctor Tomlin concluded finally that although, for a child of her age her mental development was somewhat slow, in general she was perfectly adequate both physically and mentally and that her parents should not concern themselves further in that respect.

Apparently the advice was well founded and by her third term at school, Lorna had changed personality, quite suddenly becoming more dominant. So much so that, far from being the class 'mouse' that she had been, her behaviour became increasingly disruptive. One of her school reports even described her as being—'precocious'. She became the class clown, the one with the smart answers and the one prepared to ask the awkward questions no one else dared to ask. Needless to say, she became the one on whom the focus of all the other children tended to rest.

Lorna's recovery was slow and Doctor Tomlin was still calling to see her daily even after two weeks. He told her parents that her resistance was low and that, although the battle for control of her system was being won, she would need to convalesce at home for some considerable time to come. Each time he came Doctor Tomlin would always find time for a quiet and private chat with Lorna on her own. On these occasions he would inevitably ask if there was anything troubling her—anything she couldn't tell her parents about. The answer was always a resounding, 'No'.

Unfortunately the same prognosis of improvement could not be applied to the political situation in and around Lorna's home; the battles in that context were more than metaphorical. Street violence had erupted again and RUC patrols, made their presence felt on every corner. After dark, armed men made regular sweeps of the area around Lorna's district effectively creating a curfew across the Province, Incidents between Loyalists and the Republican forces increased and riots of one sort or another became regular week-end events and whatever their beliefs, people on both sides of the political divide appeared to contract out of public life. Most restricted their movement outside of their homes, only to that demanded by basic necessity. People went to work and came home again and once home they stayed indoors. And, understanding that no-one was safe from the assassin's bullet or the fire-bomb, the social life of the Province was again leached away, leaving nerves taut and tempers frayed. Caution was everyone's watchword.

And for the first time, the depth of concern felt by Lorna's parents for the safety of their family was communicated to their offspring. By now the other children had recovered from their bouts of cold and had returned to school but prevailing conditions dictated that their attendance was irregular. Each day, the pre-school warnings were followed in the evening by the post-school investigations.

"Did you all walk together? Did you wait for one another? Did you avoid The Police? Did you speak to anyone?"—And so it went on.

A siege mentality developed. The tone of the TV news became the fulcrum about which their lives turned. They watched and listened and any hint of trouble to come caused the children to be kept at home the next day. The same was true for Lorna's Father's business. His shop was situated near to the border of a Loyalist estate and two of his fellow shopkeepers had already had their premises destroyed by fire-bombs. It seemed that political and/or religious affiliation was supreme and suspicion of transgression was enough to generate a violent reaction. Tension was therefore almost unbearably high.

As she still shared the same bedroom with her parents, Lorna soon became privy to the extent of their worries. She listened to the arguments from her Father, "It's all well and good and probably the safest option to keep the shop closed," he said, "however, sides of beef and joints of pork have a limited shelf-life and if bills are to be paid, a certain level of trade is essential."

In this regard, like her Mother, she found her Father's confidence worrying. It seemed that each successive week brought a further deterioration of the situation. One Friday evening, a neighbour only four doors away was hit by a ricocheting bullet and the following night another family from the corner house had their car set alight. That same week-end Auntie Agnes phoned from Ballymena to say that Uncle Tony had been arrested. He was released two days later but Lorna learned from the late-night whispered conversations she overheard that he had been beaten badly during his interrogation by the police.

It was nearly six weeks before Lorna was up and about again. At last her colour was back to normal and the cough, the terrible rasp that had shaken her rib-cage had been reduced to the merest tickle. Doctor Tomlin eventually told her Mother that she could return to school, "To begin with," he said, "for mornings only." However, he added the precaution that if the cough came back, or if she felt at all weakened, she should return home immediately. Lorna was sufficiently recovered to recognise a carte blanche when she saw one and in her mind's eye she underscored her most unfavoured periods from her class timetable of lessons. She decided, these would undoubtedly prove the most vulnerable should she experience a relapse.

That same night, shortly after dark there was an explosion outside of the Police station and in the wake of the bomb, the sound of car engines, running feet and occasional gunshots disturbed the quiet. The chaos spilled over into the following day and Lorna and the other children were kept at home. Her Father nevertheless went to work, even in the face of objections from her Mother.

"If I don't get those pies made today all that meat I minced will be wasted.'

He told her. She continued to argue but he was adamant, claiming that they were already in danger of spending that little savings they had made.

"We can't go on dipping into the money for England now can we. And we don't want t 'find ourselves across the water without money. God knows how we'd fare if we were left at the mercy of the English."

He promised to take care and to come home as soon as he could. It was the first time in living memory that he did not keep a promise.

It was four o'clock in the afternoon when the police called to tell them that the shop had been fire-bombed. Lorna's Father, they said, was in the emergency ward of the district hospital.

He was to stay there for a considerable time before he eventually died of his wounds . . .

CHAPTER FOUR

1969

The News: Protestant leader Ian Paisley is jailed for three months for unlawful assembly. Northern Ireland yesterday elected Bernadette Devlin, (22 years of age next week,) as the Westminster MP for the Mid-Ulster constituency. The result is a triumph for the Province's civil rights movement

Diary: December 17th 1969

It's not fair. Me Dad's dead and none of me friends are talking to me. If the Republican Army blew him up, everyone seems to think he must have been a traitor. Bessie told me—so. Patrick says it was a dreadful mistake—but they shouldn't make mistakes—not with people's lives. They're getting as bad as the bloody British. I hate them all. This is going to be the worst Christmas in my life.

* * *

She stood beside her Mother's chair during the priest's visit. Silent and attentive, she struggled to understand all that he said; battling to make sense of a religious message suddenly alien to her present needs. The other children had been farmed out to relatives and friends, leaving Lorna the eldest at twelve and a half years old as the solitary witness on their behalf. Her Mother had told her it was the responsibility of the eldest child and, reluctantly, she accepted it as such

In defiance of the approaching Christmas, for days the house had been dark and dull. The curtains were drawn and the big mirror in the hall was turned to face the patch of clean wallpaper behind it. All the pictures in the house had been draped and conversations that were held were conducted only in hushed tones. The family was deliberately cocooned against an outside world; deliberately distanced from anything that might represent the norm. The sameness of the last two days made Lorna feel as though time had stood still, as though a gap had been created and life as she knew it was unaccountably suspended.

There had been a stream of visitors arriving in ones and twos to sit briefly in the front parlour. Long faced visitors in best suits and Sunday frocks who tapped at the front door almost as though they did not want to be heard. Some of them, particularly the women, hugged her Mother and whispered words of support but it was only when they turned to face Lorna that their tears began. Ever after she would always think of herself as a 'poor fatherless child'.

By contrast, the behaviour of male visitors was strangely ambiguous. They looked uncomfortably estranged, seeming not to know what they were expected to say or how to act. Some tried to communicate their sympathy in the strength of their handshake, hiding the dampness in their eyes behind large white, pocket-handkerchiefs and a lot of nose blowing. One or two of them did not even drink the glass of whiskey her Mother poured for them but sat instead, upright and silent, swilling the contents of the glass in endless circles. The strength, that Lorna had been taught was a male province, proved to be a mirage and for the first time, the young girl began to question the traditional notion of masculine fortitude. However, to make matters worse, privately Lorna's confusion was aggravated due to her inability to shed a tear. Capriciously she found herself imagining that life might even be better without her father: a horrible and shaming notion.

As near neighbours, many of the visitors would have normally come in by the ever open back door, now however, their arrival needed to be formalised: an observance of mourning practice in a specialised cultural tradition. In that context, Lorna's job was to answer the front door and then to provide an endless supply of tea, served in the best china. Her opinions were not sought during the conversations that followed the tea and she did not offer them. In the interim she stood silently at her mother's left shoulder listening to a litany of praise for her Father; a continuous and often repeated eulogy that called on anecdotal evidence of his sweet nature and generous disposition. Much of the time, the mourners described events that had happened long before she was born and therefore portrayed the actions of a man she hardly recognised. This served only to further enhance the girl's feeling of displacement.

In terms of what was expected therefore, her behaviour was deemed perfect. She acquitted all the functions required of her and proved a model for the role she had been given. Subconsciously however, her mind was in turmoil. The images of her Father's dying moments surfaced uncontrollably leaving permanent imprints in a recurring nightmare; a series of jagged fragments like electric shocks to stun her reality. She could not cry and did not know why not. Seeing the tears around her, she began to question the quality of her conscience if not her loyalty. Incomprehensibly and despite herself, there were even moments when she felt relieved.

The priest sat forward in the big armchair, his fingertips pressed together and his eyes focused intently on those of the widow sitting opposite. He had arrived in the evening after the Benediction service and consequently he still smelled of incense and candle wax. He talked of God's grace, which was apparently needed to bear the trials of life; and of a meaning that was hidden from the living, despite the apparent unfairness of events. There was a certainty he said of the dead man's reward in heaven. He said that good souls will always triumph over those who are evil and that despair was now the most dangerous of enemies.

"Y 'must look to the good Lord for faith. Y 'must pray all the harder for guidance and y 'must never give in t 'feelings of revenge." he muttered.

The word revenge struck a chord in Lorna's half-listening ear and, as she contemplated it, there was a real sense of relief in the prospect of getting back at the stupid ignorance of the bombers. She saw them in her imagination—whoever they were—suddenly at her mercy. Alongside unbidden, she also saw memories of her Father at work, knife in hand, in the act of disembowelling the carcass of a pig. The thoughts merged without encouragement and the result hardly disgusted her at all. Without realising she did so, she interrupted the priest.

"I'd like to rip their insides out." she said quietly.

The priest stopped in mid-cliché.

"What was that Lorna—did y 'say something?"

His question opened the flood-gates. All her guilt, the bile and the venom, the hate and the hopelessness that had festered beneath the calm surface of her silent childlike stillness was suddenly released.

"Yer God's a sadist if y 'ask me Father. And the longer people like you go round telling victim's families to tolerate the killing, then the longer it'll go on. They deserve t 'have their insides torn out; their eyes burned from the sockets; their legs broken with hammers; their teeth smashed and . . . ."

"Lorna!" Her Mother's damp cry stopped the flow.

CHAPTER FIVE

1970

News: Warring factions in Belfast woke to find themselves separated by a six feet high barbed wire 'peace wall' today. Royal Engineers, supported in places by the Royal Ulster Constabulary, are building the huge barricade between the Protestant stronghold near the Shank hill Road and the predominantly Catholic area of Falls Road. At the same time a traffic curfew was imposed on the riot area, allowing only essential vehicles, ambulances, fire-engines, clergymen's cars—through heavily guarded checkpoints. Lieut. General Sir Ian Freeland. GOC. Northern Ireland Director of Operations, dismissed suggestions that his troops were creating a "Berlin Wall" situation.

Diary: October 7th

Like other Friday nights lately we are shut up in the house trying not to listen to the sound of guns and explosions. This has become a terrible place. Terry Keenan was only nine and he was shot dead through the kitchen window and old Mrs. Gannon had her front room burned black by a fire bomb. Were these mistakes as well? Sometimes I can't sleep for thinking about it all . . . . I have nightmares all the time.

*   *   *

It was almost the end of the following year before the remnants of the Donnelly family actually made their migration to the British mainland. It proved a year of endless good-byes that had begun with their final farewell to the man that had been their Father. Lorna's Mother had determined on the day of the funeral that she would take them to start the new life that her husband had planned. She decided that the children should have all that their Father had wanted for them, a firm decision made, despite the prospect of the continued upheaval and the obvious restrictions of a limited budget. Given her situation therefore, it was a brave decision, a covenant she said she made in her husband's memory.

The sale of what was left of the shop fittings, the savings, the insurance money and the prospect of resuming her career as a typist were what made the move possible and, although she knew it was still a gamble, Lorna's mother was determined that no more of her family would ever again fall foul of the terminal prejudice found in their homeland. A passage was booked and plans made to leave Ireland that winter.

Probably due to Lorna's long absence from school through her illness and her subsequent irregular attendance due to the Troubles, Bessie Devlin was the only one of her friends to come to see her off. They had always been the best of friends but on this occasion they found it hard to make conversation. Instead, they stood together in the passageway of the house and held hands. Although normally, they would have been embarrassed to exhibit their emotions, capriciously on this occasion, in the way only young girls are able, they needed the opportunity to demonstrate their feelings. When the time came for Lorna to leave in the taxi, they wept and hugged one another.

Typically, at this last moment, literally when Lorna was about to get into the cab, they both found things they wanted to say. In a sudden rush of words, breathless in their eagerness, they promised always to remain friends, to write to one another and never to forget birthdays. But it was only when the door of the vehicle was actually closing that Bessie made the most shocking announcement.

"I don't suppose anyone told you Lonny—but y 'should know that Sean O'Malley's brother got knee-capped. A punishment fer his treachery they say."

The door slammed and the car moved off and Bessie's face, pale and damp was gone before Lorna could digest the news. However, the significance of the words soon became clear. Consequently, throughout the rest of the journey to the docks, Lorna sat in silence—yet another guilt-ridden isolation.

She could only wonder if her accusations about the O'Malleys had played any part in deciding the terrible act of punishment. Surely, she reasoned, if Bessie had not believed that it was partly her doing she would have mentioned it sooner. On the other hand—maybe it was just the last thing she remembered. There was little consolation in the latter and the conviction grew that she had been guilty of instigating a terrible retribution—and all for the sake of a kiss. She was not to know at the time but her farewell to her friend Bessie would mark the last time they would share one another's company. Before her twentieth year Bessie would die in a Loyalist bomb incident: another innocent; another meaningless death.

The Donnelly family took the overnight boat in the cold damp of a winter drip-mist and, still confused, Lorna saw the last of her Ireland from below-decks and through the steamy glass of a porthole. A last look at a darkened shore where it seemed, the snakes of prejudice had finally defeated the efforts of their national saint; where it seemed the evidence of a barbed tongue was as much a national characteristic as was the shamrock.

They landed in Liverpool early on a damp Monday morning where their meagre reception was the cold rain of an English autumn.

CHAPTER SIX

1971

News: A fierce gun battle between 1500 British troops and IRA snipers continued in Belfast today after a night of violence in which three civilians and a sniper were killed and ten soldiers wounded. Meanwhile bombs have been exploding throughout the city. The latest trouble began after a police raid had uncovered a cache of arms including 15 pistols, a rifle, a sub-machine gun and ammunition.

Diary: Only days after my fourteenth birthday and Mam is about to marry again. How can she expect me to accept this little fat man as my Father? I hate him. Has she forgotten Dad so soon? I've cried myself to sleep every night since she told me.

* * *

When she was older Loma often wondered if her Mother had been endowed with an innate tendency if not a weakness for men who were butchers. Later in life she used to imagine that there must have been an, as yet unidentified gene in her Mother's make-up. One that inclined her sympathies towards those men possessing the intricate skills to bone out a shoulder of lamb; who could carve a beast's hind quarter into corner cuts or rump steak; who had the ability to roll a breast and hand of pork or to make black pudding or pressed tongue—in short—men who provided for the world's carnivores. It was the only explanation possible. How else could one justify the fact that within months of landing in England and only weeks after moving to Thornaby on Tees, she had promised to marry another butcher? She was a butcher-addict. In Lorna's mind it presented a curious and tragic anomaly.

Jimmy Ungerside, the butcher in question, possessed neither good looks nor anything like a substantial fortune. He stood only five and a half feet high and measured almost as much again around his middle. Several years older than Lorna's Mother and a widower himself, he nevertheless courted her like a young man in his twenties, bringing her flowers, writing poetry to her and treating her, in his words, 'Like a Queen.'

The nature of his attentions were of a kind, Lorna never imagined her Mother could succumb to. This was a 'women's magazine' type romance—crude and obvious. Clearly her Mother's needs in this respect had been well hidden which might also indicate why apparently, they had never been catered for.

Lorna had to admit to herself that, despite his appearance, Jimmy was a man of great variety and not inconsiderable achievement. His personality was every bit as complex as any in Lorna's experience. Once behind the counter in his little shop in Brown Street, he could demonstrate the skills of a businessman trader as well as the jocular good humour of an entertainer. In the shop he was a consummate showman. It was his style to talk continuously, ostensibly to the customer he was serving but actually also to whosoever was waiting to be served often a shop full of shoppers. It was a non-stop diatribe laced with a fund of information about his wares; his childhood; tips on cooking (he had been a Chef in the Royal Navy) and advice on how to choose the best joints. Generally, his jokes were innocent and inoffensive and he always maintained a well-practiced respect for his customers. His manner was cheery and his artistry with a boning knife or cleaver apparently unsurpassed in the town.

By contrast in his private life, Jimmy appeared a quiet sensitive man. He rarely drank alcohol but did not criticise those who did; he was a practicing Catholic but claimed a belief in the Ecumenical movement and, although his size sometimes made him the butt of jokes particularly amongst his fellow butchers, his own humour was dry and without malice. As far as Lorna's Mother was concerned however, perhaps his most endearing quality was in his love of children. And in respect of her own children, at least in part due to their recent loss of a male role model, it was initially a love that was quickly and wholeheartedly reciprocated by all with the sole exception of Lorna.

From the very first time he was introduced to the family, Jimmy apparently made a special effort in respect of Lorna. It was never clear if this was simply on account of her being the eldest child or the fact that, after her mother, she was the eldest female member of the family. When he brought flowers for her Mother, he would always select a particularly large bloom and present it to her. When his comments were directly aimed at her he would always speak quietly and seriously as though she was a fully grown adult and often, when no-one else was looking, he winked privately at her as if they shared a secret understanding. In the girl's mind, given the brevity of their relationship, it was a level of attention that was premature and one, she believed, that was uncalled for. Whatever his motive, his behaviour left the girl deeply suspicious of him.

Conversely, her Mother was pleased with his efforts. She always knew that Lorna would be the one who would find the prospect of a new father most difficult to accept but she saw Jimmy's strategy as a satisfactory way of winning the girl's confidence. Her initial diagnosis was correct but, as far as Lorna was concerned, the degree of assumed intimacy chosen by her Mother's boyfriend as a solution to her indifference only exacerbated the problem. Jimmy nevertheless married Mrs. Donnelly only seven weeks after their first meeting. Thereafter, immediately after the ceremony the family moved from a miserable first floor, council flat into his big house boasting four double bedrooms.

By this time all the children were all established at their new schools. Lorna at a Catholic girl's school, Newtown Convent in Middlesbrough, and only a short bus-ride away; Patrick, Peter and Theresa at St. Joseph's Primary school just round the corner from their new home. At that time the Convent still enjoyed the status of a Grammar school and access had been granted only after an entrance examination had been successfully negotiated. For the parents' sake this was strategic confirmation of the school's expectation of high academic achievement or at least that was the marketing intention. As a consequence, the curriculum with which Lorna was presented was quite different from that which she had experienced in Ireland. Now, there was a much greater intensity of learning expected and lessons were supplemented by the institution's expectation of an extensive commitment to home study from every pupil. However, even though the quantity of homework required, meant Lorna had little free time, under the new domestic regime she was still expected to help out in the butcher's shop every Saturday.

"After all," her step-father would say;" now it's a family business."

Not surprisingly, Loma disliked the extra work at the shop and especially as it implied a closer contact with Jimmy.

At fourteen years of age she had already reached puberty and, although many of the pressing questions endemic to her stage of development had been answered at least in part by her Mother, she was still naive by comparison to many of her new friends. Her life in Ireland had been at a different pace, with quite different terms of reference. The influence of religion and religious practice had been more overt and, although her peer group across the water may well have been termed precocious in respect of their familiarity with violence on the streets, in so far as their knowledge of the more usual facts of life were concerned they were pitifully ignorant.

Things were very different in England. Generally, the thinking amongst English teenagers was more liberal. It was the age of Carnaby Street and Swinging London; of mini-skirts and Rock music. Questions concerning free love and birth control were asked openly and the newspapers and magazines were full of sexual innuendo. For the first time in an age, it seemed that the stranglehold by adults on society was weakening. Accordingly therefore, Lorna's education underwent dramatic change both in terms of its content as well as the rate of its acquisition. Back home in Protestant Ulster, because of her affiliation to the Roman faith, she had been gently encouraged to think of herself as a religious revolutionary, now, suddenly the focus of the current revolution was defined by different parameters. Youthfulness was the favoured prerequisite, the desired status and the prizes on offer were more to do with the politics of the bedroom rather than that of the parliament.

Typically, there were some girls at the Convent who were prepared to dispense facts of life information to their peers and in Lorna's class, a girl called Helen Bonar, provided this service. Helen was a big girl, already well developed and full of confidence. At week-ends, much to the envy of other girls of her age, she was allowed to wear make-up. The proud possessor of indulgent, free-thinking parents, Helen was given a considerable amount of her own way and, however much the nuns may have disapproved, after school and on Saturdays and Sundays, Helen could do as she wished with her time. She was able therefore to demonstrate a self-assurance that belied her age. She could and would answer any queries from the girls relating to the opposite sex, particularly those concerning the male or female anatomy or the act of sex itself. Rumour had it that she had had first hand experience but no-one, at least not in Lorna's hearing, had ever found the courage to ask her directly if that were true.

For some unidentified reason when Lorna started at the school, Helen adopted her and soon became her closest friend. It was a mutual attraction that may have been simply that of opposites, of the informed for the uninformed; of the devout believer for the cynic; the experienced alongside the innocent. Whichever it was, the match was immediate. They were introduced at morning break on Lorna's first day and by the end of lunchtime they were inseparable. By the end of that week the teaching staff had also noticed, so much so that one of the Senior Teachers, a nun called Sister Monica, saw fit to place a judicious telephone call to Lorna's home. Under the guise of pastoral care, she intended to ask Lorna's Mother how Lorna was settling into her new school and, if she happened to let slip her concern at Lorna's new friendship with the Bonar girl, then that would be entirely accidental. Unfortunately for Sister Monica it was Jimmy who took the call and his response was not what had been expected.

"Y'know Sister," he said in his quiet way," Lorna's Mum and I think she is very grown up for a kid of her age. She had to deal with her Dad's death recently and we think that her judgement and her sense of responsibility are pretty good. So don't you go worrying about her making new friends, If Lorna likes the girl, then there must be something good about her. But thanks for telling us just the same."

Years of dealing with awkward customers in a commercial setting had made Jimmy into one of life's most articulate pavement politicians, especially when it came to complaints. His maxim was that the customer should always leave with a smile on their face and where that proved impossible—with a flea in their ear. Sister Monica had met her match.

The call had been made mid-morning on the Saturday, a time when business in the shop was most brisk and Jimmy had had to leave Lorna to serve the customers in order for him to answer the telephone. The subject of the nun's concern was therefore only yards away when the call came through but far too preoccupied to pay any attention to what Jimmy was saying.

Due to the constant flow of customers through the tiny shop however, it was late afternoon before Jimmy had the chance to mention it to Lorna. At the time they were having a well-earned cup of tea in a quiet spell near the end of the day when the opportunity finally arose, relaxing in the back shop just before the clear-up operation started. The necessary scrubbing down the block and washing up the knives and the trays and the final sweeping ritual to clear the floor of sawdust, signified the imminent closure of the butcher's shop. A painstaking procedure that was laborious for Lorna but nevertheless one that she welcomed.

Sipping hot sweet tea, Lorna sat on an old wooden chair and Jimmy was propped against one of the preparation tables in the back-shop when he broached the subject.

"Do you know a Sister Monica—a teacher at your school?" he asked innocently.

The response was immediate, "Yes I do." Lorna said emphatically, "She's the one always going on about behaviour and nagging everyone—a real busybody. She'll keep you in after school for the slightest thing."

She paused, suddenly realising how odd it was that Jimmy should be able to name one of her teachers. "Why do you ask?"

Jimmy glanced up over the rim of his mug and sipped the hot tea again before answering. "She phoned this morning. Wanted to speak to your Mum." he said.

The effect was instantaneous.

"Oh God no." Lorna exclaimed," What did she say?"

"Well from what I could gather, she thinks you've been getting in with the wrong crowd. Do you know someone called Helen?"

"There's nothing wrong with Helen—and I don't care what that old cow says, Helen's okay."

"Here hold your horses, I didn't say she wasn't did 1?" Now he was grinning. "But, and it's a big but, if she got to tell your Mum that this Helen was leading you astray. You can imagine what your Mum's reaction would be, can't you?"

Lorna pulled a face. She knew exactly what her Mother would say.

"You're not going to tell her are you Jimmy? Don't tell her please. Helen's the best friend I've got at school and she really knows her way round. She's great. If Mum gets wind of a complaint from old Monica, she'll stop me seeing her, so don't say anything—will you—please?"

Jimmy smiled. He put down his cup and went over to sit next to the girl on the arm of the chair. He put an arm round her shoulders and squeezed her.

"I don't grass on my friends," he whispered in her ear, "—and you're one of my best friends Lorna. The last thing I ever want is to get you into trouble. Okay?"

She did not like him being so close, she objected to his familiarity and she certainly did not think of him as one of her best friends—but—he was doing her a big favour, so she couldn't really object too much.

"Thanks Jimmy." she said in a small voice.

The response appeared to please him and his grin grew bigger still.

"Fine," he said," and as you'll discover when you know me better, I'm a good friend to have on your side."

As he spoke he squeezed her again.

"Now then, as I've looked out for your interest's young lady, how about giving your new Dad a big thank-you kiss?"

Before she could comment, still less object, he leaned over her and put his warm dry lips to her cheek. She waited for a second, a long horrific second, and then she tried to pull away. His arm was still round her shoulders and his weight pressed her back into the chair, movement was impossible. She panicked. "Don't—Jimmy—don't please . . ."

Memories of another kiss flooded back . . . it was Sean O'Malley's vice-like grip at the school gates.

His quiet laugh sounded loud in her ear, reverberating through his contact at her cheek. But at last he pulled back.

"Hey take it easy. No harm done. A little kiss for the favour I did you with Sister Monica isn't much to ask—is it?"

She shook her head and forced a smile, silently promising herself to stay well clear of him in future. Fortunately he was unaware of the depth of her reaction. He put a paternal hand on her shoulder and said, "You're a nice looking girl Lorna and you'll grow into an even better looking young woman—so—you'll have to get used to men wanting to touch you and kiss you. You'll be popular. And there's nothing wrong with that. It's natural—and if it's natural then there's no harm done."

She did not know what to say so she remained silent. Typically, he took her silence as acquiescence and stroked her arm . . .

"And don't go round thinking that older men are all bad either." He whispered, "Older men—like me—could teach you a lot."

CHAPTER SEVEN

1971

News: February: A British soldier was shot dead during rioting in Ulster tonight, the first to be killed since British Troops moved into the Province in August 1969. He was killed as his unit moved into the Ardoyne district of the city. Sporadic bombings and attacks on troops and police continued throughout Northern Ireland tonight with innocent bystanders including two girls and a youth—being injured by machine-gun fire as they made their way home through the Belfast rush-hour traffic.

Diary: I've begun to enjoy school—at last. Helen Bonar is my best friend—she is so cheeky it takes away my breath sometimes. I still hate working in the shop on Saturdays and Jimmy is as big a pig as ever—don't know how Mam ever got mixed up with him. I sometimes wish! I could see Bessie again. She never answered my letter and I can't bring myself to write again—just in case she doesn't want to hear from me. I still pine for Ulster—but I'm glad we don't live there now. It sounds even more like a war zone—it must be horrible.

* * *

It started—or at least she seemed to remember it starting, on the day that Jimmy's dog, was killed in a road accident. Apparently eight years previously Jimmy had saved the animal from certain destruction at the local dog pound and it had been his constant companion ever since. It was not an attractive dog and, if appearances were to be believed given its physical characteristics, its heritage was as mixed as the colours in its coat. Jimmy however, thought the world of it. He constantly retold the tale of how it had leapt at the metal grill of its cage immediately he had entered the pound.

"I knew that was the one for me," he would say with meaning, implying heavily that forces he did not understand had brought them together, forces he wanted his listeners to believe that were of a supernatural type," he just looked at me and we both knew."

Whatever the truth of Jimmy's assertions, there could be no doubt that his relationship with the creature was founded on a close mutual attraction. Sad Lad, the name aptly chosen for the pet, slept at the foot of Jimmy's bed, it sat next to him at the dinner table and whenever Jimmy moved the animal glued itself to his heel. He would watch his master with slow mournful eyes, anticipating the next requirement on his services with an ever attentive enthusiasm as though eternally grateful to his saviour. Even when Jimmy opened the butchers shop each morning, the dog would accompany him, posting itself as a sentinel at the door where it could dutifully inspect the customers as they entered.

The relationship between the butcher and his dog however, was quite different from that which the dog chose to share with the rest of the family. It was almost as though the deep well of appreciation felt by the animal for its master exhausted all its good intentions. As far as the rest of the household was concerned, the animal was bad tempered and bad mannered to the point of total irrationality (although no-one expected anything approaching rational behaviour from a dog) this was most especially true when its nose was in its feeding bowl. When it fed, Bad Lad made a variety of warning noises, some, aimed at any creature that might seek to share its dinner; others when anyone approached within five feet of its dish. It would issue a continuous rumbling growl followed by an open-mouthed slobbering sound not dissimilar to the noise of boots walking through deep mud. Most disturbing however was its habitual flatulence. Consequently, throughout the day its loud ripping farts provided a source of amusement for the children and an embarrassment for adults. To make matters all the worse, the noise effects were accompanied by a pervasive stench that proved easily resistant to air fresheners, pot pourri and the most compelling of disinfectants. In this last respect, Lorna and Theresa used to whisper, joking together that the dog and the man shared noticeably similar personality traits. They would laugh and giggle at the dog's eating habits and, although their stepfather thought their behaviour was out of affection for his pet, in actual fact much of their amusement was prompted by their imagining how Jimmy would look doing what the dog did.

'It eats like a pig and even walks the way he does." Theresa would say with tears of enjoyment shining her cheeks. And, on the first occasion that they saw the animal make sexual overtures to its owner's leg, such was their mirth that they had to leave the room for fear of their secret being discovered.

No one knew for certain what the age of the dog might be only that he was fully matured. The occasional gray flecks on his snout seemed to indicate his autumn years had arrived but Jimmy would have none of it.

"He's still nowt but a pup." he would argue defensively.

It was obvious however, that Bad Lad had lost much of his natural agility. His arrogance in the face of boundary infringements by others of his kind was now merely bravado. He still retained a deep bark and continued to bustle aggressively when challenged but, in the months before his accident, he seldom sought to actively engage with any interloper. Suddenly it seemed, much like his master, his performance lacked conviction.

It was about ten o'clock on a Saturday morning when Bad Lad went missing. Lorna was first to notice his absence and at Jimmy's request, she went to look for him. It was a task she did not object to as it released her from the shop. Also, despite the fact that she would normally try to avoid the company of both man and dog, Lorna found that whilst she despised the one she still had some sympathy with the other.

She was home within half an hour. She had spotted Bad Lad at the rear of a local pub rooting amongst the bins and had called to him from across the road. The lorry driver had had no chance to stop.

Some measure of Jimmy's affection for his pet might be judged by the fact that he actually closed the shop for an hour in order to recover the animal's body. Loma led him to the scene and he wrapped the victim in a blanket and carried it home through the streets, the tears running unashamedly down his face the while. Passers-by, many of whom were customers of the butcher, stopped to watch and although one or two of the teenagers sniggered at the sight, most nodded their sympathy or shook their heads at the apparent tragedy. The animal was eventually laid out on the backyard table and, watched through the kitchen window by Lorna, Theresa, Peter and Patrick, Jimmy took a clean floor cloth and gently wiped the fur free of bloodstains

What's he doing Ma? "Patrick asked.

"Shush Patrick," his Mother replied;" can't you see he's upset."

Patrick was unimpressed and soon wandered off to play elsewhere. Peter however, his face glued to the glass, was seen to cry softly alongside Theresa. Even Lorna began to feel sorry. She had never witnessed her Stepfather exhibit quite so much tenderness before. Normally it was difficult to gauge Jimmy's responses. In the girl's eyes his usual show of affection was always shallow, betrayed by a display of shiftiness in his manner and his use of exaggerated and unnecessary language. Now his behaviour concentrated her feeling of guilt and almost made her regret her opinion if not her treatment of the man. Indeed, he was so affected that she determined to express her sympathy to him privately and at the soonest opportunity.

That evening after supper, Jimmy declared solemnly that he would take the animal to his allotment for burial and, without knowing why she did so, Loma immediately offered to accompany him. She could see that her Mother approved the offer even if her brothers and sister looked surprised.

Jimmy's allotment was a good ten minutes drive away and they made the journey in total silence. Bad Lad was wrapped in the blanket from his basket and, despite the obvious threat to hygiene, the carcass was placed on one of the wooden trays normally used for delivering joints of meat and laid it in the back of the butcher's van. Lorna had not visited the allotment before and was therefore surprised to find it quite so well kept. There were neat rows of vegetables, some supported by canes in a weed free plot of carefully tended garden. A picket fence defined the area and at one end a garden shed housed a sundry collection of tools and garden implements as well as an old settee. They carried the dead animal between them on the meat tray all the way to the shed.

"Put him down here Lorna love and I'll get a spade." Jimmy muttered.

He opened the brass padlock on the door with a small key and pulled back the hasp.

"We'll plant him near the shed—so I can keep his grave nice." He added.

The dog was duly laid to rest in a small oblong plot originally intended to accommodate a few rows of onions and Jimmy erected a discrete marker made from an off-cut of planking. He told Loma that he would inscribe his pet's name on it with a soldering iron, when he had more time.

The burial over, they stood for a minute regarding their handiwork and Lorna was quite shocked when she noticed that the butcher had tears in his eyes. Suddenly she again felt sorry for him. However much she might despise him in normal circumstances, to see him react with such a depth of emotion over the loss of his dog, touched her. Quietly she put her hand in his and squeezed his fingers. His grief was infectious and she found herself crying softly alongside him. It had been her intention to sympathise and act as a support but her actions only seemed to make things worse. Jimmy cried all the more. Now he sobbed openly and, even though he tried to quell his outburst with a large white handkerchief, his big frame heaved and quivered and the tears continued to flow.

Lorna was at a loss. Her eyes dried quickly but the openness of his sorrow increasingly came as a shock. Her only experience of a similar situation had been after her Father's death and it seemed to her that Jimmy was undergoing the same kind of feelings. Consequently, she felt a responsibility to try and alleviate his suffering. She wanted to say something, words that would help make it right but she did not feel equipped with sufficient vocabulary. Instead she put an arm round his waist and whispered," There—there." It appeared to have an effect and after a moment or two he calmed down and dried his face for the last time. Finally he turned to her and gave a weak smile," You're quite a Lass—thanks Pet."

For the first and only time, Lorna imagined a bond between them. She smiled back and suggested he should wash his face before they went home," You wouldn't want Mam to see you in that state now would you?" she asked.

He nodded obediently and led the way back into his little hut. After he had splashed water on his face, he sat down on the threadbare settee to dry himself on an old towel. She stood nearby, watchful in her new capacity. He folded the old piece of towel and laid it on the arm of the chair.

"I owe you one love." he said quietly," Come here."

She went to him and he hugged her. She felt him sigh, a sign she thought that meant he was recovered. He looked into her face and kissed her.

It was during the kiss she realised his attitude had changed. His lips started on her cheek but then, without warning, slowly slid round to encompass her mouth. Instinctively she moved her head but he persisted. She tried to step back but he held her. He sat back in the old settee, dragging her with him. Now his hands began an inevitable progress and she felt the warmth of them on her bare legs. The panic surged but her arms were held tight to her body, suffocating her movement. He was so strong. It seemed that it was no effort for him to hold her with one arm and to pull her across to a half sitting position on his knee.

She screamed only once but the sound was choked back when, in response, he gripped her throat in his big hand, the one that circled her shoulders.

"Don't be silly Lonny. Just lay still Pet . . . . it's nice. You'll like it—and better me than some spotty guttersnipe in some back street—there now!"

Jimmy used her that night. For more than forty-five minutes she trembled as he touched her, the more so when he made her touch him and the whole thing was made the worse by the fact that he talked to her continuously. He tried to convince her it was his responsibility to introduce her to sex; that she would be grateful to him later when she grew up and, that this was only the first of many occasions when he would come to instruct her. He said that she should not discuss it with her Mother and that his wife had asked him not to tell her when it happened—but that she knew it would happen. Before he released her he also said that he would provide the same service for her sister—and her brothers, "One big happy family." he said.

Before that evening Lorna had regarded Jimmy as nothing more than an inconvenience, an impediment to her free will and a trial that had to be endured until such time that she could leave home and make her own way. After the episode in the garden hut however, the hatred started. A deep and enduring alienation that would make her wish the man dead—worse than dead. Even in her juvenile mind there was a level of understanding that described his behaviour as being subnormal. And it was not simply his treatment of her that caused such a depth of feeling but the fact that she knew she could not tell anyone, a knowledge that made her begin to despise herself. The hatred was accompanied therefore by a sickening revulsion more profound than any emotion Lorna had ever experienced.

When they returned home that night her Mother had supper ready but Lorna could not bear to eat alongside her stepfather. She feigned an upset stomach and went to her bed. Her Mother came to see her later and sat at the side of the bed. She told her eldest daughter how much Jimmy had appreciated her help and valued her sympathy over his dog and how she herself hoped that this might be the beginning of a new relationship between them.

"I know you and Jimmy haven't always hit it off Lonny," she said, "and that is understandable. I knew he could never take the place of your real father—but he does love you—all of you."

Lorna snuggled down beneath the blankets, hiding her face as much as possible but did not respond. Was it possible that her mother had sanctioned

Jimmy's actions? Did she really know what he had planned? She did not trust herself to say anything but her Mother seemed not to notice.

"Jimmy tells me you helped bury the dog near his hut," she added, "thank you for being so caring."

She leaned over and kissed the top of the girl's head, stroked her hair lovingly as she muttering her good night and then left the room.

It was hard for Loma to properly accommodate what had happened. Even her behaviour was confusing. Perhaps she could have fought him harder—could she? She might have run off, causing a search to be made and drawing attention to the situation—perhaps? There was just the possibility that if she had made a complete confession to her Mother, she may have found a sympathetic ally—but she hadn't. In actual fact, she had almost frozen with fear when he had grabbed her. Her limbs had become heavy, almost too heavy to command and it felt as though she had no control over herself. She viewed the occasion, as if from a distance, almost as a disinterested observer rather than a prime participant. Jimmy was a pig but she knew that with every second that passed, every delay that occurred, the chance of exposing him for what he was diminished.

It was only as she finally drifted off to sleep that she thought for the first time about his promise to use her sister and brothers in the same way. A threat that horrified her, making her shiver in fear for them. If that were to happen, she promised herself, she would be forced to do something drastic. She chose to believe however, that it had been an idle threat and that Jimmy would never to dare to assault the others. Consequently she persuaded herself that her own needs had priority, a complete reversal of her usual protective role.

It was several nights later before Jimmy started to visit her bedroom on a regular basis and some time before the nightmares started again.

CHAPTER EIGHT

1972

News: A terrifying wave of shooting and bombing has engulfed Northern Ireland following the reintroduction, after 10 years, of the Special Powers Act regulation, allowing for internment without trial of political subversives. By last night (Aug.9th) at least 11 civilians had been killed on the streets of Belfast. They included a Roman Catholic priest, two women and a boy of fifteen. At Claudy, near the border with the Irish Republic, a member of the Ulster Defence Regiment died in an ambush. At Armagh, a civilian died in hospital after a gun battle between troops and a passing car . . . A statement issued on behalf of the Commander, Land Forces, Major General Robert Ford, said," Since early this morning the security forces have been engaged in a constant war of attrition against terrorists armed with automatic weapons and petrol and gelignite bombs."

Diary: I never thought I would ever say so but thank God for school. This is the only place where I feel comfortable. Home is a nightmare. I daren't write down the things that happen there. Next month I will be sixteen—1 pray to St. Jude, patron of lost causes that things will be different.

* * *

The gymnasium at the Convent school stood apart from the main buildings, occupying a position in the centre of the grounds. It was connected to the Upper School block by a long corridor that bisected the playground. Access by Lower School pupils from the opposite side was therefore, across an open space consisting of part lawn and part tarmac. The entrance on the side for the younger children was, by way of double doors which were shielded from the elements by a timbered vestibule. This refuge proved to be a favoured lunch-time location where small groups of girls often met in private to share their secrets. The dining hall was sited on the ground floor of the Lower school and each day two sittings were accommodated there. Younger children ate first, leaving the longer session afterwards for those over fourteen years of age. Members of the teaching staff doing a lunch time duty were divided equally between the sittings.

Not surprisingly, Helen Bonar found the vestibule at the far end of the gymnasium to be a convenient spot in which to hold her daily surgery. After the first sitting, she would arrive there each day with a small group of favoured petitioners and acolytes to dispense her worldly wisdom. As the same people were to be found regularly in attendance, the sessions soon acquired the character of a private club or secret society. Admittance to this inner circle therefore became a matter of status and it was not too long before a procedure had to be invented by incumbent members, in order to filter applications. Helen argued that this was necessary due to the limited space available but everyone, including Lorna, understood that access to the vestibule was more a matter of a pupil's face fitting the desired profile than numbers.

Typically, the selection process took account of each applicant's attitude to the school's authority. They did not, for example, admit 'snitches' or 'swots'; they considered a declared interest in boys to be a healthy response—and anyone saying that sex was a sin was automatically declared persona non grata. Finally, the procedure aimed to take into account the applicant's experience with boys—if you'd never been kissed—properly kissed with full tonguing, then there was little use in trying to make your way into Helen's group. Conversely however, if you were boastful enough to claim that experience described by the Church as 'carnal knowledge', Helen would veto the application. So far only two girls had tried that tack, obviously imagining that such a claim would endear them. They were not to know that, as regards her area of expertise, Helen was proprietorial in the extreme.

It soon became obvious that the development of, what became known as the Vestibule Club, substantially and increasingly changed the nature of Helen's counselling activities. Whereas, at one time she was only too pleased to answer questions and to give advice to anyone who might ask, as the club became more and more exclusive, she was more likely to smile wistfully in the face of such questions and say that she shouldn't talk about such things.

"Why don't you ask Sister Mary that?" she would reply, knowing full well that no-one was going to raise matters about sex during Religious Education lessons.

Needless to say, the Vestibule Club's cliquishness left many pupils feeling thoroughly rejected. And although membership was still seen as being desirable, criticism of the Club's practices became common. It thereby attracted a reputation far in excess of its actual importance and it was not long before staff started to become aware of its potential for disruption

In actual fact much of what took place in the vestibule was merely gossip. The girls would spend their time exchanging anecdotes, salacious tales of rape and the like, often culled from the pages of less than desirable periodicals and newspapers. They would air their views on cases of indecent assault and sometimes take votes on which punishments were seen as most appropriate. However, if any Parliament had seen fit to pass the more imaginative motions approved by the club, public executions and mutilation of prisoners would have made an immediate comeback, leaving any number of the male offenders deficit in the reproductive organs department. It seemed that the more shocking the story, the more extreme the violence then the greater its success with the group.

Consequently with the passage of time and as the limits of imaginations were stretched, an element of competition crept into the discussions. The girls showed off, vying with one another to find the most outrageous tales and the more disgraceful the account, the more explicit the descriptions, the more they were appreciated.

Lorna and Helen sat in judgement over these affairs together but, unusually, the girl from Ireland always deferred to the other's opinion. She had come to hero worship Helen, imagining that she represented all those qualities of maturity to which she herself aspired. By now they were literally inseparable. They had even engineered to sit next to one another in class; they shared their breaks and lunch-times and spent more and more time together out of school.

Helen nevertheless, found it difficult if not impossible to understand Lorna's sense of duty on Saturdays.

"But why do you have to work in that awful shop every week? "She would ask belligerently and no matter what Loma said, it did nothing to convince her friend. Finally, after continuous attempts to persuade Lorna to renege on the job had failed, she suggested that she came along herself to help at the butcher's shop.

"1 suppose it's a case of Mohammed and the mountain," she said mysteriously, "and anyway, if I help out perhaps you will be able to get away all the quicker at the end of the day. We could go to the pictures eh?"

Lorna did not want to deflate her friend's enthusiasm, but she knew secretly that Jimmy would not let her go until it was six o'clock, the time he normally closed up. She also knew that it was unlikely that her Mother would give permission for her to go out on a Saturday night, even with a girl-friend. 'The town's always full of drunks at the week-end.' was one of her Mother's favourite complaints and she would often as not add that young women were asking for trouble if they went down town when the drunks were about. It was a theme that her Mother had recently adopted more and more often of late. A prelude to other warnings about the appetites of young men and how her daughter should never place her trust in any of them.

"If she did but know it," Lorna boasted to Helen," I probably know more about men than she does."

When Saturday came round that week, Helen was as good as her promise. Granted, she did not arrive at the shop until ten o'clock, by which time Loma had already done two hours work but when she did arrive, she quickly won Jimmy's respect by the level of her effort. Nothing was too much for her. She wiped dishes and tidied the window display; she worked the mincing machine and did not balk, even when she was asked to collect chicken innards in a plastic bag. In the afternoon she even started to give change at the counter. Jimmy was full of admiration and to amuse his customers, he kept introducing her as his new girlfriend. Lorna found his comments offensive but determined to say nothing.

Helen played up to his chat and seemed to enjoy all the attention. At some point she whispered to Lorna that serving behind the counter was a bit like being on stage. She was always talking about being an actress and the shop appeared to satisfy at least some of that inclination.

"I see now why you do it," she said, "I could get hooked on this myself."

Lorna was glad of the company but as the day progressed, she became concerned at Jimmy's attitude to her friend. His attentions and his comments became increasingly suggestive. Since the episode when he had kissed Lorna, he had attempted to be familiar with her in public on a number of occasions. He always wanted to lay a hand on her shoulder when she stood near to him, on her back as she passed by and once, when he came up behind her as she was wrapping up a customer's purchases; he had leaned into her, pressing himself against her bottom. His frequent attempts to kiss her had met with total resistance but he devised a strategy to legitimise his efforts. He suggested to her Mum that all the children should kiss both their parents before they went to bed.

"It's nice to show your feelings," he had claimed," and there's nothing wrong in kissing your Dad goodnight."

Her Mother had thought it a sign of genuine affection for his inherited family and supported him in his request. Even when all four of her children protested, she argued on his side. The nightly kiss had therefore become institutionalised and the children's objections were overruled. Their reluctance was seen as mawkishness and a sign of ingratitude inappropriate to their new condition.

Peter was the only one to persist with his objections in public and each time Jimmy kissed him, he would make an exaggerated show of wiping his cheek before he kissed his Mother. But this performance tended only to amuse the adults, their laughter emphasising his embarrassment. Little Theresa also hated the contact and several times Lorna had found her crying into her pillow.

"I don't like him anymore," she told Lorna one night," I don't like how fat he is, I don't like his smell and I hate it when he puts his mouth over mine. He's disgusting."

And whilst she was relieved to find that her feelings about the butcher were not unique, Lorna had a foreboding of more difficult times ahead. Secretly she knew that Jimmy's attentions, his kisses and his touching, were unnaturally sexual. He often came to her room late at night, " . . . to tuck you in . . ." he would say but it proved ever more difficult to get him to leave. She could not in all conscience bring herself to express her complaints to her Mother. All too easily they could be seen as a betrayal. Her Mother had been happier in the last few months than Lorna could ever remember her being and she did not want to ruin that. Nevertheless, through her conversations in the 'vestibule', the girl had gained some understanding of where Jimmy's behaviour might lead. Two of the other girls who met there had talked about being touched by male relatives. According to Helen who was as explicit as ever, they had experienced what amounted to an indecent assault, one by an uncle and the other by her older brother. Significantly, neither of the girls had found a convenient way of letting their mothers know. It was all just too embarrassing.

Not surprisingly, although the whole of the Vestibule Club had been sworn to secrecy, Lorna never found the courage to tell them of her own fears. She and Helen shared the most intimate detail of their various desires and feelings but her ongoing concern about the butcher's behaviour was a taboo subject.

"Here don't stand there daydreaming." Jimmy remarked as he stroked a large blade across his steel.

Having been caught up by her personal concerns, Lorna had stopped pushing meat scraps through the mincer and he had noticed from across the other side of the shop.

"That one is in a world of her own most of the time." he said, shaking his head.

This time he made the comment to one of his customers, a well-dressed, elderly lady with a big nose.

"You're lucky to get 'em to work at all these days,' the woman replied, "My niece wouldn't raise a finger not even if I burst into flames. But these two are proper little grafters though. Mind, I didn't know you had three daughters."

Jimmy laughed an affected, diplomatic sort of laugh.

"I don't." he answered, "just the two and two sons. Mind you, I wouldn't object to adopting this one."

As he spoke this time he put his hand in the small of Helen's back and placed his cheek close to hers.

"She's a right little cracker. Works like a Trojan and smells as sweet at any rose."

Helen just grinned but the old woman gave her a long look.

"At her age a rose shouldn't need quite so much make-up though. Some might think it provocative." she said critically.

Jimmy sprang to her defence.

"Each to his own Ma, I happen think it suits her—and what's more, it's nice to see young lasses trying to make themselves presentable for the public."

The old woman seemed unconvinced and as she left, she muttered something about girls being old before their time. The door closed behind her and Jimmy made an insulting remark under his breath.

"And don't you go taking any offence at her Helen. She's a silly old boot. She's well behind the times—probably just jealous of your lovely complexion. Now—when we finish up tonight, I think Lorna's Mum would like it if you stopped for tea. Eh? What do you say?'

Helen's immediate agreement caused Lorna to stare hard at her friend. So much for going out to the pictures, she thought. But Helen seemed to have forgotten all about the arrangement.

Just after five o'clock Jimmy indicated that they should begin the evening clear-up and he began the task of emptying the window display. Lorna and Helen tidied the shop, washing surfaces, putting the working parts of the mincer to soak in the back-shop sink and clearing away any scraps of bone or fat. Lorna ran a bucket of hot water from the ascot heater and added a generous measure of Domestos before wiping over the block and as she set about it with the scrubbing brush, Helen started to sweep the floor.

At the end of the day, most of the cut meat on trays was relocated in the counter top freezer but the larger joints, including a leg of beef which had hung throughout the day from one of the rails, were transferred to the big walk-in fridge in the corner. Moving the leg of beef took considerable strength and help was needed with the big hook when it was re-hung. As there were already several other carcasses of pigs and lambs hanging in the fridge obscuring the space, Helen, stepped inside to hold the hook at the ready. Lifting the beef caused Jimmy's face to turn red and by the time he had staggered across and into the fridge, he was panting like the proverbial 'broken winded old horse'.

Lorna was still busy scrubbing the block but she heard Helen's saying how strong Jimmy must be to carry such a heavy weight. A moment later, after the sound of the hook taking the strain, she heard her school-friend squeal. For a second she thought Helen may have trapped a finger or been jammed between the carcasses, common enough accidents in such a confined space but the giggles that followed soon made it clear what was happening. Lorna's stomach sank, if Jimmy was making a pass at her friend, the secret of his nightly visits might be exposed. She felt her colour rise and a wave of guilt immersed her. Helen finally emerged a moment later and her face was flushed. She was a little breathless and clearly excited.

According to Jimmy, the vast majority of effort involved in running a butcher's shop comprising a one man business, took place behind the scenes. The necessary preparation of small-meats—sausages, pies etceteras, he would claim was a specialised skill. However, the purchase and storage of the basic product, carcasses of lamb, mutton, beef and pork, whether frozen or bought on the hoof also took considerable organisation.

"Fresh meat has a limited shelf-life," he would say, "and its storage needs careful consideration."

Consequently it was the Local Authority Health Inspectors that caused him his biggest headache. Any shop involved in the sale of cooked meats alongside uncooked meats had to observe the strictest code of hygiene. Cleaning and disinfecting machines and work-surfaces, storage containers and tools, therefore took considerable time even after the doors had been closed to shoppers and, in this last respect especially, it was argued that no self-respecting tradesman would dare to cut corners. Inspectors insisted that the commitment of sole-trader's needs to good practice must be absolute. As far as hygiene was concerned, Jimmy trod a tightrope. He did only just as much as he had to and complained at every turn about, what he saw as, the unfair work load.

Increasingly he was in competition with the supermarkets that stole his customers through undercutting his prices. They had no problem with matters of hygiene, the investment that they had made in new appliances and their advantage in having more staff made the task of keeping the meat counters clean, easy.

The option of personal service however, was the one remaining advantage retained by the small shop owners like Jimmy and this was his greatest strength. He was an excellent salesman. On a one-to-one basis and in the context of customer satisfaction he had no peer. The same was also true of his butchering skills. His boning knife left no scrap of meat and his joints were cut with the precision of a surgeon. Unfortunately the development of his business did not depend solely on these skills and a second set of inspectors—those from the Inland Revenue—regularly caused him a different kind of headache.

Although Jimmy was in some sense a sharp operator, his skill as an accountant was less than perfect. He was seldom able to make good sense out of columns of figures and, like many others in small businesses, preferred to do most of his deals in cash. He found himself therefore, in a continuous dialogue with Inspectors from the Inland Revenue, causing his business to be constantly under strain. Needless to say, under the brave exterior of his performance behind the counter of his shop, he lived in continuous fear of unwelcome visits from both public heath officials and from tax investigators.

Saturdays were a crucial time they were the busiest days and the day when the largest stock change took place. It was only after calculating the profit from Saturday that Jimmy was able to estimate the viability of his week's work. However, it was also on Saturday evenings that he entered the financial information in his accounts book, and this was an event that he did not look forward to.

Having had a good day in the shop that Saturday, when Jimmy accompanied Lorna and Helen back to the house, he seemed pleased with himself but his mood changed as soon as he opened his mail. He usually left before the post was delivered each morning and the evening ritual of opening his letters was always done before the kitchen fire with a mug of tea in his hand.

"Buggar me, "he exclaimed, clutching an official looking letter." they only want to charge me . . . . well . . . a lot of money. A fine—they say for evading tax."

As he spoke he stomped across to the table and slapped the headed paper on the wooden top. Helen was in the process of being introduced to Lorna's Mother as Jimmy made his exclamation.

"What's the trouble now Jimmy?" Lorna's Mother asked.

"The trouble is that those bastards at the Tax office think they can screw even more money from me. Well they can go to hell. I'll fight this—yes that's what I'll do. I'll give old Jenkins the accountant a ring."

Before Lorna's Mum could say anymore he stamped past her into the passage where the telephone sat on the hall table and began to dial a number. Surreptitiously her Mum indicated the stairs, "Might be better if you girls made yourself scarce for a while. Why don't you take Helen up to your room Lorna "I'll call you when tea's ready?"

This advice was delivered in a half whisper and it was obvious to the girls that the new Mrs. Ungerside wanted time to smooth the domestic situation in private. They went quietly up the stairs.

Once in Lorna's room, a tiny box-room at the back of the house, Helen sat on her bed as her friend closed the door.

"He can be a right swine sometimes." Lorna said.

"Funny eh he was as nice as pie in the shop." Helen said.

She giggled and winked as Lorna turned to face her, "Nicer in fact. Did you see?"

"See what?"

"He couldn't keep his hands off me all day. Every chance he got he was touching . . . ."

"Oh God I'm sorry Helen. I should have warned you about him. He can be creepy and . . ."

"No." her friend interrupted, "Don't worry about it. I didn't mind. It's quite nice to attract an older man."

Lorna pulled a face. "Older men you can keep all that they may have—and this 'older man' happens to be a dirty old man, a dirty old fat man at that."

Helen laughed, "Lorna sometimes you're still a little prude."

"No I am not. I just object to a step father who gropes me every chance he gets."

"Well I didn't mind at all. He grabbed me in the fridge you know—kissed me—tongue and everything."

"He didn't?"

"Yes he did—and he tried to get his hand away. But I stopped him. Well, a kiss is one thing but . . . ."

"The dirty bastard I should tell him."

"Hey don't do that. He didn't mean any harm," she smirked and lay back on the bed, "I suppose some men are bound to find me irresistible."

"Helen please—stop it. He's my stepfather; he's married to my Mother. Listen to yourself. You sound like a prostitute."

The accusation rapidly brought Helen to a sitting position again.

"What a damned cheek. You sure it's not just jealousy. You said yourself he'd tried it on with you—which was news to me by the way—and I'm supposed to be your best friend. Never mentioned that did you?"

By now Lorna had perched herself on the stool that sat in front of her little dressing-table and for a moment or two the two girls faced one another in silence through the mirror Lorna was the first to look away.

"I'm sorry Helen," she said at last in a small voice, "but he gets me so mad. You realise of course, he's a pervert."

"So fancying me makes him a pervert eh?"

"No of course not but trying to arouse girls so much younger than him is perversion—and it's also illegal." she paused to see if she was having any effect, then added," I don't know quite what I should do about him."

This time the reply came quickly.

"Nothing—that's what you should do my girl. If it ever came out that he tried to touch me up—and that I laughed about it—Christ Almighty. You just say nothing. Anyway, you wouldn't want your Mother to know that he'd been in your knickers—would you?"

"He hasn't" Lorna lied, her face flushing with guilt, "and he never will—

Please God. But we shouldn't let him get away with this."

Loma was almost as furious with her friend as she was with Jimmy. She could not comprehend how she could allow such a slimy middle-aged man get anywhere near her. And to imagine that she would approve of his actions was beyond her understanding. However, the disagreement caused both girls to feel slighted and for the first time in their relationship they felt awkwardness between them. Casual conversation seemed almost impossible but, even as the thought crossed Lorna's mind, Helen bridged the gap.

"Hey, do you realise—we're arguing over a man." Her laugh was infectious. "Now how's that for being an adult. Not yet sixteen years of age and we're fighting over a man in his fifties. I always told you we were more mature than the others at school."

Loma could not help but smile. In a funny kind of way Helen was right. Most girls of their age would have ended up in tears. Secretly however, she hoped that no one else would end up in that state—especially not her

CHAPTER NINE

1973

News: A Loyalist vigilante group, styling themselves 'The Ulster Freedom Fighters', have claimed responsibility for a series of sectarian murders in Northern Ireland.

After two men—one a 17-year old-youth called Daniel Ruse—were shot dead in Belfast, a caller to a newspaper described one of the killings thus: "We gave him two in the back and one in the head. There will be more." The Defence Minister Lord Carrington, refused to comment today on a claim by the convicted bank robber—Kenneth Littlejohn—that he had been employed by M16. Littlejohn made his allegations at his Dublin trial at which he was sentenced to twenty years. Some Ulster MPs said last night that the Littlejohn affair might help to explain the planting of bombs in Dublin—leading to anti IRA laws—and called for an inquiry into Intelligence activities in the Republic.

Diary: There are things I fear that I dare not write down, but discovery is more likely than ever before and the constant fear of it makes a sweat break out all over my body. I have prayed for guidance—for help and for a solution but no-one listens. There is no-one to tell, no-one to talk to, and no-one with which to share this dreadful secret. Life is unbearable. Help me St. Jude; I really am a lost cause.

* * *

Loma was to take her 'A' Levels early. She had worked hard and her teachers forecast good results. Consequently, she had been offered conditional places both at Warwick and Durham universities these being her first two choices. Unfortunately, as far as her teachers were concerned, during the period of the examinations, she appeared to suffer a sudden and unforeseeable lack of confidence, resulting in a performance far less than that which everyone knew she was capable. Indeed the difference was so marked that after the last English paper, her tutor Mm. Jenkins called her to her study to discuss the reason.

Mrs. Jenkins had taken a special interest in Lorna's progress mid over the years had devoted much time to ensure a satisfactory academic outcome. Needless to say she had been shocked when Lorna appeared to falter. It was her estimation that only something of major importance could have distracted the girl and she was determined to discover the cause.

"I had a glance at your last paper," she said as soon as Lorna was seated, "and I must admit that I was surprised and disappointed. What has happened Lorna? The questions should have been perfect for you—but you tackled them as if you'd never considered them before."

Lorna sat in silence offering neither excuse nor explanation.

"I can't help if you don't tell me what might be wrong." the teacher added. It was a tortuous moment for the young seventeen year old. She knew full well that the quality of her answers had been below par, more importantly she also knew why.

Since just before her sixteenth birthday Loma had begun to menstruate. However, she had been well prepared for the change in her body chemistry.

As was her usual practice, her friend Helen had provided a wealth of information and advice but it had been her Mother who had been the greatest help. She had ensured that her daughter could anticipate the event from the most balanced perspective and in the process, for the first time their relationship had prospered. It was a step nearer to full maturity and, given the factual basis of the information communicated to the girl, an occasion to be appreciated rather than feared. Or at least that had been the theory. Neither Helen nor Lorna's Mother were to know that it was the increased possibility of pregnancy that was the root of the girl concern, prompting her continuous nightmares of conscience.

Lorna's Stepfather Jimmy had continued to rely on her enforced silence and persisted in visiting her in her bedroom, at least once each week. By now these appearances, always in the early hours of the morning, had become almost institutionalised practice and, as the perpetrator well knew, once established it was easier for the girl to tolerate them than to raise objections. For Loma, the nausea associated with Jimmy's demands had been subsumed by her need to protect her Mother from the knowledge of his perversion. However, with the development of her new physical status and through being better informed about such matters, her fear of the likely consequences increased. Now, each month was another crisis to be overcome, each relief short-lived and each contact more repulsive than the last. To make matters all the worse, her paternal rapist refused to use any kind of protection and between obscenities would whisper his boasts of the fact in her subservient ear.

The arrival of puberty had focused Lorna's thinking about her situation and she seemed to spend much of her time reviewing the history of Jimmy's abuse of her. It had started soon after his marriage to her Mother and for some time thereafter the considerable shock she experienced as a consequence, immobilized her emotions. More recently however, a subtle change had developed. Due to the frequency and regularity of his visits, the occasions had acquired a kind of normality and, however much the girl's revulsion usually, within the time parameters of his visits, there were periods when she had almost begun, to enjoy what he did to her; an ambiguity, prompting her to hate herself almost as much as she hated him. Not surprisingly therefore, the preparation necessary for her examinations suffered. She could not concentrate still less could she rely on her memory.

Nevertheless, given her record of achievement, she might have managed still to satisfy the promise of her potential except for the fact that only four weeks before the first paper she had discovered that she was pregnant.

Who to tell and how to tell them became the all consuming consideration of all her day-time thinking. The most natural repository of her trust should have been her Mother but that was impossible given Jimmy's involvement. She considered, trying to keep his name a secret but concluded that the blame she would accrue in apparently having agreed to a sexual liaison with some other person would be unfair. Why should she, as the victim accept responsibility for the actions of a child molester, she argued. But if she told her mother the truth then all her previous efforts would have been for nothing. She might have confided in Theresa had their relationship been sound but she knew her sister would immediately report the fact to theft Mother. It was an insoluble conundrum.

That afternoon, she sat in Mrs. Jenkins's study listening to her tutor probing for an acceptable reason for her failure. Clearly her tutor was sympathetic and it suddenly occurred to her that this was the person to ask for help. She had exercised patience when Lorna had been slow to grasp the subtleties of more complex texts; she had argued her case when the Principal had threatened to discipline Lorna for a minor transgression and, most recently, she had spent considerable time and effort after school to ensure all the required assignments were completed.

"I'm pregnant." She said suddenly.

For a moment Mrs. Jenkins was silent then she came round the desk and sat close to her pupil. There was no purpose in further subterfuge, so when her teacher asked about the father, Lorna told her the truth. It was her first opportunity to tell her story and she did so in great detail, holding nothing back. Mrs. Jenkins listened without comment and when she did respond there was no hint of criticism or judgement. In her usual practical way, she itemised the alternatives, making a brief estimation of the consequences in each case and when she finished she took Lorna's hand and said, "Whatever you decide to do Lonny, if you want me to help—I will."

The relief was just as if a huge weight had been removed from the girl's shoulders and quietly, she began to cry.

"What do you think I should do Mrs. Jenkins?" she asked finally.

"You're a clever girl Lonny and you have the opportunity of a good career—but—should you opt to keep the child, life will prove very difficult for some years to come." She paused to offer the box of paper tissues. "I know you were raised with a strong religious conviction but—given the circumstances—I think you should consider terminating the pregnancy."

It was the one option Lorna was most afraid of voicing. The notion of abortion was contrary to everything she believed—and yet—it was the one way out of her misery without hurting her Mother or bringing disgrace to the family.

Mrs. Jenkins told her that she knew of a private clinic in London where such a procedure could be carried out discretely and that she was prepared to design a cover story, sufficient to persuade her Mother that Lorna was away on study leave. She even offered to help finance the operation.

"There is only one condition Lorna," she said," you must stop your Stepfather. However you do it, he must be made to understand that he no longer has any access to you. If you want me to, I will speak to him.'

As good as her word, that same day Mrs. Jenkins telephoned the shop and asked Jimmy to call into the school for a chat. Imagining that he was being treated as the natural father, he promptly agreed and an appointment was made for five thirty the following day. Initially Lorna had said that she would like to be present when Mrs. Jenkins spoke to Jimmy but her teacher persuaded her that her presence would limit what she could say. Conversely, Mrs. Jenkins, with a wary eye on any possible legal reaction, chose to have Miss Lincoln, a member of her faculty, present as a witness and Lorna was asked to wait in a nearby office. The victim of Jimmy's attentions was never told in any real detail what actually transpired that afternoon. She saw him arrive and forty minutes later she saw him leave. After his departure Mrs. Jenkins came to see her and said simply that in future she would not be bothered by him ever again. She added that, in recognition of his responsibilities, Jimmy had kindly offered to pay for any treatment or allied expenses Lorna may accrue when she went to London. The girl was amazed at the result and again, her feeling of relief left her tearful. It was only two days later before Mrs. Jenkins announced that the arrangements for her operation had been agreed with the London hospital. A letter was sent to Lorna's Mother telling her that her daughter would need to attend a series of seminars specially designed for those students contemplating a career in teaching. The letter also stated that Jimmy had already agreed to foot the bill.

Within seven days the emergency was over without ill-effect. Given the time to think about her future, Lorna also decided to pursue the idea of a teaching career. Her results arrived during the summer holidays and although they were less than she had hoped for originally, they proved sufficient to gain her a place at a Teacher Training College in Chorley in Lancashire. She would study there for a Teaching Certificate and follow this by an extra year to take her degree. Neither Lorna nor her Stepfather ever referred to the change in their relationship still less to his visit to the school. The public image between them continued in exactly the same vein as before, the only difference being that his behaviour towards her was increasingly distant. He avoided even the most innocent physical contact and never again indulged in the suggestive banter that was previously his standard benchmark. Needless to say his nocturnal visits stopped completely. Consequently, for the first time since her Mothers marriage Lorna was able to rely on the privacy of her own space and she would remember the time until her departure to Lancashire as being the happiest she ever spent at home. Sadly about this time her friend Helen Bonar moved with her family to live in Colorado in the USA. This was a significant loss for Lorna and at a time when she was especially vulnerable.

CHAPTER TEN

1975

News: December 12th.

The Balcombe street siege ended peacefully today—six days after four IRA gunmen took a husband and wife hostage in their Marylebone flat. TV viewers saw police, wearing bullet proofed flak jackets and training pistols on every move, bring Mr. John Matthews aged 54 and his 53 year old wife Sheila to safety and take the hooded gunmen into custody.

Diary;

Just a few more days and we break for Christmas—deo gratias. I never imagined that working for a teaching degree could be so difficult or so all consuming. Thankfully, I seem to be making good progress and have decided already to concentrate on working in the Secondary sector. I had a nip of whiskey before going to bed and it helped me sleep—soundlessly and without the usual nightmares. Perhaps scotch is the solution to my night-time menagerie of dreams.

* * *

Tom liked the look of the girl, for a start she was tall and blond but more importantly, she filled the dress in all the right places.
"This is Connie," Paul said, "Connie—Tom."

"Hi." Tom grinned, taking the hand offered, immediately noticing the ring. That she was married and did not hide the fact was unusual. A married woman on the prod—some might see as a stimulus others, a sign of trouble. Tom decided that for the moment at least she was simply a date. As far as dates were concerned, Paul was a fixer and, as the recipient of the fixing in this instance, Tom was grateful. His new friend had a talent for arranging double dates and if that were not enough—for 'blind 'double dates. However, it was a convenience, as much dependant on their mutual need for economy as it was on their friendship. Since they shared a room in the lodgings, it made good sense to share the cost of dating and, with the difficulty of having to make the first move taken out of his hands; Tom was pleased to acknowledge his friend's aptitude. Paul was always at ease in the company of women. He brimmed with confident chat lines and maintained a level of eye to eye sincerity that would have enabled him to sell veal chops to vegetarians.

The teacher training college in Chorley was sited conveniently, just off the market place and, although it catered primarily for mature students, mainly married women starting late careers, there was nevertheless, a large cohort of females under the age of twenty-five. This was a private and readily available reservoir of sexual hope, as easily accessible as turning on a tap. (Paul's description) His friend had a perverse skill in coining phrases that likened women to public utilities. And, although he was a model of consideration in their presence, capriciously in the company of his male friends his references concerning his female companions were sometimes caustic often derogatory and inevitably vulgar.

Certainly, the college did have something of a reputation and one that was established long before Paul had arrived there. If the rumour factory was to be believed, marriages of students at the college would be tested to breaking point no matter what the constitution of the individual year group. Infidelity, it seemed, was a virus from which no-one was immune. Indeed, it was claimed (by Paul of course) that any number of females entrants made Chorley their first choice, simply in order to enjoy freedoms they may have missed in their youth. He never made a point of saying so but the same was also true for many male students, Tom included.

In fact however, Tom was from a very different mould. Chorley had not been his first choice and, at least initially, his familiarity with carnal pleasure had been limited to occasional fumbles in the back row of his local cinema with girls from his Sixth Form class. Consequently, although he had acquired the skill of loosening blouse buttons in the dark with one hand, to his continued embarrassment the intricacies of bras straps continued to elude him. To his surprise he found that his lack of experience was often seen as an advantage by the women of his more recent acquaintance. Their preference it seemed was for young men with less than average experience. Given this advantage and through the diligent organisation of his room-mate in arranging dates, his popularity amongst the population of female students had grown quickly. Albeit ten years or so late, it was his first taste of the Swinging Sixties.

In actual fact, Chorley had been the only college to offer Tom a place. His 'A' Level results had not been as good as expected and in the scramble to leave his family home in Durham city, he had been only too grateful to accept their offer. His main subject was history and his period, the Eighteenth and early Nineteenth Centuries. His special interest was that time known euphemistically as the 'Enlightenment' and his thesis was planned to include much about the French revolution. However, despite the fact that the college was an institution commissioned to train teachers, or that he had reached his second year without mishap, Tom remained uncertain if he had the capacity or the patience required to teach: a doubt that was not shared by his tutors who continued to believe that he had more than the necessary potential.

Connie, he discovered, was studying Science, a fact with which he became more thoroughly acquainted as the evening wore on. Throughout the movie, a popular science fiction epic, she was kind enough to give him a running commentary regarding the possibility of travel at speeds faster than light and, in a stage whisper; she discussed Einstein's theories on the subject and hypothesised about alternative dimensions. Later that night in a friend's flat, even as Tom helped her undress; she continued to lecture him on Quantum Mechanics. It proved a soulless coupling. The preoccupation of her casual chatter made close contact impossible and provided an effective immunisation against sexual passion.

An early lecture caused Connie to leave the flat before Tom was awake. He had not intended to spend the night but frustration had tired him out and he had fallen asleep despite himself.

He found the bathroom empty, save for the collection of underwear and tights that festooned the hanging space and, even though he felt it was a bit cheeky, he ran a bath. The hot soapy water made him feel much better and he set to with the shampoo to wash his hair. Consequently his face was covered in suds when the door opened.

"Oh sorry," the voice said," didn't know we had visitors."

It closed again before he had cleared his eyes. He had a vague recollection that someone had told him the flat was shared but he couldn't, for the life of him, remember who the other girl was. Guilt got him to his feet and, although the towels were still wet, he dried himself as best he could and dressed quickly.

He found the girl in the kitchen when he came through. She was dark haired and very attractive. When he opened the door she was just in the process of pouring coffee. She glanced up catching his eye.

"Hi—fancy a coffee? "She asked.

He hesitated. "Don't want to interrupt your breakfast." he replied.

"Well," she said impishly," as there's no hot water left I may as well take my time—black or white?"

He felt himself begin to blush but nodded and said that that black would be fine. He sat down. Without asking, she laid a place for him and served him toast on a white plate. "There's honey—but no jam or marmalade . . . ." she said sitting herself opposite. "As you can see we have a lot of visitors. A disparate collection some might say."

He ignored the reproach and accepted the hospitality in silence, feeling like he was being organised. A moment late she spoke again, this time just as he sipped the hot coffee.

"By the way—I'm Lorna." she said grinning, "I share this little palace with Connie—and a host of her occasional transients . . . , many of whom regularly use the hot water without so much as a by your leave."

He paused, the cup still to his lips and then he stood up, pushing back the chair.

"Okay." he said," Enough's enough. I'm sorry if I used all your hot water, I'm sorry if my predecessors ate your jam and your marmalade. I apologist for dating your flatmate and for staying overnight—but if you have a gripe, you should take it up with her. Manners don't cost much you know . . ."

She kept eye to eye contact and answered back immediately, "Not as much as hot water anyway."

He flushed again and felt his temper rise.

"Fine if you care to tell me how much I owe you, I'll settle my bill before I leave."

She continued to grin and suddenly he wanted to be out of there. He strode to the door but before he reached it she began to applaud him. Clapping like he had performed for her. He stopped and turned again.

"If you ask Connie nicely, "he snapped, "I'm sure she would even be able to fix you up with a blind date—maybe even someone who enjoys an argument . . . ."

There was a moment's silence, just time enough to appreciate how ridiculous the situation had actually become, and then they both laughed.

By lunch-time that same day Tom and Lorna had become friends. She discovered that he was also from the north of the country and that he was the son of a publican. In return, she had described her life as a child in Ireland and later the move to Thornaby on Tees, only a stone's throw from his own birthplace in Stockton. They got on so well together that they spent the rest of that day exploring their various likes and dislikes arguing politics and swopping favourite recipes for Italian food. Tom's very dry sense of humour was matched by Lorna's cynical and often irreverent observations, many of which shocked him but often as not, still managed to reduce him to tears of laughter.

She was by far the most attractive girl he had met since coming to Chorley and, if the attention she gave him was any indicator, he imagined that she must like him too. They went out in the late afternoon to a local pub and although she drank only half pints of cider, by early evening they were both quite merry. At closing time they strolled back through the streets arm in arm, chatting about their courses and their friends.

"Have you known Connie long" Lorna asked him casually?

"About twenty-four hours." he replied, grinning, "She was a blind date."

Lorna was quiet for two or three steps and, for a moment or two, Tom thought he could detect a note of disapproval.

"I've got this mate," he said defensively, "I share a room with this mate and really fancies himself. He's always fixing me up with strange women".

"Did you know she was married?"

The awkwardness was emphasised again and he wasn't sure where the question might lead. "I saw her wedding ring when she was introduced."

"So you did know?"

This time the interruption left no doubt about Laura's attitude. The question was accusatory. Before he could decide on an answer she continued," You certainly knew—before you went to bed with her."

He muttered something about free choice and not being the guardian of Connie's morals but although they still linked arms, the space between them had suddenly opened up. He glanced at her and saw she was frowning, staring down at the pavement, as they walked along. "Well—just so you don't get the wrong idea," she said," I don't make a habit of sleeping with anyone I've just met and I take the idea of commitment seriously."

"Okay," he answered, trying to lighten his reply," then I promise not to try

And seduce you straight away—not for another hour or so anyway."

She did not laugh.

They stopped outside the flat and Laura turned to him. Her face was half lit by the street lights and he could see from her expression that his attempt had failed.

"I'm sorry Tom—I mean if you think I'm some kind of prude. Maybe when you get to know me better you'll understand . . . ."

"Hey—explanations aren't necessary," he said quietly, "it's me who should be apologising. Sometimes I let myself be swept along by my flatmate. I'm not really a Don Juan." She found this funny and smiled the first smile in minutes.

This was his first indication that his companion was not caste from the same mould as many of the other female students he had met up with. Surprisingly perhaps, he was not disappointed or frustrated by her response. In a novel kind of way he was even pleased. That night, the first of many they spent together, they kissed and he left her on the doorstep.

Back at the lodgings, Paul was mortified by Tom's attitude. It was beyond his comprehension that his friend should spend an evening with an attractive girl and not have his way with her.

"Christ almighty," he declared, "you let her get away with that kind of shit. You need your head examining. What you should have said was . . . ." Tom was making coffee during this lecture and as he poured the boiling water he suddenly began to appreciate just how juvenile Paul's protestations were.

"I don't think you should give advice about women Paul," he said," you hardly have a string of such brilliant successes yourself—and anyway, Lorna is different from the slags you date."

"My God," Paul exclaimed," that's all the thanks I get is it. Suddenly the country hick is the all time expert in humping women. Well in future friend, you can fix up your own dates."

He stomped off to his bed, leaving his cup of coffee steaming on the kitchen work-top.

Things between the two young men were strained for some time after that night. Paul hardly spoke when their paths crossed and he spent more and more time away from their accommodation. Any comments he did make were snide reflections of his own preferred agenda and, although Tom tried to ignore them, increasingly they became an irritation. He knew it was a situation with a predestined consequence and secretly he began to look for somewhere else to live.

Conversely, the time he spent with Loma rapidly became the most important in his daily routine. He tried to engineer it that they met each lunch-time and sometimes at break-times between lectures he would even go looking for her in the canteen. They spent most evenings together and although neither of their budgets would permit too many visits to the pub, or the cinema, they were content enough in one another's company simply to go for window shopping walks round the town. Occasionally, if the weather was reasonable, they would take a short bus ride out into the surrounding rural areas and walk back through the country lanes. The rain, they discovered, was one of Lancashire's prevailing characteristics and if they decided to walk very far, inevitably they had to take some kind of protection from the downpours.

Crouching beneath an umbrella and sharing a plastic Mac however, proved a further aid to their special friendship. And whether they sheltered beneath a tree or shrubbery, in a shop doorway or under its canvas awning, their innocent tactile awareness of one another was enhanced by their clinging contact and cheek to cheek touching. It was nevertheless some ten weeks into their relationship before Tom was invited to share Lorna's bed. Ten weeks in which they had grown to know and to begin to understand each other's most intimate thinking—almost.

They both enjoyed talking, that much at least had been obvious to both of them from the start. Indeed it was often the source of jokes and teasing between them. But whereas, Tom was an open book, always keen to discuss his background and offer anecdotal evidence about his family and his home environment, Lorna's conversations tended to dwell exclusively on issues. Information about her childhood therefore remained sketchy and anything that did slip through her disciplined filter system was clearly only an edited highlight. Therefore, despite the fact that they had become close and that a complex of trust had developed between them, Tom knew that Laura still held some things back. Apparently, there were areas, memories perhaps which she herself had not yet accommodated, that she preferred or needed to keep private.

The local cinema in Chorley sometimes showed old movies, the kind that only enthusiasts for film really appreciate. It appeared to be part of the management's marketing strategy to offer their audiences different seasons in which they could concentrate on individual star's or director's performances. Clearly the movie house was struggling to remain viable. The growing competition generated by video recorders and the availability of films for hire must have wreaked havoc with their budgets, making their future unstable. There was nevertheless a small clientele, mostly derived from the student population, who valued the seasonal offerings and who continued to patronise the cinema. Tom and Lorna belonged to this group. Not surprisingly therefore when they saw a series of films in which Jimmy Stewart played the leading role on offer, they determined to see as many as they could afford.

On the first Wednesday they watched 'Where the River Bends' and the following week on the Saturday 'Vertigo' but it was a Sunday night late showing of 'This Wonderful Life' that did the trick. Before its timely conclusion, the old black and white film had reduced most of the audience to tears several times and Loma and Tom were no exception. They left the small theatre smiling and hand in hand, sharing a feel-good factor of epidemic proportions. Outside in the dark, she linked her arm through his and pressed her face to his shoulder as they walked back to her flat. Within the hour they were in bed together.

Although neither appreciated it at the time that first encounter, squashed together in Laura's single divan bed, was to prove seminal to their relationship. The first thing that Tom became aware of was that, for whatever reason, Laura was terribly a nervous lover. Not for her the casual abandon that had been Connie, for Lorna it was a serious business from the start. This was confusing for Tom but initially, he put it down to her sensitivity. And although she had told him that, whilst she was not very experienced, she was certainly not a virgin, nothing could have prepared him for the degree of timidity—almost fear—that she exhibited that night. Ostensibly, she was at least as keen as he to consummate their relationship, in fact it was at her invitation that he stayed overnight. Unfortunately, once the prospect of sexual contact became immediate, she froze rigid, shrinking from his touch, suddenly in floods of tears. Sensing that the ambiguity of her state was even more frustrating for her than for him, Tom simply held her close whilst she cried into his neck. She refused to discuss the cause of her condition but she was effusive in her thanks for his consideration. Needless to say, although they spent that together, they did not have intercourse.

During the hours of darkness she told him about her abortion and the delay it had caused in her accepting the place offered at Chorley. In a small voice she said that the trauma brought on at least in part through her religious beliefs, had left her stricken, unable to function properly and that, as a consequence, she had stayed on for an extra year at school, in the process taking more 'A' Level exams. The delay had been justified to her Mother by her Tutor, who simply argued that Lorna was not yet ready to leave home.

The next morning Lorna was up before him and by the time he appeared at the kitchen table, she was her old self again. With Connie still hovering in the background however, it was difficult to hold any kind of private conversation. Consequently, they left her to make whatever assumptions she might without adding any qualifications. They walked to college together but at the first corner they met up with three other students from Lorna's group, so the discussion Tom had intended was again delayed.

The talk amongst the group was all about the coming examinations and it was not until they were on the college steps that Laura turned to Tom.

"Will I see you tonight?' she asked.

"Course you will," he replied, conscious again of her unusual nervousness, "if you want to."

She smiled brightly, obviously relieved and kissed him quickly.

"I'll be finished by four—meet you in the bar eh? "She said.

Hearing Tom agree to the date, the others laughed and walked on. Lorna hurried to catch up with them.

CHAPTER ELEVEN

1976

BBC News. January.

Troops from the elite Special Air Service were today ordered into the "Bandit" country of South Armagh where 15 Protestants and Catholics have died in sectarian revenge attacks this week . . . bringing the total Ulster garrison to about 15,200. But last night the violence continued. The body of a man in his late twenties was found in Donegal Road, a Protestant area of Belfast . . . . Downing Street said last night that SAS troops would be used in County Armagh," for patrolling and surveillance tasks for which they are particularly suited." There was a mixed reaction last night to news of the SAS deployment. Mr. Gerry Fitt, SDLP MP for West Belfast said," My immediate reaction is that people in Northern Ireland . . . would apply the same standards to the SAS as they do to the CIA, and that is an indication of how people feel."

Diary: June . . .

Given the troubles back home (in Ireland) I feel guilty about being so happy. Tom is wonderful company. I didn't really believe that any man could be so sensitive, so caring or so loving. My only real concern is that he is becoming serious about our relationship rather too soon. I have mixed feelings about marriage (even to Tom) and would prefer to wait a good while longer before making a lasting commitment—just to be sure—I think!

* * *

As usual the end of term party was held mainly in the bar but the celebration spilled over into most of the rooms on the ground floor. A five man group played in the dining hall, one of three employed to provide the music throughout the night. The difference between them was not one of content but rather that of noise level. One was loud, another very loud and the last threatened to burst ear-drums.

Tom and Lorna arrived just after nine and by then the drinking had become serious. According to Tom' definition, it had reached its first level of stupidity. As a self-proclaimed expert on the art of alcohol ingestion, apparently he had designed a scale by which he would evaluate different levels of drunkenness. It was one subject about which Lorna thought he could be very boring, especially as he tended to expound his theory only after he himself had swallowed four or five pints of bitter. As they came through the main doors into the entrance hall they were greeted by the sight of Henry, a fourth year B.Ed student, standing on the newel post at the foot of the stairs, delivering a lecture on Surrealism. Harry was an art student, famed so far for, what some regarded as, an obscene painting that now hung in the students' union office. He was one of those people who were always talking, usually arguing and inevitably the disruptive focus of much attention because of the intransigence of his views.

He's still conscious of what he's doing though," Tom remarked as they drew near, "but a couple more drinks and he'll reach stage Two—then he'll have his clothes off."

"Tom—don't start all that again." Lorna replied trying to hurry him past.

Harry was just up the "Dali owes everything to Carl Jung "part, usually the lead up to his argument that the need for the Surrealists' work was rooted in society's shared psychosis that had nothing to do with Art but everything to do with its need for therapy. An argument rehearsed many times before in the bar and one which Tom had opposed on every occasion. This time, due to Lorna's insistence, the conflict was not permitted to develop. Other than three acolytes however, three raw new recruits from the First Year who hung on his every word, Harry attracted little more than a few seconds attention from the majority of the crowd. Some shouted derisory comments as they passed others just shook their heads.

"And one day he may be a teacher." Tom quipped ironically as they passed.

The hall was full. A mass of heaving bodies gyrating to the music, many in acts of coupling that might be seen by more sceptical observers as a sexual encounter without the sex. Tom found a table near the temporary bar set up at one end of the hall.

Tom should have guessed as much. The man sitting, chatting to Lorna turned out to be Paul. Since he had moved in with Lorna Tom had seen very little of his previous flat-mate but as soon as realised it was Paul chatting up his girl-friend, he felt his temper rise. 'Typical,' he thought,' Paul could catch the scent of an unaccompanied woman from two hundred yards,'

Loma was the first to see his approach.

Tom love," she said as he placed the drinks on the table," Paul was just . . . ."

He didn't let her finish.

Yeah I know. Paul was just sniffing around because he thought you were on your own. He's like a dog on heat.

Paul just grinned but Loma sighed, a minor version of her longest-suffering-most-misunderstood sigh.

"Actually he came over to invite us to his engagement party—next Saturday." she said.

Tom continued to grimace, he took his seat and then asked sarcastically if meant engagement—as in a job.

"You've got yourself a job then have you?"

"No me old mate," Paul smirked," it means that me and Julia are planning to get hitched."

He had clearly intended that his news should have a dramatic effect on his friend but Tom's reaction spoiled it.

"I thought you'd be pleased," Paul continued, apparently still searching for approval," let's face it, you were always telling me to take life more seriously."

"He says the same to me." Lorna added supportively, glaring at Tom.

It was clear that she was ganging up with Paul and Tom didn't like it at all.

"Okay—okay," he said reluctantly," point taken." he paused and offered his hand cross the table. Paul took it enthusiastically," Congratulations you old sod. Must admit, I never thought you'd settle down."

They all laughed and Paul looked surprisingly pleased. The reconciliation caused Lorna to put her hand on Tom's arm and smile. She hated any kind of confrontation.

"I can recommend it," Paul said grinning," so when are you two going to make it official?"

Lorna saved an embarrassing moment by claiming that just for the present they were both far too busy to think about marriage. The fact that Tom had never asked her was therefore well disguised.

It wasn't until some time later, whilst Paul was dancing for the third time with Loma that Tom began to wonder where Julia was. Surely, with an engagement so close, he wouldn't come to a college 'do' on his own? By then he had downed the statutory three pints of John Smiths and he was beginning to wish that his ex-flatmate would make his exit. He wanted some time with Loma on his own. A moment or two later his wish was granted, Lorna appeared from the crush on the dance floor. She looked flushed and bounced down next to him with a big smile.

"Phew," she said," so how about you and me having a creep around the floor then. Or do I have to find someone else to dance with me?"

He leaned over and kissed her on the nose.

"I see," he said," now that you've stomped poor Paul into the floor you come looking for new blood eh?"

She laughed.

"Cheeky sod, your buddy has had enough of me it seems. He's gone off to seek pastures new."

"Yeah," Tom replied," and talking about that, did he say where his intended was? I mean, it's a bit odd him coming here by himself—isn't it?"

"He's a bit odd altogether," she said quietly," but to hell with him let's us have a dance eh?"

Some time later Tom found himself standing in the Gents next to Barry, a student from his History group and a sometime friend of Paul. They nodded to one another and engaged in polite urinal conversation. The subject of Paul's engagement party came up and when Tom asked if Barry might be going to attend. Barry looked amused.

What engagement party? "He asked scornfully.

I must admit, I was surprised myself," Tom answered," he told me that he and Julia were getting engaged. Just shows how wrong I was . . . ."

Barry interrupted, laughing as he fastened his zipper.

"That's a good one," he said, "I suppose that's why Lorna slapped his face in the middle of the dance floor—sort of a congratulations slap eh?"

Tom's questions followed with predictable urgency and Barry was only too pleased to give him the full rendition. It appeared that he had seen

Paul and Lorna dancing together several times but, during one of the slow numbers, she had suddenly stepped away from him and slapped his face.

"And when I say slapped, I mean she really gave him it hard right across the face." Barry said." Everyone turned round to look. I suppose he was gripping her bum just a bit too tightly and she . . . ."

He was not allowed to finish the torment. Tom's index finger arrived with some force under his chin to stop the flow.

"Okay Harry, I get the picture—but watch your mouth when you tell the tale. I catch you slagging off Lorna and we could fall out."

Tom marched off, he was furious. It was obviously apparent that the engagement party was just another of Paul's chat up lines: the latest ruse to get his way. And, to make matters worse, he had allowed the gutless, lying bastard to dance with Lorna. More to the point however, why hadn't Lorna told him about the incident he wondered? He pushed his way through clumps of students back to their table.

Lorna was talking to a friend of hers, a girl from the Second Year, about the English course. Consequently Tom had to wait until the girl left before he could have his say and, fortified as he was by then with several pints of Bitter, his accusations were wildly exaggerated. For once Lorna was not prepared to make allowances. She had dealt with the situation to her own satisfaction and as far as she was concerned that was the end of it. It took only a few minutes before they were head to head in a full-scale row.

* * *

"Why the hell do we do it?" Tom asked his companion.

It was the early hours of Sunday morning and he was sitting on a bench near the park, sharing his last bottle of Newcastle Brown Ale with a tramp. His new found friend shrugged his shoulders and stared at the bottle, Ever since Tom had joined him, the old man had not been able keep his eyes off the bottle. It was not too often that someone came along and offered him drink. More usually they wanted to buy him a cup of tea or a bag of chips. On the other hand it was just as rare to find anyone who could match his own capacity for alcohol. They had finished five of Tom's six bottles together and last one was open.

"I mean, "Tom went on," so we have a row—but then I get pissed. And I mean pissed. D 'you know . . ." he tried to focus on his companion," it's years since I drank as much as I have tonight how about you?"

"Giz a gulp o 'that then . . . , if n, y 'don't mind Mister?

It took several seconds for the message to get through but when he realised he was being asked for a drink, Tom passed the bottle without hesitation. The man drank greedily. "Oy I said Oy—don't drink it all y 'bastard. Fair do's."

Reluctantly the swallowing stopped and the bottle was returned three quarters empty. An' she goes and starts to make eyes at all sorts of shits. I mean—why. It's nonsense. She's the girl I want to marry—for God's sake. She shouldn't be having all those creeps grope her like that." He paused and finished the bottle off. The old man watched, hoping that another might magically appear from Tom's overcoat.

"Y 'got another? "He asked finally, patience exhausted.

"Tom studied him again.

"Another what?"

"A bottle."

* * *

When the telephone rang Lorna was in a deep sleep. She had danced all night. After Tom had stormed off she had stayed on the dance floor until the band went home. She had been furious at his outburst and was determined to enjoy herself whether he stayed or not. Much later, alone in the flat she had been tearful. In fact she had cried herself to sleep.

The voice on the phone said that they had a man in custody at the Police station, a drunk who insisted that they call her number. Did she know him? Did she want to come down and collect him?

"We've no interest in keeping him here any longer than absolutely necessary Miss." the policeman said. "He was only picked up because he was found climbing half way up the side of the Town Hall . . . . could have killed himself."

She knew who it was without being told and, despite the aggravation, she was glad to know where he was. She took a taxi to the station and had him released into her custody, by then it was six am.

Later back at the flat she dumped the figure onto the settee where he immediately fell into a deep sleep. Unable to rest herself, Lorna made a cup of sweet weak tea for herself in the kitchen—a traditional treatment for shock she thought. But, she decided, she should not have been shocked still less surprised. It was not the first time Tom had sought solace in a bottle after one of their tiffs. He may not have Irish blood, but it seemed he had certainly acquired some Irish habits.

She was so tired she did not remember lying down on the bed but must have done so, waking a couple of hours late to find Tom beside her. She watched him through half closed lids—a boyish face, pale beneath his darkened thatch of hair. On an impulse she leaned across and lightly kissed him on the lips. The effect was instantaneous and a moment later she was pressed back into the pillow under the full weight of his body. Excitedly his tongue probed and his hands searched and, without appreciating it her more normal resistance was absent, she responded in a sudden and unpredictable passion. Clothing was pulled back urgently and the coupling, although fiercely enacted, proved a satisfying release—a remedy for their heightened feelings and a balm for the hurt. In terms of their physical resolve, they had never before been quite so close—or so vulnerable to one another.

CHAPTER TWELVE

1978

News: February 17th; at least 14 people died tonight when a bomb exploded at the Le Mons restaurant and hotel near Belfast tonight . . . . flames swept through the building, killing people trapped in the wreckage. Many guests leapt from windows, their clothes on fire. Many people are still missing, so the death toll could rise. Many of the victims are children.

Diary:

The commitment 'thing' with Tom has become an issue. I am determined to have a career of my own and, although I hate the idea of losing him, Tom will have to take second place. God that sounds hard. The crazy thing is that! I think I'm in love with him—but I just can't . . . . really can't, go along with marriage right now. Perhaps he'll wait? I hope I can.

* * *

She was out of sorts with herself, she concluded. The final exams had gone well enough and there were four or five job interviews fixed for the coming weeks, so there was nothing of any substance to complain about—but that seemed to make no difference. She had heard herself being unreasonable with everyone around her. Picking arguments and deliberately misunderstanding things said—especially with Tom. It was stupid, almost to the point of being incomprehensible.

Privately she knew that he was on the verge of suggesting marriage and, despite the fact that the thought thrilled her, there was another voice in the back of her head telling her to refuse. Virtually all her waking moments were spent trying to analyse the confusion she felt. The idea of marriage had never been a consideration until Tom came along. She had half decided years ago that future should be devoted to career rather than family—but Tom had changed all that. Their association, the depth of their friendship, not to mention the quality of their sexual adventure had forced her to reconsider. But the doubts remained. Lorna had had several boyfriends during her time at Chorley although none of them had been serious relationships. She had always been the one to end them and each time the end had been presaged when she imagined a deepening commitment in the offing.

That afternoon she sat idly in front of the television half watching an old black and white gangster movie. Tom was out having a pint with some of his cronies from the football team. A last drink before the college closed for the summer recess and before they all went their separate ways. She supposed it was the advent of another major change to her pattern of life that caused her need for self analysis. Every time she had ever reached a new crossroads, there had been a mandatory review, almost as though she was afraid of taking whatever next step that might be needed. She got up and made herself a cup of tea. As she poured the hot water she found herself thinking about being at home in Ireland. It seemed a lifetime ago, almost the life of someone else.

Standing at the sitting room window sipping the hot drink she looked down onto the street below. She liked being above the hurly-burly of the street, it made her feel private, distant and aloof. At the house in Belfast, the close proximity of the other terraces had always left her feeling claustrophobic. Her bedroom there overlooked back-yards, tiny square spaces with dustbins, dogs and outside lavatories: grubby spaces where the effluent of neighbours' daily life overflowed. Often, she had felt guilty looking down into those yards. They were—or should have been the most of private places, screened from curious onlookers—private almost in the same sense as ones toilet functions—or ones sex life.

She suddenly became aware of another headache and she went to the cabinet for painkillers.

Tom got back to the flat just after four pm. He was in a good mood and suggested that they went to the movies that evening.

There's one on at the flea-pit that I bet you haven't seen—The Seventh Seal, a really dark piece with Death playing chess on the beach.

And he went on about it at some length.

The last thing she wanted was to go and see a film and she certainly did not want him to describe the plot in such detail even if she had. She was trying to tidy the kitchen when he came in and typically as he spoke, trying to infect her with his obvious enthusiasm, he followed her about, getting under her feet and blocking the small space. Eventually she could stand no more of it.

"Oh for Christ's sake Tom—if the bloody movie is so good—then go and see it yourself. By yourself if you like."

The outburst stopped him in his tracks. She knew it was uncalled for but she could not help herself. "And please—please stop following me round like a lap-dog."

He stood by the kitchen door looking hurt and surprised and for a moment she almost apologised.

"What the hell is wrong with you?" he asked after a moment's pause, 'I only suggested a night out."

She busied herself at the sink, careful to avoid eye to eye contact. "Well, I don't feel like a night out. Okay?" she snapped back. "Fine we'll stay in then." He said quietly.

For the next half hour or so neither of them spoke. She stayed in the kitchen, washing and re-washing surfaces and drying pots that didn't need drying whilst Tom sat with the newspaper in the sitting room. At Six o'clock he called through telling her the BBC news was on TV. No matter what either was doing, normally everything stopped for Six o'clock news. This time however, she did not even bother to reply and a moment later he appeared again at the kitchen door.

"Did you hear me Love—the news is on . . . . ' he said again.

"I heard you the first time." She replied, keeping her back to him, clutching her tea-towel as it were a life-belt.

He waited only a second and then came across to where she stood. She did not hear him approach and was surprised when his arms circled her waist and his face pressed close to hers.

"Come on—tell me what's bothering you?" he said. "What's the trouble?" He laughed and whispered, "I hope you don't get moody like this after we're married."

She shook free of him and stepped away, turning for the first time to face him.

"That is the trouble Tom . . . . it's all about being taken for granted."

He waited without trying to answer the accusation and after a moment she continued. "Look—I guess I've been thinking about this for some time—and—what with the exams over and everything—well—I think we need to talk."

He folded his arms silently and they faced one another across the small space, like dogs vying for the communal bone. "Go on," he said finally, "get it off your chest then."

"Well for a start—I never agreed to . . . . I never said we should get married."

Her delivery was rushed, a speech that had been rehearsed in her mind and she was glad to get it out at last.

"And—well, maybe we should have a serious think about the future anyway. I mean—we don't want to tie ourselves down too soon—do we?"

"Well clearly you don't." He said.

'Look—it's not that I don't like you—I like you a lot as it happens. But I'm just afraid that—we might be jumping in with both feet before . . . .'

"Fine,' he said interrupting her," so what do you want to do?"

By now the awkwardness she felt bit deep into her stomach lining, causing nausea. A condition made up in equal parts of self-revulsion and the shock that she had initiated an irreversible action. Uncontrollably her face flushed and she found herself near to tears. Nevertheless, having made a start, her determination increased. Having begun to express her doubts and despite her physical reaction, she was increasingly certain that she was doing the right thing by both of them.

"I need some time," she said quietly, "and space."

*   *   *

Tom left the flat that night. He stayed only long enough to pack a small bag with a few things. Before he went, he laid the keys silently on the kitchen table.

Everything that needed to be said had been said and, although he stopped momentarily at the door, he added nothing. The door slammed shut and Loma Immediately dashed to the bathroom where she retched violently into the hand-basin. Her throat was dry and the action released er tears.

CHAPTER THIRTEEN

1979

News: March. A terrorist bomb today killed Airy Nave, a Tory MP who was a senior aide to Mrs. Thatcher, as he drove out of an underground carp-ark at the House of Commons. As Tory spokesman on Ulster, he advocated a tough line on security to combat the IRA and had known he was a possible target. Police fear his assassination may be the start of a terror campaign in the run-up to the General Election.

April: Four policemen are killed by a 1000lb bomb; the IRA's most powerful yet.

Diary: December 2nd.

When I got the letter from Mam about Jimmy! I must admit I cried—not for him of course but for Mam. If anyone could be improved by being dead, in my view it would be Jimmy—God forgive me for saying so. Having lost one husband to the troubles was bad enough—but to lose another, so soon after just a few years—that must rank as a tragedy. Mam deserved better, but even for her sake I'll find it difficult to go to the funeral.

* * *

Lorna only agreed to go back for her Mother's sake. She knew it would be a long journey in a dirty train—from one grubby railway station to another. But it was the least she could do. It had been easy enough to get time off from her school but having only been in London for one term she felt badly about asking for such a concession. She had suffered a kind of breakdown after being at the school only a few weeks—nothing too serious the doctor said. But she was advised that she must handle stressful situations more carefully.

It was a damp December morning and at Kings Cross railway station, despite its much-vaunted face-lift, the wrinkles still showed beneath the new plastic skin.

She found railways stations frustrating places. Their intended purpose as a place of transition was inevitably defeated by the unreliability of the human flotsam; by the debris they left; by unintelligible announcements and by a public too confused or too stupid to know which platform they needed or what time their train might arrive or leave. Railway stations remained the best of marketing tools—for the use of the private car.

She struggled to cross the obstacle course. The litter, blown by a desultory breeze eventually sought shelter in corners, climbing into pyramids and clutching wall surfaces, monuments to carelessness. And then there was the aimless herding of misdirected travellers: drifting wanderers. They swarmed in disparate groups; heads raised searching the Departures notice-boards; impeding those who already possessed the knowledge; tripping over carelessly abandoned luggage and all the while spilling tea from cardboard cartons. And there were the clutches of lost children, the older ones wearing brave faces, the smaller ones tearful and calling out for their parents. These waifs were continuously endangered by mechanised luggage convoys that snaked across the concourse trailing dozens of tiny caged carriages in their wake.

Undoubtedly, the railway station with its overflowing rubbish, its smell of diesel fumes mixed with fast order food and its population of displaced persons was a uniquely British tradition but it was one she could have well done without.

She stepped up into a carriage and found a seat, settled herself and collected her thoughts, thoughts about the funeral. At least there was order to be found in the Christian ceremony associated with death, she decided. The service, often a Requiem Mass, a well-practiced proscription; the journey by car to the cemetery and the hierarchy of mourners; the burial—a neat finality covered by a headstone to mark the spot. There was a precision evident that she enjoyed a well-ordered structure in which the debris was carefully put in its place and everyone knew where they should be and what they should do.

'A place for everything' she thought, reciting to herself her Mother's favourite cliché. The notion of planning an outcome reminded her of Jimmy's butcher shop and the inevitable chaos of his daily practice. The hours she had spent searching out hidden smells, scraps of meat, fat pieces having been swept lazily in to nooks and crannies; tiny mounds of bloody sawdust abandoned behind the counter and all those forgotten joints of mutton, left to moulder in the big fridge. The big fridge: scene of despicable acts and a place to be avoided at any cost.

As a young girl, although a reluctant Saturday worker, she had lived in a constant anxiety almost as much about salmonella outbreaks, as in fear of being caught in the fridge by Jimmy. Not that she had any strength of protective feeling for the butcher himself. Indeed, at that time she would have been only too pleased to see him dragged off to face the courts and a long prison sentence However, even as a teenager, she understood that the shop provided a living for her Mother, her brothers and her sister. And, without the financial umbrella of the business, she knew only too well that the old insecurities would return. Consequently she hated their dependence on Jimmy and she hated him, almost as much for his lack of hygiene, as she did for his foulness in other ways.

The inter-city express left the station six minutes late. Some time later an announcement over the public address system made a perfunctory apology and a promise of time that would be made up during the trip. The disembodied voice however, lacked any conviction and the resignation on the faces of her travelling companions seemed to indicate they were used to disappointments in this regard.

"Promises—promises." The thought made her squirm.

An image of her small single bed in the back room at night. Jimmy's voice, penetrating the dark, waking her from a deep sleep. His hand searching beneath the covers. A cold clammy hand—a hand she had first encountered in the allotment hut—touching, stroking, feeling for her.

"Shush—shush now. We don't want your Mum to hear us—do we Pet." He would plead.

The wall at the far side of the bed inevitably arrested her retreat and then there was nowhere else to go.

"Hold still Loma—there—just hold still. It won't hurt, I promise."

It always seemed like an age before she could speak and when she did, the sound was like someone else's voice.

"Don't—I don't want you to—don't—please don't."

His chuckle was the same one he used so often in the shop when faced with a difficult customer but in the darkness the menace implied was exaggerated. The hands would find her, tugging back the flannelette nightie as she remained frozen in shock.

"There," he would whisper," there you are." and the reality of his body became a nightmare. "Now be a good girl for your friend Jimmy and he'll promise to buy you something nice."

To her shame, she had always been a good girl for Jimmy.

Whenever Lorna recalled Jimmy's visits to her room, she hated herself that little bit more. Her adult self could not forgive the little girl for her lack of resistance. She could never understand why she had been so terrified that her Mother might hear. She knew now that the power her step-father exercised was illusory, completely without substance; a confidence trick and, much like the man himself, a complete fake. The memories however, had been the root of nightmares that continued to plague her sleeping hours even into adulthood. More troublesome still were the occasional flashbacks she would experience when she was awake. These were irrational and, despite her reading on the subject, they continued to reside beyond the spectrum of her conscious control.

She stopped pretending to read her novel and glanced for while at the passing scenery. The sealed envelope of the compartment was claustrophobic but the silence was comforting. A middle-aged man sitting across the aisle suddenly stood up. He caught Lorna's attention.

"Would you mind keeping an eye on my brief-case?" he asked," Just going down to the bar."

He was well dressed and she knew the type, she thought but she smiled back and agreed. He muttered his thanks and left, swaying in harmony with the train as he made his way down between the seats. Her thoughts returned to her Step—father.

This would be her last contact with Jimmy. A welcome one in respect of its finality. Her system however, still echoed with the effect of him. Because of him, she felt that her ability to give love had been seriously impaired and the complaint was chronic. As she had matured the memories had become more prevalent, giving rise to her recent problems and making the deficit appear more pronounced. The giving that had once been a characteristic of her personality had disappeared all but completely and a brittle selfishness developed in its place. It was nevertheless significant, that in tandem with the evolution of her new hard edge, her career had prospered. It seemed that those above her in the hierarchy at work approved her willingness to stand her ground and within a year of receiving her teaching qualification she was catapulted into a Head of Faculty post.

The train was due to arrive at Darlington station at 12.32 hours, just in time, ten minutes later, to pick up a connecting local train that would take her to Stockton. By the time it arrived, the brief case had been collected by its owner who, apparently once fortified with what smelt like whisky, had then attempted to chat her up. His new found confidence proved hard to dent and Lorna's polite refusal to a proposal for a dinner date was initially swept aside with alcoholic arrogance.

"But why ever not? "He had asked, as though her continued refusal signified she did not fully appreciate the honour he wished to bestow on her. The scene was witnessed silently by several other travellers seated nearby, a fact that appeared paradoxically, to encourage the man in his persistence. Well used to a captive audience however, Lorna responded with a practiced application of acid.

"Simply because I don't allow middle-aged drunks to pick me up on trains." she replied.

The smiles of satisfaction and encouragement she received from those seated near enough to hear her, provided the final curtain to the man's performance. Thankfully he did not join the same train as her at Darlington.

The only other funeral that Lorna had ever attended before had been her Father's—her real Father that is. It had left her with a paranoid dread of such occasions. The grave, a trench of hopelessness and helplessness into which her emotions had tippled then, was only accommodated later by a thin layer of scepticism. A delicate umbrella that was just as likely to turn inside out as it was to offer protection against further dampening hurt. That moment when the coffin was finally lowered into the depths devastated any beliefs she might have previously held dear. All the questions of unfairness—and the why him and the why her—had finally exhausted her faith in her religion. Thereafter, as she matured, her cynicism had become rooted in a form of practical materialism; a 'survival of the fittest'; a dogma of 'the devil take the hindmost.'

Not surprisingly therefore, her journey north was troubled by the question of which face she could afford to wear. The people she would see, her closest relatives, knew her almost as well as she knew herself and, whatever their perceptions, they would be bound to scrutinise anything they might identify as significant change. As far as she was aware, they all still practised the Roman religion and any failure on her part to join with them in the devotions of the Requiem Mass and the burial ceremony would be bound to attract attention as we as predictable cross examination.

"Well that's the autumn gone." A voice in a Devon accent said.

Lorna had been staring at the rain as it scored diagonals across the train window and the little old woman sitting opposite offered her comment, clearly as an opening gambit. Predictably, as soon as Lorna gave the automatic nod of agreement that convention demanded, the old woman began to talk like they were old friends.

"I was just saying to my old man the other day, they can say what they like about all this global warning, but up here we still gets our share of rotten weather. Eh? Going far Love?"

"Stockton."

"Family there—have you?"

"My mother, a sister and two brothers."

"Come far have you?"

"London."

"Ah—a holiday—is it? Taking a few days off?"

"A funeral."

"Oh dear I am sorry. Anyone close?"

'No. A friend of my mothers." she paused then added," No-one special.'

"Special enough for you to come all that way. Now that's what I'd call a good daughter. It's not everyone would travel for—how long is it—four hours, it must be four hours at least, just to attend the funeral of her mother's friend. I bet she'll be pleased to see you."

The old face beamed its benediction. Laura knew that she had been successfully Pigeon-holed by the old woman. She was the dutiful daughter, going out of her way to support her mother in a time of trial; another cliché, another easy solution. For a moment she considered if she should shatter the illusion and tell the dozy old cow whose funeral it was but in the end she decided to leave the woman with her fantasy.

The smiling face opposite however, refused to leave the matter alone. "Tomorrow—is it?"

"Sorry?"

"The funeral—is it tomorrow?"

Laura sighed, "Yes. Ten o'clock at St, Cuthbert's."

The sigh was taken as some expression of bereavement and the old woman rapidly became sympathetic. These were emotions best attributed to music-hall, Lorna thought.

"Never mind Love. We've all got to go sometime. Would you believe—I'm seventy three, myself. And my old man is four years older than me. Still you know what they say—only the good die young."

Lorna struggled to smile back.

"I must have been really evil eh?"

This time she laughed at herself. A laugh that turned quickly into a deep cough. The sound of water foaming over pebbles; air struggling through treacle.

"Would you like a mint?" Lorna offered.

It was the only thing in her bag that remotely resembled medication and the old woman took one gratefully with her left hand. The other held a large white pocket-handkerchief to her mouth as the coughing continued. The phlegm made its audible progress into the constricted larynx and after a moment it was hawked with considerable force and enthusiasm into the white cotton.

"Ah—that's better. Better out than in I says . . ."

As the old woman rambled on, Lorna's attention was caught by a young man a little further down the carriage. He stared round the side of his evening gazette at the performance, shook his head to demonstrate disgust and then disappeared again. A final judgement. A man's judgement. The same man who probably poured strong beer down his throat every Saturday night until it spilled back, bringing his dinner with it, on some street corner. Traditional week-end entertainment for the typical northern male. How she hated hypocrisy.

"I said—are these extra strong mints—my dear?"

"Sorry—yes, yes, I think they are." Lorna replied belatedly.

"Thought so . . ." The old woman spat the white disc into the handkerchief. "Sorry—but I can't take strong mints. They burn my tongue."

A little while later at Stockton station, Lorna found herself helping the old woman down the step and onto the platform. It was a relief from the investigation she had continued to make into Lorna's personal life. She walked with her to the exit and promised, as was suggested, to tell her mother that her travelling companion thought her daughter was a nice young woman. "I just hope she appreciates you dear." she said as she handed her ticket to the collector, "I think you're a very considerate person and your Mum is very lucky to have one like you—Ah there he is . . ."

Her husband turned out to be equally small. A tiny round figure in a mackintosh wearing a tiny round smile. He took his wife's arm and thanked

Lorna with typical geniality before leading off his spouse, arm in arm, to an old Ford car that waited at the kerb-side.

Nice people Lorna concluded. But they did not offer her a lift.

* * *

The town had not changed. The same High Street boasting God knows how many pubs, the same Town Hall sitting amidst the market in the centre of the road. Stockton was still a busy place and, as the taxi turned onto the main road, the memories came flooding back. She passed the place where the jazz club used to meet; now a supermarket and the Globe Cinema—now entitled the Essoldo and so on. Being a Saturday the town was crowded. The open market attracted hundreds of visitors from all the outlying suburbs. It was a Mecca for bargain hunters, a shopper's paradise, a place of colour and noise of familiar smells and sounds and a focus for thieves and pickpockets. The stall-owners and salesmen, yelling prices, boasting quality, the rain and the smell of damp canvas awnings, an evocation of her youth. Closer still, stopped in the traffic she watched. Anything and everything was sold on the market: fresh fruit and veg; fresh fish and meat; pies and sausages, tripe and black pudding; a myriad of stalls selling textiles and clothing (mostly seconds from the big stores); pottery stalls, electrical goods. Second hand books and comics; household bargains including everything from soap powder to boot polish. There were plants for sale and gardening implements, cut flowers and packets of seeds, there were shoes for sale and underwear, balloons and toys, ice cream and fish and chips, hot dogs and shellfish.

Her excited grin was noticed by her driver.

"Doesn't change much does it Pet?" he said watching her. She glanced up at his eyes framed in the interior mirror.

"Apparently not . . . I used to love this place." she answered

The nostalgia, filled her with a pleasurable comfort, almost painful and she could have easily wept. So much had happened here. Yet this was what she had sought to escape from, it was all part and parcel of her home life memory. Her childhood and early youth a time capsule that was separate from Tom, and consigned to a memory box she seldom explored. She had closed the lid on that container, ensuring her trauma of shame and disgust remained secure and, more importantly—private.

They reached Thornaby Bridge and briefly, she looked down at the gray waters of the Tees. It still had a look of dereliction. For this part of Tees-side the river had a jaded past from which it had never quite seemed to recover. The iron and steel and the ship building industries had all been lost due to the economics caused by the horseshoe bend in this river, giving rise to the development of the more accessible port of Middlesbrough. Stockton's coat of arms the Castle and Anchor translated as Fortitudo et Spes—Strength and Hope, now seemed sadly inadequate. Despite the promises of local politicians, apparently there was a continuing lack of will to make serious change and Stockton remained a place that had never reached its full potential. The pollution was as bad as ever, leaving buildings along the river banks scarred and dirty, it was a failed landscape.

Once over the bridge they took a right hand turn and a few minutes later passed Jimmy's shop on the corner of Brown Street. The house that had been her home was three doors down on the left.

"Here we are then Love.' the driver declared, stopping before the terraced front door. He left the cab and carried her suitcase to the step before accepting payment. "Thanks," she said," keep the change."

He was obviously pleased and muttered, "You're a lady—good luck to you."

The taxi was still in the midst of doing a three point turn in the street when the door was opened by her Mum. The sparkle of her welcome could not hide the depletion evident in her face.

"I thought it was you Lorna," she said in a quiet voice," I'm so glad you were able to make it." She paused and then added," It's been such a long time."

The almost forgotten accent made Lorna's eyes fill and a moment later the two women were clasped in a loving, tearful embrace. Her Mother's tears, half in joy, half regretfully, came in torrents. She pressed her face in her daughter's neck and sobbed. Behind her Mrs. Kettle, the next door neighbour appeared in her piny. She smiled, patting Lorna's arm.

"She's been waiting for you Pet. Not a tear so far. Held it all back just till you came home."

Inside the small living room, Lorna found Theresa and Peter sitting together on the settee. Her sister was the youngest in the family born five years after Lorna but now suddenly she looked sophisticated, very much the fashionable young woman. She ran to hug her.

"Lonny y 'look so grown up. I'd not have recognised you really. She does, doesn't she Peter?"

Theresa's outburst was typical and Lorna was relieved to see that nothing had changed her.

"From where I'm standing, it's you whose all grown up." she said holding her sister at arm's length.

Peter stood up half shyly, smiling the same small smile that she remembered so well. He leaned past and kissed her meekly on the cheek, an intimate gesture indicating nevertheless the obvious depth of his emotion.

"I think we've all grown up," he whispered," so don't think you can sit at the top of the stairs all by yourself in future."

They all laughed.

"And Patrick," Lorna asked," where's our Patrick?"

Theresa wouldn't meet her eyes and Peter just shook his head and turned away.

"Come on you two—it can't be all that bad. Where's the big feller."

Patrick, although a year younger than Lorna, had always been the biggest one in the house, a large friendly giant without an arch bone in his body. He was the only one she could ever turn to when she was in trouble, the one who would listen without criticising, and the one which would hold her hand and supply her with his big white handkerchief to dry her tears.

"Mum," Lorna insisted," what's wrong. Where is our Patrick and why isn't he here?" She turned to find her Mother standing close behind her, one hand still on her shoulder. "Lorna—I'm sorry," she started haltingly," but Patrick's in prison."

For a moment she could not believe what had been said and stood there, her jaw slack.

"He got himself into trouble," her Mother continued," got in with the wrong crowd. Drinking and fighting in the street. Jimmy warned him it was only a matter of time . . . ."

"But what happened—I mean what did he do?"

By now Peter stood next to his Mum, his arm round her shoulders and he answered this time. "Ah it was awful Lonny," he said, "he got drunk one night and got into a fight with some feller in the High street. Nearly killed him. The man's still in a coma."

Shocked, Lorna sat down on the arm of the easy chair. This was not the brother she knew. The big sensitive lad who'd held her hand.

Finally she asked," Does anyone know why?"

"Why," Theresa's voice rose in anger," why indeed. 'Cos the fool can't control his temper. That's why. If the man dies, they'll put him away for life."

She went quiet and at that moment Mrs. Kettle appeared in the kitchen doorway with a tray of teacups and a large teapot.

"They'll be time enough for all that. Away all of you have a nice cup of tea and a biscuit. Theresa clear that table will you?"

* * *

Predictably, the funeral service started with a full Requiem Mass. Jimmy got the full treatment, the black cope and stole and the long candles standing at each corner of the catafalque, the dark wood coffin with brass fittings, four altar boys and a eulogy that could have done justice to any of the apostles. When the mass ended prayers for the dead were read over the casket; it was blessed with holy water and incense was wafted across its length. Finally it carried to the waiting hearse by four tall men. Apparently it had not been possible to obtain four volunteers from the Master Butchers' Association which would have been the normal practice. For reasons that were never explained only two of his fellow tradesmen were willing to shoulder his corpse and two more needed to be recruited by the Undertakers.

The cemetery was only about a mile away but the mournful progress of the three black cars that followed the hearse made seem much further. In the streets various older people stopped and crossed themselves as the procession passed by, a sign of respect that left Lorna feeling irritated. It was a kindness she would have normally applauded but, applied as it was, to Jimmy, it only increased her bitterness.

As they turned into the cemetery gates she noticed another vehicle parked up close to the entrance. Two men stood near by clearly waiting for the funeral party and as her car turned into the driveway she saw that one of the men was Patrick. The priest and the altar-boys led the way to the graveside and as Lorna joined her mother at the head of the deep hole, she was joined by Peter and Theresa. Patrick stood back a little to her right and she caught his eye, sufficient at least to show her pleasure at seeing him. He returned her smile briefly but looked uncomfortable.

The service was predictably short, ending with the De Profundis.

"Out of the depths have I cried for thee oh Lord . . . ? "The priest intoned.

The small congregation gave the prescribed responses in a ragged chorus, "Lord hear my prayer . . . .'

After the service ended the mourners formed a line to shake hands or kiss the widow's cheek as they passed on their way back to the cars. Jimmy's only blood relative was an aunt, a rotund figure with white hair who spoke to no-one and left immediately the service ended. It was a typically English service in Lorna's eyes, an uninspired ritual in which any sadness experienced or sympathy shown, felt to be deliberately abbreviated, almost as though those involved were half ashamed to express their feelings. A far cry from the bitter tears and true desolation she remembered at her own Father's burial.

Suddenly Patrick was at her side. His eyes were tired and he looked a beaten man.

"Lovely to see you Lonny," he whispered, "you look a treat."

She turned and hugged him but, despite his comment, he was distant, allowing her embrace but without a genuine response.

"Patrick," she whispered in his ear," oh Patrick. What are we to do with you now?"

When she pulled back and looked into his face, his eyes had filled but the expression was one of stone.

"Best forget me altogether." he answered.

"I'll come and see you." she said, "but we must talk. Can you come back to the house?" Before he could reply the plain-clothed policeman was at his elbow.

"Time to go Patrick." he said gripping her brother's arm.

"Surely to God, the lad can come back to the house for a minute?" she snapped.

The man shook his head, "Sorry Miss." he said," But we've got a tight schedule."

At that moment Peter and Theresa moved close, just close enough to hear. Both their faces were pale and strained. Theresa spoke first," His Father's schedule is even tighter. He has to come back with us." she said.

Standing at the graveside surrounded by the four of them the policeman might have been forgiven for feeling threatened. In the event it had no visible effect. He made a sympathetic face and shrugged his shoulders.

"I know how you feel Miss, but I have orders to follow and a train to catch." His grip on Patrick's arm tightened as he spoke.

"You must appreciate that he's on remand and this visit was a special concession under the circumstances."

Lorna stood closest to the man and for a second she was tempted to push him. One hard push would have had him slip back into the grave on top of the coffin. The sole reason she did not act was on account of Patrick's look of resignation. All the fight had gone out of him and he left the impression that he would rather there was no bother. Instead she kissed him on the mouth. It was not until she had turned away allowing space for the others to say their good-byes, that she realised her cheeks were wet.

When they got back to the car their Mother sat alone in the deep leather seat, gazing blindly out of a side window, her face set. Before Lorna could begin to ask, her Mother answered, "I want no more to do with him Lorna—so keep your comments to yourself."

"But Mum," she started.

"And the subject is closed." her Mother interrupted.

The final intransigence was typical and Lorna let the matter drop.

CHAPTER FOURTEEN

1979

News: August 27th

Lord Mountbatten killed by IRA bomb:

It was the middle of the morning when Earl Mountbatten and members of his family drove from their Irish home, Cassiebawn Castle down to the harbour and set out for a day's fishing in their thirty foot boat, Shadow V.

The boat had hardly left the harbour mouth when it was ripped apart by an IRA bomb. Earl Mountbatten aged 79, statesman and warrior was killed instantly. His grandson Nicholas aged 14, and a seventeen year old boatman also died in the blast.

In a statement tonight the IRA claimed responsibility for, "the execution of Lord Louis Mountbatten." and said that the boat had been blown up by remote control. The bomb contained 50 pounds of explosives. This is mass murder and nothing can justify it," declared Cardinal Thomas O'Fiaich, the Roman Catholic Primate of Ireland.

Diary:

I must try to see Patrick. I'll go to see him in prison—whatever the cost. He is the only man in my whole life (other than my Tom-wherever he is) to treat me as an equal and he deserves better than to be ignored or forgotten.

* * *

Peter drove her to Durham in his old Ford and although it coughed and belched fumes, making a noise like the sound of a 747 coming into land, it nevertheless got them there in good time. They finally parked up outside the gates in a visitor's car park along with a dozen or more other vehicles. Peter switched off the engine and lit a cigarette.

"Y 'should have let him know Lonny." he said quietly blowing smoke at the windscreen.

She said nothing, staring instead at the gray of the high walls. It would be difficult to imagine a less welcoming place. Typical of the North, she thought. The cold immutable stone stained with generations of grime, coal-dust smoke belched from the hearths of miner's cottages over hundreds of hard-working years. Coal, the root of the industrial revolution, had left its scars on each and every town in the region. Sometimes visible on the buildings in the architecture of exploitation, sometimes implicit in the character of the people. Fortunately, the tradition of subservience had given way in the face of a dry cynical humour now recognised as a local personality trait. And then there was the wealth brought by the coal, the wealth that had forged a chain linking so many of the landed gentry with the aristocracy, some with royalty itself. A wealth acquired literally off the backs of the miners. She recalled one of her father's most common sayings, "If you can't be exploited then you're unemployable." That same wealth was now a little more—just a little more—evenly displaced and Durham, along with many other towns in the North, seemed to be thriving.

"He might refuse to see you." Peter continued.

"You shouldn't smoke." Lorna concluded." You always had a weak chest.'

As if to confirm her observation he coughed, laughing and choking at the same time. "Y 'don't change Lonny. I think that's why you're such a breath of fresh air. But, I meant what I said—he may not want to let you see him in there. Y'know what he's like?"

She certainly knew what he was like. She could remember the times he would crawl into her bed crying. The long conversations in the dark; the exchange of secrets; the promises of eternal friendship. She had been closer to him than any of the others.

"He'll see me Peter," she said,' in fact he'll be expecting me."

She glanced at her watch. There was still a few minutes before she needed to join the line of visitors so she checked her carrier bag. All the advice had indicated she should take only either food or cigarettes. Cigarettes, the favoured currency inside the prison were always welcome and, as meals were so predictably poor, food had to be a bonus. Peter watched her.

"They'll dig through that lot you know." he warned, "before they let you give him anything they'll poke the cakes and handle the fruit, just to make sure you're not trying to give him drugs."

But she knew what to expect and had chosen her purchases carefully. The sponge cakes were still in their shop bought wrappers and the apples and the grapes were loose. She had even taken the packets of cigarettes out of the paper covering, leaving the packs of twenty lying loose. Her only transgression was the letter that she had slid into the back of one of the cigarette packets. Using a scalpel blade she had slit the bottom of the cellophane and the cardboard and inserted a letter. It was written on tissue paper and folded round two ten pound notes.

Smuggling anything into the prisoners was an offence and she knew therefore that she was taking a chance. However, once inside, the supervision would be such that it was unlikely that she would be able to say very much of any real significance to her brother. The letter was meant simply to bridge that gap. The money had been an afterthought. Money was always useful and, if she could make life any easier for her brother, she was determined not to miss the opportunity.

Twenty-five minutes later she had successfully negotiated the guards' cursory interview and search and found herself shunted along a cold corridor to a large room. It was a more relaxed atmosphere than she had imagined. People chatted and joked with one another, many with bags of food giving the impression of a family picnic rather than a prison visit. A dozen or more small tables were set in rows, spaced along the length of the room, each one identified by a number contained in a stand-up plastic holder, a bit like a tea-shop. A variety of light plastic chairs were stacked near the door and, as each visitor passed by, they collected a chair and went to their designated table to wait. Two guards acted as ushers at the entrance, examining tickets which had been allocated after the property search and directing visitors to the requisite tables. Four more guards patrolled the room and although the organisation was carefully orchestrated, the security was reasonably unobtrusive. Nevertheless, all the visitors were seated before the first of the prisoners was allowed to enter.

A large percentage of those who had come were clearly relatives and they greeted the various inmates warmly. Some hugged and kissed, some laughed clapping one another on the back, others only smiled tearfully, clasping errant sons, brothers or husbands in, what appeared to Lorna to be, genuine regard. Gifts were delivered and received gratefully and in some cases, food appeared confirming the impression of a picnic.

Lorna waited patiently. She watched the reunions and noted only one situation that defied the general good humour. At a corner table a man in his late forties sat opposite an older woman, possibly his mother. They held hands across the table-top, engaging in a whispered conversation that rapidly left the woman in tears. The man struggled to maintain his own composure and hid his discomfort behind a flurry of nose-blowing. Other than the obvious, it was impossible even to guess the cause of their unhappiness and Lorna was so engrossed in watching them that she did not see Patrick enter the room. He was standing in front of her before she realised.

"It's rude stare Y'know Lonny," he said quietly, 'an especially when y 'keep your big brother waiting for a kiss."

She leapt to her feet and in a moment they were locked together. Through his prison shirt Lorna could feel how thin her brother had become. All the baby fat had disappeared, leaving a torso that was finely muscled. His grip was that of steel and he smelt of cheap soap. She pulled back and stared into his face, smiling.

"And Peter said you might not want to see me."

He laughed. "That'd be a fine day. How are you Lonny? God I've missed you. Y 'look so grown up." She pulled him to his chair and sat alongside still keeping a tight hold on his hand. "What about you—y 'big lunk? If anyone's grown up it's you. Look at the size of you. He was bigger than she remembered, bigger and more angular and of unlikely proportions . . . The arms beneath the shirt were thick and the hands that gripped hers still seemed uncomfortably large. The smile was just the same lopsided grin she recalled so well but the eyes were different. The blue had faded almost to gray and the hoods, now fully developed, shielded a new and surprising hardness which was exaggerated by deepening shadows. What had been laughter lines were now furrows, scoring the pale skin as though by mechanical incision.

"You're staring again." he said guardedly.

"And sure, if I'm not allowed t 'stare at me brother, then pray tell me who might be?"

The eyes flickered and then he smiled again.

"Only you can," he replied,' only me darling sister. You've earned the right to stare as much as y want to. The question is Lonny—what d 'you see?"

Patrick knew her probably better than anyone else had ever known her and, as his question clearly indicated, his perception of her moods had not diminished despite her long absence. For a little while she did not reply but continued to study him. Throughout childhood, he had always been her dearest friend, her most reliable ally and, in times of trouble, the sole repository of her most guarded secrets. She realised that, although she had not been prepared to admit as much, one of her motives for making the journey to Durham that day was to discover if the depth of their friendship still existed.

She answered him slowly, choosing her words with care.

"I see lots of changes Patrick—scars from the past maybe. There are bits of you that I don't understand anymore—and—I want to understand. I want to understand more than anything." The question was left only as one implied.

His smile, like his response was too quick, almost as if he regretted opening the door to such a discussion and she stopped him mid sentence.

"Don't Patrick. Don't pretend with me. We've both carried too much baggage for too long to pretend to one another now."

Briefly a protective shield glazed over his stare and he dropped his eyes for the first time. His grip tightened on her hand and she thought, for one terrible moment that he was about to turn to anger. Instead he sighed, not the sound of resignation but one of relief, like the dam of his resistance had suddenly burst. Now, when he met her searching look, the brittle hardness had gone.

"D 'you still have the nightmares Lonny?" he asked.

"You know I do." She whispered.

"Mine started to happen in the daytime."

A chill started between her shoulder-blades and made the hair on her neck prickle.

"I found that a good stiff drink helped to dull them," he continued, "that is—for a while. Before I knew it, I was taking that same stiff drink with me cornflakes."

It was her turn to grip his hands. She knew precisely what he meant. Her own recent experience had provided an insight to a similar culture of uncontrollable memories.

"Patrick—you need help," she said softly,' it doesn't have to be like that."

He laughed quietly with undisguised bitterness and let her hand go.

Now you're beginning to sound like the pig doctors in here. The only help I need is to get out of this shit-hole."

He delivered the last sentence in a loud voice, almost deliberately attracting the attention of the guards patrolling the room. People nearby glanced nervously in their direction and the inmate at the next table whispered across," Take it easy Pat. They'll have you back in solitary if you give 'em half a chance."

But the die was cast. The edge had returned and Patrick sat back in the chair and looked about him provocatively. The guard nearest was only a few feet away and he reached the table quickly. He rested one hand on the back of Patrick's chair and stared down at him. "Sorry about that," Lorna intervened," we were just . . . ."

The man ignored her and interrupted speaking directly to her brother.

"Keep it down Donnelly. Another outburst like that and you're away."

Patrick looked up into the face above him and the moment seemed to stretch.

Lorna was close to panic. The very mention of professional help had acted like a catalyst, speeding the change in Patrick's mood. Tension spread round the room almost as quickly and an awkward breathless silence developed.

"Do you hear what I say?" The guard repeated.

"I hear you." her brother replied.

The guard nodded and appeared to be about to move away when Patrick added, "I can hear you and I can smell you. Pigs have a distinctive perfume—I think they call it—shite." Later Lorna best remembered the look of resignation on the face of the man on the next table who had whispered the warning. She saw him shake his head and mouth the word 'Sorry' to his wife, just as Patrick stood up. Very little of what followed however was very clear. She was not even certain who struck the first blow or when the other convicts joined in, it seemed that in an instant the whole room was in chaos. The solid sound of overturning tables, chairs flung back, the grunts and gasps complimenting the noise of blows—bone on bone, screams and then the alarm bell.

It was impossible to see precisely what happened or even to identify clearly the sequence of events. At some point Lorna found herself on her hands and knees, climbing over bodies to reach the relative safety of the corner. A haven sought by other visitors but one not achieved by all who tried. By then the door had been flung open and a horde of uniforms had burst into the room. Truncheons flailed and blood splashed, men and women were felled and even some of those crouched near the wall found themselves pushed or dragged into the melee. Patrick's outburst had triggered a mini riot involving visitors, guards and prisoners alike and it took the authorities some considerable time to quiet the disturbance and restore order.

Paradoxically, it was Patrick who was the last to be dragged out. Three guards held him, one on each arm and one who pulled him by his collar. Lorna watched in a state of shock as his blood-stained face turned at the door. A last moment of resistance halting his progress, just long enough for him to catch her eye. He grinned and shouted to her.

"See—I've got all the help I need."

A second later and he had been dragged away out of sight.

A senior officer appeared and marched to the centre of the room. He scanned the mess about him and then addressed the people left.

"Should anyone need medical attention, the prison doctor will be prepared to examine you and to dress minor injuries. The Governor will be here in a moment to talk to you but he has instructed me meanwhile to tell you, he will consider any complaints about today's events as long as they are made in writing. "He paused but as there was no substantial response, he continued, "There will of course be a full investigation and some of you may be required to give evidence—but I might add, a statement from one of my guards seems to indicate that he was attacked—and that was the start of the disturbance."

It was over an hour later before Lorna was able to join Peter back at the car

Peter drove slowly. He was a polite driver and exercised care especially on main roads, and more so still when the traffic was heavy. It was just as well that he did. Travelling along the old A1 in the evening crush few other drivers paid scant regard to safety. Nevertheless as Lorna's rendition reached its climax, Peter became more and more agitated, apparently paying less and less attention to his task. He asked his Sister to light a cigarette for him as she concluded her report. She did as he asked and slid the lighted cigarette between the fingers of his left hand so as not to distract him. As she did so however, she became aware for the first time how upset he had become.

"He'll be okay Peter—really he will. You mustn't get upset on his behalf."

"I'm not," he snapped back, "I'm just—bloody well annoyed." He drew on the cigarette and then continued, the words tumbling out, "To tell the truth, I'm more than annoyed—those fucking guards. It's a different culture Lonny. Those bastards don't operate in the same world as the rest of us."

As he spoke he accelerated suddenly to overtake a long trailer and in the process caused a small Japanese car to swerve to avoid him. The other driver shook his fist and shouted something but Peter didn't react at all.

"They're always beating him you know," he said bitterly, "Tessa and Mum don't know the half of it. Those pigs only need half an excuse." He pulled back into the first lane, "He tells me things when I go to see him on my own—things he doesn't want the rest of you worrying about. I could cheerfully kill those bastards."

Peter's outburst seemed to have exhausted him and he fell silent. Lorna did not want to press him any further. She decided if he wanted to share any more of Patrick's confidences, he would tell her in his own time.

The rest of the journey passed in almost complete silence, leaving them both free to consider what had happened in their own way. For her part, Lorna felt that she had learned a lot about both her brothers that day. She regretted not having had more time to talk to Patrick—but that had been his choice and she wondered if his behaviour was his way of punishing her for her long absence. There had hardly been time to discuss the offence he was charged with and she had wanted to listen to his side of the story. Apparently, street fights in Stockton were less common now than when they were children, living in Thornaby—probably due to a marginal reduction in heavy drinking. However, there had been few near fatalities even when street fighting was common. She decided that before she returned to London, she would play detective herself and see what she could find out.

The passing landscape between Durham City and Tees-side was largely one of neglect. The fields looked uncared for and the hedgerows had all but disappeared, those that remained had thinned to scratchy, uneven borders. It was a telling contrast with the view she had grown used to in the South. The Home Counties were lush with an air of prosperity reflected in trim lawns, tidy streets and well designed public places. She decided it was easy to see where the balance of economic investment resided. The contrast was enhanced further by the attitude of the people. In the South largely there was an apparent respect for the Police and for the rule of Law. Those institutions representing authority were generally accepted as necessary. Peter's outburst had been vehement, surprising her with the depth of his feelings but, in his case, she decided it was uncharacteristic. She was pleased nevertheless, to see that he had maintained a close relationship with his elder brother. As children the boys had been separated as much by the difference in their interests as by their personalities. Patrick was always the sportsman, the outward looking one, the leader and at least superficially, the brighter. He lived out of doors as much as possible, arriving home only at meal times, inevitably dirty. Peter on the other hand was the home-bird, content to read his books in the quiet of his room rather than playing football in the street. He never needed to be reminded to wash his hands before meals, or to clean his teeth and he was the only person in the family who didn't complain when he was asked to do the washing-up. Their Mother described him as 'sensitive' and made allowances for him that she would never consider for any of the others. For example, when Peter declared he could no longer tolerate the taste of cabbage, his decision was accepted without question. He was thereafter provided with special portions of broccoli or beans. None of the other children would have publicly attempted such a sacrilege. Privately however, the question of their 'forced cabbage'—which was how they came to describe it—was the subject of intense debate.

Lorna was pleased therefore, that the grown-up Peter was willing to allow his brother a similar consideration despite the debate. "Perhaps"—she thought, "forced cabbage was a thing of the past"

CHAPTER FIFTEEN

1979

Diary: December 10th.

The atmosphere at home is tense whenever I mention Patrick's name. Mum seems to have closed her mind even to the possibility of his innocence and Tessa refuses to discuss the business. I am finding it hard to keep off the drink whilst I am here—sometimes I could kill for a large scotch. Today I will pay a visit to the pub where the fight took place. Perhaps I can find another strand of the truth that the Police have missed. We need something, anything, to justify Patrick's release. Please God I find it.

* * *

The landlord made it obvious that the Junction was not the kind of pub that expected young women to arrive unaccompanied, still less to buy their own drinks at the bar. And, despite the fact that it was lunch-time and there were only two other customers in the bar—two male customers—when she arrived, Lorna was studiously ignored. She remembered the culture well. The demeaning patronage, the protective possessiveness, the feeling of being owned and somehow therefore of being less than capable. She crinkled her ten pound note noisily and the fat man turned.

"Did you want something Pet?" he asked—like he didn't know. She bit back the anger and smiled.

"A drink—please."

Sighing as though having to deal with a naughty child, he levered himself off the bar, shook his head in resignation at his two cronies and waddled over to the alcove that described the lounge bar.

"I hope yer not driving sweetheart?" he said as he approached," I wouldn't like t 'be responsible for you losing yer license."

She maintained her smile with difficulty.

"A large gin and tonic please—and no, just to put your mind at rest, I'm not driving."

He poured the drink with theatrical care as though he had never performed the service before, all the while avoiding direct eye contact.

"Ice and lemon?" he asked finally looking up.

"Please."

As he worked Lorna was conscious of the stares of the other two men. They stood, leaning on the bar-top with half-empty pint glasses before them. One of them, the younger one, caught her eye and smiled. "You'll not be wantin too many of them Pet,' he said jokingly." His Geordie accent noticeably stronger than that of the landlord. "Else we'll hafto be carryin you owt."

Showing solidarity his companion joined in with his laugher. The landlord took up the point. "Naw lads, she's sensible young woman—but, if she doesn't mind me saying so—next time she fancies a lunch-time drink, it'd be better to come in with her boyfriend."

He turned then to face her direct and added," No offence Miss, but people round here a just a little bit old fashioned—if y 'see wat I mean."

Now she laughed, and she could see by their expressions tat all the three men were suddenly uncomfortable.

"And do you have many fights in here?" she asked.

The question took them by surprise. The two drinkers frowned looking confused and the landlord, by then counting her change at the till, turned to study her more closely. He was the first to respond.

Don't tell me—you're with the constabulary—yes?" The nervousness in his voice was obvious.

"It was a nasty one a few weeks ago wasn't it?" she went on," that feller is still at death's door—or so they tell me."

She sipped her drink giving them time to consider the situation. She did not have long to wait. The younger man opposite emptied his glass.

"I'll be off then Gordon. Maybe see you t 'night." he said and with that he turned and left. His companion was less worried.

"Aye. I hear he's still in intensive care. As far as ay 'm concerned he got what he deserved. A nasty sod that one. Right Gordon?"

Gordon counted out her change and nodded," Right enough. He's alus lookin for trouble. And when he gets out he's barred from the Junction that's fer sure."

"How about the other one, the Irishman?" she asked innocently.

"Patrick—oh he's a good lad. Got a temper on him—but he's okay." Gordon paused and then asked," But I thought your lot were satisfied. I told the other CID Inspector all this."

Loma affected an old fashioned expression," He may be satisfied—but that doesn't mean I need to be," she said enigmatically. "There were other witnesses—yes?"

"Oh aye—the place was full."

"And do they agree with you—I mean about this other feller deserving what he got?"

"I suppose so, d 'you think so Charlie?"

The other man grinned.

"There's many of 'em would have liked to give him a kickin themselves. Yeah—everyone agreed."

"So when does Patrick come up?" Gordon asked.

She ignored him again and asked instead if they had all made statements. It appeared that six had been taken, apparently all testifying to the provocation and aggression of the victim. With a little encouragement Charlie amplified his own account, telling her how Patrick had been challenged several times about his step-father.

"That feller in hospital—Wayne Stoppard, he's a right red-neck—kept taunting the Irish lad about Jimmy Ungerside, his Step-dad. Seems that when this Jimmy was a young man himself, he'd been arrested for molesting a little lad. No charge was laid but according to Wayne who got it from his Dad, everyone said he was guilty as hell." Loma felt herself go cold.

Well, I mean, "Charlie continued," even if it was all true, it was nothing to do with Patrick, Just a nasty thing to go on about. A couple of the other fellers told him to shut his mouth but he took no notice and when Pat ignored him, he threw beer over him. That did it. Ill tell you what Miss, I wouldn't like to have had a beating like Patrick gave Wayne. And he was cool as a cucumber the while he was—just methodical. A careful smacking—his face then his body. Christ what a mess he made.'

Charlie drained his pint.

"I must confess we all thought Pat'd killed him—poor sod. What d 'you think he'll get?" Gordon answered," If Wayne dies—the least he'll be charged with is manslaughter. If not, he might get off with actual bodily harm. Could be as little as six months—or as much as life."

Lorna nodded sagely, as though she had already known the detail.

Before she left she bought Charlie a pint and thanked him. She was actually grateful for his account. It had thrown new light on Patrick's behaviour explaining his outburst. It had nevertheless amused her to see the total change in their attitude as soon as Gordon and Charlie began to believe that she represented the Police. Suddenly she was not just some air-head female; she was a figure of authority. The usual expressions of male superiority, the 'pet' and the 'sweetheart' all stopped and she became 'officer'.

Outside it was raining, a cold, slanting, and needle-damp from the East under a quickening sky. She walked across the bridge heading back to Thomaby, feeling the wet penetrate her thin coat. The river had risen and for a moment or two she stopped to look down at it. Its surface was still thick and heavy but now it moved quickly, hurrying the pollution it carried down to the sea. The factories she remembered from her youth had mostly disappeared but unfortunately the buildings replacing them were no less grim. The river edge, as far as she could see, was wasteland—an area of scrub, still used as a convenient dumping ground for old mattresses and bedsteads, broken bicycles and black plastic bags of rubbish. Traditionally it was the repository for dead pets and, it seemed, as long as they were contained and made unidentifiable in the black plastic bags so popular now, no-one thought to complain. What the eye doesn't see—and all that. Much like Jimmy.

The bald exposure of Jimmy's past had come as a shock and she wondered critically if her Mother had known before the marriage. The thought was unworthy and she felt guilty for even considering it. There was no doubt that he was a child abuser when Lorna and Patrick were children—but when he himself was young? He must have gone undetected during the greater part of his life. It made her feel physically sick, Child abuse had long since been recognised as one of the most abhorrent of crimes, well beyond the willing understanding of most of the population. And, whilst it was attributed to men who were unknown faces in the newspaper, it could remain simply a theoretical exercise in hatred. If the perpetrator was known however, passions rose and the communal feeling of disgust acquired new and sometimes violent proportions. Patrick must have imagined that the ghost of his own childhood had been long since laid to rest. To hear the same accusations made public must have exposed a nerve and struck at the root of his security. Not surprisingly then, his reaction was violent. Poor Patrick.

CHAPTER SIXTEEN

1979

Diary:

I have sent a long letter to Patrick's lawyers. If the new information isn't sufficient to sway the judge then nothing ever will. God knows why no one else has gone to the same trouble. Poor Patrick lies in that awful place and all they do is think the worst of him. Odd isn't it—they are prepared to see the worst in Patrick but think that Jimmy was a really good guy. Enough said!—Whilst moral shrapnel is clearly no respecter of previous good character, nothing must disturb those explosive issues on which false respectability is so tightly packed.

But enough of all that. I must get myself together and go back to work. The term is almost over and there are all kinds of things I should have done. Sadly the impetus behind my career ambitions seems to have dissipated. I need to reinvigorate my effort.

* * *

This time the sun was shining. A late winter sun, slanting through the trees outside her bedroom window making dappled patterns on the fading carpet and long shadows. The curtains glowed and the silence was absolute. The quiet disturbed her and she was not sure why. It was almost too quiet. A holiday quiet, a time when children did not want quiet, the quiet of late boring afternoons when nothing happened—when she wanted something to happen—anything. (Get out of the room. Don't lay there. Listen to me) She could remember feeling drowsy, her face against the cool of the cotton pillowcase, the smoothness of thin sheets against her bare skin. (Don't go to sleep—whatever you do don't go to sleep) But whilst there was a physical ease and a sense of comfort, her mind raced, objecting, not wanting. There was a feeling of anticipation—a fear of what was about to happen. (Oh God not again she thought—not again. Don't let her do it again)

The time frame flickered and it was dusk. Longer shadows now. The sound of traffic died away. Children went home for supper and men walked home after work. Soft footsteps on the stairs. (Get up and hide. At least lock the door. Leave the room. He would never attempt anything outside of the room.)

The door opened slowly and he stood there. The smells of the butcher's shop, sawdust, freshly cut meat and sausages filled the room underscored by the sweeter stench of offal. Nausea set in and the girl in the bed squirmed. She would not look in his direction, turning instead to face the wall, hoping he would leave, wishing he would think that she was asleep. For a moment the observer's voice was still, apparently more horrified even than the girl in the bed, struck dumb by what was known to happen . . . happened . . . happening. (No—no—not again, not again. Please not again.)

Panic echoed between the two, accelerating with each rebound. The one frozen with fear, rigid against the wallpaper beyond help, the other in a hot sweat of distant concern—hopelessness.

And then the scream.

* * *

She awoke sitting, the loudness of her voice still sounding in the small room. The duvet a tangle beneath her calves, the sheet pulled back and her body pumping sweat. Her hands quivered and the muscles in her face and neck twitched and jumped. She breathed deeply and wiped away the last tear.

It had been a bad one. Much worse in its effect than anything she could remember in recent years and the thought uppermost was that she still needed help. She swung her legs round the side of the bed, grateful for the cold of the linoleum under her feet, relieved by air from the open window. Slowly her breathing resumed its normal rhythm and the balance of her thinking was restored. She realised that the nightmare had evolved. Now she experienced both the memory of the event as the victim and witnessed it as a concerned observer of her own past. She was both the child and the adult—the worst of both worlds.

Fighting the depression she felt, she stood and put on her dressing-gown. She needed a cup of tea or preferably a stiff drink she thought. She needed to talk to someone who knew about these things and for a second she considered telephoning the hospital. She resisted the idea in favour of self-help. A little while later she sat at the kitchen table under the sixty watt bulb sipping hot sweet tea laced with whisky, a concoction that soothed as much as it numbed. She was annoyed with herself—at her lack of control—her nightmare had reached a new level of intensity even in the face of her recent treatment. She decided that the knub of her anguish—at least her conscious anguish—was the disappointment she felt at not being cured. Despite the doctor's warnings that treatment over a much longer period was needed, she had believed secretly that after the trauma related to the episode in school had passed, her routine would return to normal. All she had ever wanted was a normal life—to be just like everyone else.

The second cup of tea was a sixty-forty mixture with the whisky having the edge and as she sipped it, her thoughts turned to Patrick again. Theirs was and always had been the most special relationship. His was the shoulder she cried on when no one else understood, when no-one could be trusted with her problems. Their views and questions and ultimately their rejection of their inherited religious faith had been arrived at during their regular whispered discussions usually when the others had gone to sleep. All the more disconcerting for her to witness his strange behaviour at the prison. In her mind she reconstructed their conversation again, trying to find new significance in what he had said, trying to see if he was sending her a message, a secret sign that she alone should understand—but the task defeated her. She knew then that she would have to go again to Durham. She could not return to London with the matter left unresolved.

Just as she emptied the cup the kitchen door opened and Theresa entered.

I thought I heard someone," the younger girl said yawning," guessed it would be you. Is there any tea left in the pot?"

Without her make-up and still in the early stages of waking, Theresa looked like a little girl again—very young and very innocent. She poured herself a cup of tea and sat opposite her sister, her elbows propped on the table-top.

"So," she asked, "what's the problem now?"

There was a note of resignation in her tone, as if she were the more mature one, as if she had always been the sounding board for Lorna's continuous quandary. It made the older girl smile.

"Bad dreams I guess.' she answered.

"A guilty conscience?" Theresa asked.

"About what?" There was a criticism implicit in the question that Lorna quickly reacted to. "You name it. You've plenty to choose from."

"I think you'd better explain that."

The younger girl adopted a provocative sneer," That's easy—you leave home under a cloud, after the mysterious seminar in London. You have no contact with anyone for years save for the occasional Christmas card and then you turn up; giving the impression that you can sort out all our problems—problems, the cause of which you have no notion. D 'you want me to go on?"

Lorna struggled to keep her temper.

"Please do—get it all out."

"Okay. Look at the way you behaved at the funeral—like Jimmy had done nothing for any of us. Like you were doing us all a big favour just by being there. You upset Peter then you go to Durham and upset Patrick. Honestly Lonny—you need to get down off you high horse and remember where you came from. I'm not surprised you can't sleep."

The attack came as a shock to Lorna. She had imagined that she and Theresa had a good rapport, that being sisters, they shared the same family concerns.

The comment about Jimmy was especially irritating. The stupid girl had been used, just as the rest of them had been and for her now to claim some sort of sympathy—let alone gratitude to the man, was almost unimaginable.

"I'll choose to believe that you have a short, if not a convenient memory Tessa. However let me remind you about dear Jimmy

Before she could put her argument Theresa interrupted angrily," Don't bother slagging him off. I've heard it all before Lonny. Once upon a time all you could talk about was Jimmy's behaviour. You infected all of us with your senseless venom. To be honest, I came to believe that it was all founded on jealousy."

Jealousy?"

"Yes. You couldn't stand it when Jimmy turned his affections to me. You were green with envy. It's time someone told you the truth, if only to stop the hypocrisy."

For a moment Lorna almost slapped her sister's face. Instead she drained her cup, banged it down on the table before responding, this time in a louder voice.

"Turned his affections to you," she said cynically,"—you silly young cow. Jimmy was a child abuser, a pervert who should have been put behind bars years ago. I kept quiet for Mum's sake and, if you did but know it, I tried to warn you what he was like long before he sneaked into your bed. If you enjoyed him, you're welcome to him you fool but at least recognise what he was. You might be interested to know that he had been in trouble with the police as a young man for exactly the same thing. And as far as jealousy's concerned—forget it. He was and is my eternal nightmare."

Theresa's white face was streaked with uncontrollable tears, she actually dithered with fury and for a little while she could not speak. When she did, her voice was raised by an octave.

"You broke Mum's heart you know. She knew how you'd teased and tempted Jimmy; she even suspected that you'd seduced him. Jimmy used to tell me how it happened and . . . ." Lorna stood up suddenly, stopping her sister's tirade as she did so. Her chair fell back with a crash behind her and she leaned forward over the table breathless with renewed anger.

"Did he also tell you how he'd screwed my school-friend Helen Bonar? Did he tell you how he'd assaulted Patrick—and Peter and God knows how many more unsuspecting underage children. Tessa you're a stupid slut you . . . ."

Before she could finish the kitchen door burst open and Peter stood there.

"Enough." He shouted," Let it be. The whole street can hear you."

* * *

The next morning Lorna left before her brother and sister were up. She telephoned for a taxi and after finishing a cup of coffee in the kitchen, she left. Her Mother came down just as the kettle boiled and it was obvious from her attitude that she had heard at least some of the argument the night before. She looked tired, sitting quietly at the end of the table as Loma prepared the drinks.

Eventually Lorna looked her in the face.

"Sorry Mum. I'm really sorry." She said," The last thing I ever wanted was to upset you." Her Mother sighed and looked tearfully at her daughter.

"It's me who should be apologising Lonny. Deep down, I knew what was going on. I—I just didn't know what to do—ever. Either time."

The admission was as shocking as it was pitiful and for the first time Lorna realised how weak her Mother was. She was as much a victim as the rest of them. She went over and put an arm round her, resting her head against her Mother's.

"It's all in the past now Mum, best forgotten. I should never have made it an issue with Tessa."

"I'm glad you did."

Lorna looked at her, curious about her comment.

"I'm afraid your little sister was—well she was distorted by it all. That's the only way to describe it—distorted. You may not want to hear this—but she liked it. She even encouraged it. You were the only lucky one—getting well away. Poor Tessa never really understood."

Lorna felt nauseous. It confirmed all that had been said in the kitchen the night before.

"Then she should get some help Mum," she said," if her values are so twisted—she might do anything. Look—"she pulled a card from her purse and handed it to her Mother," Get her to see this doctor. Mention my name and I'm sure she'll get an appointment quickly."

The tears rolled down her Mother's face but she took the card.

"I'm going back now Mum," Lorna added," I'll try to call in and see Patrick on the way and I'll write to you from London."

At the door they hugged and kissed before Lorna got into the taxi and her Mother stood at the door waving until the cab turned the corner.

* * *

During much of the following twelve months that last conversation between Lorna and her Mother became an incendiary that burnt intermittently bright in Lorna's mind. It proved an internal debate that was interrupted only by the pressures and demands of work. An inverse relationship in which such interruptions also seemed to fuel the intensity of her memories as they returned but that prohibited any accommodation of the facts. Consequently, the pressures of work seemed to become more unmanageable whatever the degree of the effort she invested. An outcome as capricious as any she could imagine.

As promised, she did write home but only once. However, the letter was never answered and consequently, Lorna wrongly assumed that no one wished to reply. Distance, providing a convenient buffer for her emotional involvement, enabled her to leave the matter unresolved and she satisfied her conscience by promising herself that she would pursue it more fully at a more appropriate time. It was decision she was to regret. Nine months later she received a phone call from Peter telling her that her Mother had died suddenly of a heart attack.

The news came at a time when Lorna was already feeling fragile. Since returning to her job, the movement for greater accountability in schools had led to an atmosphere of increasing constraint, making her responsibilities on a day to day basis, all the more onerous. It fell to her to communicate the new recommendations to staff and, to make matters worse, it was implicit also that she should explain and justify them. As a new Deputy, she was used to operating in the no-man's land between the Head teacher and the rest of the teaching staff and she had long since appreciated that, whatever her own feelings, she was inevitably obliged to translate his policy decisions into acceptable practice. The problem therefore was not in applying the principles of her management role but rather in the increase of the difficulty factor associated with that role. Now, every meeting she attended proved contentious. Staff resistance turned to enmity, multiplying in direct proportion to what they saw as outside interference and the ethos of the school suffered badly as a consequence.

Much of this may have been better manageable had she not already been under such personal stress prompted by her private problems. The situation was further accentuated by staff reservations about her professional capability. She was young—too young to be a deputy—some said. She imagined the exchange of looks between certain Heads of Department to be derogatory, their comments to be patronising and their attitude generally to be one of pained tolerance. Not surprisingly therefore her response became all the more strained and all the more dependent on the favours of an American called Jim Beam. The sour mash whisky was her only respite.

The news of her Mother's death was the last straw.

On the day in question, she had worked the whole morning with a particularly difficult lower ability group of fourteen year olds. Nice kids but with an average reading age more appropriate to children three years their junior. A group who, whilst they might know the intimate detail of every character in a multitude of TV Soaps, had yet to experience the possible delight of the written word. During mid-morning break that day, she had listened to complaints from a concerned parent and intervened in a dispute between the PE. Department and Joy Pritchard who was responsible for Special Needs programmes and during the lunch-time break, she was booked to chair a meeting of the Curriculum Committee to discuss yet more new proposals for change.

Peter's call arrived just after the lunch-time bell and the secretary found her, just as she was about to sit down in the Lower school dining hall with her fish fingers chips and beans . . .

After taking the call, she returned to the dining hall where she sat for several minutes without speaking whilst the food, only tepid to start with became cold. It took a little while but pupils on a nearby table soon noticed her immobility and when she did not respond to their questions, they became concerned. One of them went to report the strange behaviour to the office staff and returned with the secretary. She reassured the children and helped Lorna to her feet. Clearly all was not well. Locked in a recent memory of her Mother, Lorna moved as a sleepwalker, eyes glazed and almost completely immured from her real environment. Her condition was diagnosed by the school nurse as being one of considerable shock.

It was twenty-four hours before Lorna fully regained a sense of place and time. A whole day spent sitting alone in her flat, perched uncomfortably on the edge of an armchair facing a blank television screen. One of the Senior Teachers had driven her home and her doctor had been called. After a cursory examination, her minimal response to his questions, allowed him to assume it was only a temporary trauma and in the tradition of a busy locum, he wrote her a prescription for more sleeping pills and left. His scribbled note was still grasped in her hand when finally she came round.

There were several aspects of that last conversation with her Mother that continued to disturb Lorna and it was these she had dwelt on during her long silence. By far the most shocking was the admission that her Mother had known about Jimmy's abuse. That she could ignore it was incomprehensible and what did she mean when she said " . . . Either time . . . ?"

She must have known it happened more than just twice. Equally, given the

As though she had long since granted a perverse dispensation to her new husband. And it was the passive toleration of such behaviour that had made Lorna feel delirious.

This time however, her long silence was not accompanied by insensibility or disassociation, the grains of consciousness had remained throughout. It was as though the mixture of emotions suddenly experienced: the loss, the frustration of questions that would be left unanswered and the appreciation of her Mother's complicity were too much. At a stroke, the news had flooded her mind, breaking the dam between the subconscious, half-digested worries that had been held in abeyance and the conscious need to continue to operate in the real world. It was only when a level of accommodation had been reached, inevitably a slow process that she could function again. She threw the doctor's prescription in the waste bin and packed a case.

* * *

This second funeral service was an even more desultory affair than Jimmy's had been. According to her Mother's wishes, the body would be returned to Ireland for burial. However, given Patrick's continued incarceration, the rift between the sisters and Peter's determined refusal not to return to the land of his birth, it was left to Lorna to make the arrangements. A ceremony was nevertheless held in the local parish church prior to the body being moved but only served to emphasise the ambiguity of a funeral without an internment. To make matters worse, the friction between Lorna and Theresa proved to be a barrier that could not be breached. Lorna was greeted formally by her younger sister but was made to feel unwelcome, an act of self indulgence that obliged Lorna to take a room at a bed and breakfast hotel nearby rather than stay at the house. Much to his discomfort, Peter was left therefore to act as intermediary, a role for which, through his natural timidity, he was badly suited. And, although Patrick was allowed to attend again, this time he was more distant than ever, refusing to talk to any of the rest of the family including Lorna. He had finally been sentenced to twenty months in prison for Grievous Bodily Harm. Fortunately, his victim had survived and the court had considered his provocation in the sentencing. Nevertheless, according to the police, it would be several months more before Patrick could be considered for parole. Lorna tried to talk to him but, after his refusal to see her last time, she guessed he would refuse any contact. She was proved correct.

As she had been left to organise the export of the body and its burial, Lorna spent much of her time filling in the requisite forms and making arrangements over the telephone. She decided to accompany the coffin herself and, because of the atmosphere between her and Theresa, she ensured that the trip would take place as quickly as possible. She could see little value in delaying it. Consequently, only twenty-four hours after the church service, the undertakers delivered the casket to the airport where it was loaded into the hold of a British Airways flight, bound for Belfast.

Fergal and Molly still lived in the street and had kindly offered to host the occasion of the burial. They met her from the airport and although the meeting was sad, there was an element of home-coming evident in their presence and for Lorna it was like 'touching base' again.

CHAPTER SEVENTEEN

1979

News: August: At Warrenpoint Co Down, an IRA bomb containing more than half a ton of explosives hidden in a hay-cart, exploded as an army convoy drove past. Fifteen soldiers were killed and eight more, "very seriously," injured said an army spokesman.

A helicopter was damaged in a further explosion, but managed to fly the wounded to hospital. A gun battle ensued between troops and IRA men across a nearby loch. The death toll was the worse suffered by the army in any single incident and brings the total of soldiers killed in the Province since 1969 to 316.

* * *

It had been at Tessa's insistence that the wake was held. Peter was against the idea. In his view there was something primitive about celebrating your Mother's death with a party, something darkly unfitting and he wanted nothing to do with it. Lorna was briefly absent due to a curriculum meeting that she had been asked to host back in London. The plan was that she would return only in time to accompany the body back to Ireland. Had Patrick been there Peter was sure he would have objected to the wake and if Lorna had been present there would have been no question about it—but they weren't there and in their absence Tessa took charge. Peter was surprised at the steely determination his little sister showed, he had never seen her quite like this before, so sure of herself, so certain that she was right. It was a side of her that either she'd kept hidden or one that had just suddenly emerged. Whichever it was, he didn't like it.

When his Mother had suffered her final attack it had been Peter who tried to resuscitate her, who had finally held her hand as it grew colder. He had been awakened by a noise that night, a strange noise, like someone gargling. Having been deeply asleep, it had taken him several seconds to register where it came from and when he rushed into his Mother's room next door to his own, he'd found her in the final stages of what he rightly thought was a myocardial infarction. Peter had trained as an ambulance man and naturally therefore, on this occasion his reaction was instinctive. He made sure the airways were clear and he raised the patient's legs on several cushions before attempting to massage her heart and inflate her lungs. But it had been too late and when Tessa appeared at the door he was sitting alongside his Mother, tears streaming down his face, holding her hand and crooning a bedtime lullaby that she once used to sing to him.

His younger sister did not seem to be affected to the same extent. She was sorrowful apparently without the trauma. Her lack of reaction left him uncertain if the need to make the necessary arrangements had served as an occupational therapy sufficient to hide her bereavement or if she was actually immune to the deeper feelings he experienced. Her suggestion that there should be a wake left him horrified but his arguments were swept aside with the justification that, as she had organised everything else, the choice should be hers and hers alone.

In the ten years or so since they had settled in Thornaby, Peter's Mother had made a variety of friends. Some were as a consequence of the business, other shop-owners and farmers however those she had valued most had been from the Irish community. For reasons it was never clear, the North East coast had attracted a fair sized group of immigrants from across the water and this included several priests from the two largest Catholic churches, as well as a number of other families. Many of the husbands and fathers worked in the building industry, one or two successfully running their own contracting businesses and, needing a reliable labour force, it was this group who were mainly responsible for encouraging other young men to migrate to the British mainland.

There were two places where the Irish community tended to congregate for social occasions, the Knights of St. Columbia Club situated behind St. Mary's church and the Irish Working Men's Club located in a single storied building just off the High Street. Jimmy Ungerside and his wife had been members of both clubs and had been regular visitors, particularly at week-ends. Not surprisingly, those friends originating from these two places thought that Tessa's idea of a traditional Irish wake was a laudable notion and they threw their support behind her. Peter could do no more than concede. He nevertheless observed that Tessa was careful to promote the occasion of the wake before her elder sister was due to arrive. Lorna would have been quick to scotch the idea.

The night that the celebration took place saw the little family house crowded to capacity. The open coffin had been sited on the dining-room table and that room was lit only with long church candles, a flickering light that occasionally made the face of the dead woman appear to change expression. Unfortunately, certainly from Peter's point of view, the crowds of mourners produced such a crush that, before the night was over, glasses of drinks were being balanced all around the corpse. Had she been able to comment, Peter was certain that his Mother would have disapproved most strongly however, his own objections were ignored.

Typically, the visitors drank too much and it was not long before groups of men were being sent to the off-license to buy more alcohol. By this time someone had seen fit to play records of a collection of maudlin Irish songs that were designed, both to produce nostalgic tears in the eyes of the listeners and to prompt those still coherent to join in the various choruses. The ensuing noise, the crowds and the overpowering sink of beer eventually sickened Peter. The respect they had all claimed to have for the deceased was forgotten in a selfish quest for the oblivion they sought. It seemed to him that his helplessness was magnified all the more by the confusion of the melee and in the end; he quietly retired to his bedroom to be away from it all.

For a while he lay on his bed, his face pressed into the pillow with the door firmly closed. He badly wanted to speak to Lorna but as the telephone was downstairs that was impossible. If he could only have been as strong as she was, he thought, then none of this would have happened. With the realisation of his own weakness, he suddenly experienced a terrible feeling of desolation. He was, he thought, a poor excuse for a man without doubt the runt of the litter and the one with the greatest need for help and assistance. In the true meaning of the word he saw himself as being forever dependent. In his mind's eye he scanned what little there was of his life's achievements and the conclusions confirmed his worst fears.

For a while he stood before the wardrobe mirror and scrutinised himself, trying to make an objective assessment of the young man before him.

"Tall and thin," he told his reflection, "dark hair, pale complexion but a weak chin. Aesthetic looking at best—feminine at worst . . . . You haven't even ever had a girl-friend." The last remark was made loudly, a confession to shame himself. "What will you do now—now your Mother is dead?"

The mention of his Mother brought back the tears and the tears emphasised his feeling of self-loathing. On an impulse he left his room and went next door into his Mother's room. There was clothing stacked in neat piles on the bed and a collection of personal bits and pieces laid out on the dressing table—clearly Tessa's handiwork. In a moment of anger he swept his arm across the dressing table top, sending everything onto the floor. He spun round then, intending to similarly disrupt the piles of dresses and coats and underclothes that lay so neatly on the bed, but he stopped himself. There was nothing to be gained by vandalism. It was a sterile expression of weakness. He told himself he should go downstairs instead and eject the drunks, kick their arses into the street and Tessa along with them. But he knew he would not do so.

He sat on the bed feeling confused and disappointed not knowing how he could ever express the depth of his empty anger. His hand fell onto a pile of lace, silky underclothes, beautiful smooth things that felt cool to the touch. He held up a satin slip—almost a work of art. Before he knew what he was doing he had removed his shirt and jeans and pulled the slip over his head. It felt good. Quickly, he slipped out of his underpants and slid into a pair of fine silk knickers. The image he presented to the dressing-table mirror was quite different from that he had watched in his own room. With the female clothing suddenly he acquired a new confidence.

CHAPTER EIGHTEEN

1980

News: Belfast. Anne Maguire, the death of whose three children in 1976 sparked off Northern Ireland's Peace People movement, was found dead with her throat and wrists cut in her Belfast home today. Foul play is not suspected.

Diary February: It did not feel like a homecoming despite the fog, the rain and the wind, atmospherics that are forever in my imagination the Irish soup. Indeed I felt like a stranger. However, the authorities were just as intransigent as I remembered, making me wait for over two hours before issuing the permit to allow Mam's body back. I was horrified when they insisted on opening the coffin. A precaution they claimed to ensure it was free from arms or explosives—bastards. The place has changed. A transformation most apparent in people's faces and their lack of humour—their lack of sympathy. Northern Ireland has hardened itself—perhaps necessarily—against the abuse it suffers daily. All sides in the conflict have much to blame themselves for. It was such a relief to find Molly and Fergal still in the house next door to my birth-place.

* * *

The dog kept on barking. "You're a bastard!" Tom muttered. He squatted in the shadows of the wall watching the street that crossed in front of him. The street light round the corner cast a yellow triangle, defining the boundary of his anonymity. The light and the dog challenged his security. Suddenly one of the men behind him coughed. A shallow sound that echoed, bouncing off the silent brickwork. He glanced back and saw Private Wayne Holier make an apologetic shrug. The four man army patrol was on its way back to barracks after their nightly tour of the back-streets in West Belfast. It was a front-line duty. In that location, a couple of hours creeping about were enough for anyone. Each of his team was fully kitted and, although the heavy bulletproof vests caused them to sweat, they were glad of whatever protection they could get. Intelligence would have them believe that the terrorists had only two sniper rifles but who could say what was true. And whilst the vests would stop most bullets from regular weapons, the sniper rifles could send large scale, armour piercing shells through anything—vests, bone, muscle and sometimes even brick walls given the right conditions.

The dog's barking ended in a squeal. Clearly Corporal Jimmy Burt had found it. The men behind Tom grinned. So much for the English as animal-lovers, Tom thought. Belfast was populated by dozens of homeless dogs and typically, they would follow the soldiers at night, barking at them, whether for attention or food. Any number of serious incidents had therefore been prompted by stray dogs. They gave away both the presence and the position of the patrols consequently it was common practice to cut their throats.

Jimmy returned silently and took his position again at the back of the column. They crossed the street and, with a wave of his hand, Tom sent two men to walk the opposite pavements. Wayne joined Jimmy and Paul stayed behind Tom.

The procession moved slowly. In each case the lead man swaying, staring hard and watching all those blank windows, those empty doorways. The men behind riding rear-guard, made crabbed progress, it was for him to study where they had come from. The movements had been refined, a choreographed precision hard won by countless casualties. Not surprisingly, it was easier to operate in an empty road rather than one full of people. Pedestrians were hard to accommodate in the security context that the soldiers practised. Conversely however, empty roads at night brought their own problems.

The street joined a main road—the road to the barracks and the soldiers' pace quickened. Tom skirted a parked van and signalled Paul to follow suit. Vehicles were often used to house explosives, bombs waiting for the predictable appearance of the English. Access to the barracks was severely limited and it had proven to be a fact of life that the nearer the barracks therefore, the more likely an attack.

A group of late-night drinkers passed by, muttering their objections, one of them spitting in the gutter to demonstrate his feelings. They were ignored. The road bent and the floodlit high walls of the Army HQ stockade appeared in the distance. Now they broke into a trot: an orderly increase in pace. Twenty yards further on, somewhere south of them the low desultory c-err-ump of an explosion sounded. Tom could see Jimmy grinning under his helmet, obviously glad that the disturbance was now someone else's concern. Weren't they all?

As if by magic the gates opened at their approach and a second later they were all safely back inside the stockade. Tom reported to the duty officer in charge and then went to his room to change. After a shower he went to the Officers Mess and treated himself to a welcome pint of beer. Up until Belfast he had enjoyed his career in the Army. He liked the proscription. No thinking needed and only decisions to make, when he was told to make them. Life was predictable, secure. It was just as he'd been told it would be—like being part of a huge family. Once the workings of the hierarchy were understood, even here in Belfast, there was little to worry a young officer—other than staying alive.

"And was it a good tour?" Gerry Watson another lieutenant asked.

"Not bad—fucking dogs though."

"Yeah, we had four last night,' Gerry said, "one of them, a big Alsatian, nearly took Geordie's hand off."

"You got any leave coming?" Tom asked.

"No. Not till Easter."

"You'll not get off at Easter unless it's a compassionate . . . . It's all hands to the pumps at Easter—one of their silly seasons."

Another explosion sounded as he spoke. This time it was much closer and almost everyone in the room stopped to listen. Sure enough a few seconds after the bang, there was the sound of gunfire.

"Those are AK 47's," Gerry observed, "not our lot anyway."

Almost immediately his analysis was contradicted when the distinctive sound of army weapons opened up.

"Aw shit," Tom muttered, "let's hope we're not called. I've just got in."

As if on cue, at that moment Captain Evans strode into the room. He saw Tom immediately. "Need you Tom," he called out, "kit up and I'll meet you at the gates in five minutes. Okay?"

"And the lads too?" Tom asked.

"Leave 'em be. We'll join Red Patrol they're on stand-by."

Although it sometimes felt like a lifetime, Tom had joined the Second Parachute Regiment only two years before, after cutting short his academic career. Despite having gained a teaching qualification and a degree, during teaching practice he had never felt comfortable in the classroom and his degree was only a third. Even so, he may have settled for teaching, if things had gone better with Loma. He liked to tell himself and anyone else who would listen that his aptitude was for commanding men and that he did not understand women. Whenever the affair with Lorna was referred to, as it was only occasionally and then, only by very close friends, he would say it was destined to fail from the beginning. It was a lie that no one believed and privately, hidden in his most secret heart of hearts, the fact that he had lost Lorna was the deepest regret of his young life.

"What's the flap Sir?" Tom asked as he climbed aboard the troop carrier.

"Murder and mayhem Tom—what else." Captain Evans replied, "Let's face it; if the buggars were having any other kind of party we wouldn't get an invite."

Some of the men laughed. The vehicle careered round a corner throwing Tom almost into the Captain's lap. He struggled back to his seat and grabbed the support strap.

"Okay but where are we going?" Tom persisted.

"Denby Road—do you know it?"

It sounded familiar but Tom could not place it.

"Sorry.' he replied, shaking his head" . . . What's the SP??"

"Major Grieve with a patrol of six—fired on, ambush style—two men down. And the cheeky bastards are shooting it out with the Major, even as we speak."

It was obvious by the speed of the carrier that someone thought it was a real emergency. Including the Captain and Tom, there were eight men on board plus a medic in the front with the driver: heavily armed soldiers all of whom were chomping at the bit.

The troop carrier screamed to a halt and simultaneously the back doors were flung open. As each man left the safety of its protection, automatically they adopted their part of a defensive grid position, weapons pointed outwards, alternately crouching and kneeling, eyes and gun muzzles scanning the landscape. Evans called for the Sergeant to hold the position and he pulled Tom to one side.

"Take a quick gander round that corner Tom—and—for God's sake don't get yourself shot." Denby Road was wider than most and from Tom's vantage point despite the dark; he could see that about thirty yards away a group of men were firing on a terraced house. The guns flashed, challenging the dimness of street lights. The light-toned chatter of automatic weapons was punctuated by the heavier sound of the patrol's disciplined single shots. Windows in cars parked nearby were shattered and the brickwork of the house where the soldiers had taken refuge was pitted with shell scars.

"They've got the Major pinned down in a house Sir," Tom reported, "three shooters that I can see, set up behind parked cars."

The Captain deployed his men quickly. He sent Tom with three soldiers to block the other end of the street.

"And when you have to open fire Tom—please don't hit any of our fellers. We'll try to drive the lunatics towards you so we'll be in your line of fire. Okay?"

Tom nodded and led his group off at the double.

The Captain's attack had been spotted almost as soon as he turned the corner and, from the other end of the road, Tom saw one of the terrorists beneath a large Ford, laying flat on the tarmac; turn his weapon in their direction. The Captain's relief force was immediately halted—a stand-off. At Tom's end of the road the houses had bay windows and rather than wait, he decided to advance using the bays as cover. He moved his men forward slowly, two on either side of the road. As they drew closer he could see the bodies of two soldiers laid immobile on the pavement and the legs of another protruded from the open doorway of the house where Major Grieve had taken cover. Clearly the ambush had caught the patrol completely by surprise.

So far unseen, Tom had time to study the situation. It was impossible to say where the terrorists had hidden originally. However, they must have been confident of a quick victory if they broke cover to complete their attack. He scanned the house fronts. He found the size of the terrorist force surprising. Not like them to send only three men to hit a patrol of six. They usually liked the odds. Now however, the pincer movement was almost complete. The three men shooting at Major Grieve were covered on three sides. Their only escape route lay to the rear, through the house that stood immediately behind them.

As if reading Tom's mind, the Corporal across the road signalled, telling Tom that they needed to gain the high ground. He pointed at the upstairs of a nearby house. Good thinking and Tom acknowledged as much. Unfortunately, it was when he moved forward the next time, sliding round the next bay window to implement the plan that he was spotted.

One of the terrorists had turned to reload, sitting with his back to the Ford his face hidden in the shadows. Now he faced the other end of the road and he saw Tom's move. A second later, still half exposed, Tom and his companion came under fire. The soldier with him was hit in the first volley. Two rounds in the neck almost took the young man's head off. He was dead before he hit the concrete. In anything but such a densely populated urban location, Tom would have thrown a grenade. He could have finished all three gunmen in a few seconds but standing orders prohibited such a move. Instead he crouched, flattening himself against the brickwork, trying to keep his head lower than the glass. Bullet ridden chips of concrete from the pavement scattered around him and the windows smashed, hurling shards of glass, He felt the warm flow of blood across his cheek where a splinted caught him. Suddenly from the dark, the soldiers across the road opened up and the pressure was relieved as his attacker pulled back out of their line of fire. Given a moment's grace Tom slipped through the front door behind him. He found himself in a dark passage. A woman's face appeared from the distant kitchen.

"Oh God no," she muttered, obviously terrified.

"Sorry Love," Tom said hurrying to the stairs," I need to use the front bedroom."

It was a small house and he had no difficulty in finding the room he wanted. Exactly as he'd guessed, the big bay window overlooked the scene below. It was a scene of almost total chaos. He stared through the lace curtains.

"Please—please don't smash the house up." the woman said quietly from behind him. She had followed him up the stairs and now stood at the bedroom door ashen faced. Tom had no time to explain, still less to reassure her. He looked down with a clear view at the three assailants, switched his weapon to automatic and opened fire. The glass shattered, the fine lace curtains burst into flame and the three men crouching behind the old Ford car took the full brunt of his three second burst. It was all over.

The woman behind him screamed an empty low sound more like that of an animal in distress than a human. He tore the curtains down and stamped the fire out.

"Sorry," he said again," couldn't be helped."

She rushed forward trying to help put out the flames, all the while moaning fearfully. Tom stepped back. He looked down through the broken glass and saw Major Grieve emerge from across the road. The soldier advanced on the car carrying his service pistol. The two men remaining from his patrol also appeared. One was pale-faced and bloody, his left arm hanging useless. In the distance the Captain's men came running but before anyone else could reach the scene, Tom saw the Major approach the three terrorists. He stopped where they lay. One, a badly wounded man, rolled slowly onto his side and said something, without hesitation Grieve pointed his pistol and shot the man in the face. He turned the gun on the other two and fired one round into each of them. Tom could hardly believe his eyes. He heard the Corporal yell something and, out of the corner of his eye, saw him come running.

At the foot of the stairs he saw two more women standing, looking towards the front door which now stood open to the dim street outside. Tom hurried down.

Now there would be hell to pay. All the accusations of 'shoot to kill' would be dredged up again and the traditional face-saving consequences would apply to everyone involved. "Excuse me Love," Tom muttered, pushing between the women.

The nearest turned and he caught her eye as he rushed past. He was two steps on before he realised. Disbelievingly, he stopped and turned back. Lorna stood with her arm round the other woman.

"Lorna?" he asked, still uncertain.

She stared for a moment, equally prepared to deny what she saw.

"Tom—Tom is that really you?" she asked finally in a very small voice.

"Lorna—what the hell are you doing here?"

He blurted his question without thinking, even as he remembered. She had told him all about her childhood, living in Denby Road. This was her part of the world, the world she had tried so often to describe to him. The one she had run away from after her Father's death.

"I could ask you the same." She said.

Captain Evans's voice broke the spell. He called for Tom from the doorway and Tom answered automatically, tuning again as he spoke. At the front door he stopped and looked back. Was it really Lorna he asked himself? But sure enough she still stood there three yards away staring after him.

Later on the experts would argue that it was because he stood still in the half light of the open door that he made such a good target. Others would say he was chosen because he had defiled the house of one of their locals. Whichever it was, he became a focus for the other member of the ambush team, and the one Tom had earlier suspected might be out there. A single shot rang out and Tom spun in the doorway falling, dead weight to the floor. The returning fire came from three separate sources simultaneously, almost before Captain Evans shouted the order. It was a swift retribution shattering the whole upstairs window frame of a house opposite before doing the same to the head and upper torso of the assassin.

Tom retained no memory whatsoever of the actual event. One moment he was staring down the passageway into Lorna's green eyes and the next he was on the floor, helplessly gasping for breath. The time frame jumped and Tom looked up to see Lorna, now suddenly close, now in tears, calling his name, then screaming for help. He blinked, it seemed and the Captain appeared, his hands tearing open the tunic front, forcing wads of combat dressings into his shirt and muttering all those pointless platitudes, those expressions of support, the lies one always gave to the dying.

"It s not that bad Tom I've done worse shaving—hang on—keep looking at me—the medic will be here in a second. Come on Tom stay with me—don't slip away—Tom, Tom. You young bastard stay with me."

In one mind-set, the detached part of him assessed the situation and drew the obvious conclusion. He had been hit somewhere in the upper torso, probably the left lung, so he would be bleeding massively internally. He had a less than evens chance of survival. What a bastard, he thought and he could see himself relax falling into trauma. The unresisting part of his thinking was very different and he couldn't see what all the fuss was about. He was comfortable laying down there on the floor and he was so pleased to see Lorna. It had been such a long time. He could feel her gripping his hand and he tried to smile to reassure her. She'd always worried about him. He made himself say her name, as much to confirm the reality of her presence as to actually communicate with her.

"Lorna." He said and she came closer, so close that he could smell her perfume. The same perfume he always smelt on her underclothes that she always hung out to dry in the bathroom. Then a black curtain came down.

* * *

He was fortunate. At least that was what everyone told him. And, if it was lucky to have a hard-nosed bullet chip one's collar-bone and send a fragment to collapse one lung and another to lodge deep in a chest muscle, then that's what he was . . . lucky. And of course there were various conflicting opinions about what constituted his good fortune. For example

Captain Evans would tell him repeatedly that his luck had arrived in having the immediate attention of a Medic.

"Not every soldier has a Medic on hand to stop him bleeding to death." he would say.

Whereas the doctors told him that had the fragment that punctured his lung turned only a matter of two or three degrees, it would have ripped a piece out of his heart and then no Medic in the world could have done anything to save him. They were therefore convinced that his luck depended on the angle of the shot. Even his Commanding Officer, Colonel John Hepworth had a theory. He came to visit Tom on day three of his confinement in hospital and, Tom believed, from the best of motives told him that, if the assassin had switched his weapon to automatic his luck would have certainly run out.

There was some evidence to support all these notions. However, Tom would always believe that he was lucky, simply because he had found Lorna again. Major Grieve on the other hand, was not so lucky. He had executed three men in full view of a countless number of witnesses. And, although there may, in his own mind have been some justification for his actions and certainly some sympathy for them on behalf of those army personnel present, the civilians who saw what he did, naturally felt quite differently. Major Grieve suffered a nervous breakdown. He was brought before a court-martial and only escaped a jail sentence because of his obvious state of mind. He was therefore discharged through ill health with a recommendation that he should receive psychiatric care. It was as generous a result as anyone might have hoped for and, although it did not satisfy that section of public opinion traditionally and, most felt, justifiably biased against the occupying forces, by the time the Press got hold of the story, the result was a faites accomplis.

After two weeks Tom was transferred to a hospital back in England. It took time for the wound to heal and for bone and muscle to mend. It took even longer however, for Lorna to accommodate seeing Tom again.

All the feeling of previous hurt and the baggage that she carried over from their affair, as she liked to call it, was suddenly freshened. The same questions were posed again, the same arguments rehearsed in her mind. This time however, she had the benefit of distance and time. It had been years since they split up, years in which she had proved her independence, demonstrated her abilities and made her own way. Now there could be no question about her career options. They were established fact. The integrity of her feelings for him was another matter.

That night, the night of the shootings, she defied the opinion of her relatives and the advice of friends and spent the night by Tom's bedside. His Colonel had been most understanding and had done his best, easing the red tape to enable her presence in an army hospital on the base. Not a decision that was easily come by, given the circumstances. As a consequence she had tolerated the indignity of the searches, the cross-examination by an officer from M16 and the armed guard that accompanied her throughout her stay. She closed her mind to trivia and focused all her attention on Tom.

For some time after surgery, the doctors were not convinced that he would live. They suspected that, despite the evidence of X-rays, there may still be tiny splinters, possibly the size of a hair's width, lodged in other vital organs. And, as if to confirm their fears, several times in the recovery room, his heartbeat became irregular and his breathing laboured. On one occasion, shortly after the surgeons had finished, he haemorrhaged and had to be rushed back into the theatre. It was nine long hours before he stabilised and another twelve before he was off the critical list. Eventually the doctor described the situation to Lorna.

She had waited, as instructed, in the small room down the long corridor. The small room that was made all the smaller by the presence of the large, uncommunicative soldier left to watch her. After what she had seen that night, the feeling of restriction, of being helpless to affect the outcome had left her nerves frayed. No one had even seen fit to offer her so much as a cup of tea during her vigil and by the time the doctor finally appeared she was in a state of third stage anxiety.

"Difficult to say." the doctor replied in answer to her question," If the internal bleeding has really stopped—then he may have a good chance."

"And don't you know if it's stopped?'

"The trouble is one can't ever be sure—not with a gun-shot wound." He paused and then added, "And of course we don't know how he'll deal with the trauma. A terrible shock to the system—a bullet wound like this."

In fact Tom dealt with it just as he dealt with everything else, with philosophical detachment. He accepted the cosseting and the attention albeit reluctantly and he settled into convalescence as if it were an army project, under orders, requiring him to lay still and recuperate as quickly as possible. Consequently, to everyone but Lorna's surprise, his progress was rapid. However, despite his healing rate, in its infinite wisdom the medical arm of his regiment decided he should be transferred to a hospital back in England. They argued that there were insufficient resources on hand in their base, to provide proper care and that the bed may be needed for other emergencies. For the first time since he had arrived in the Province, Tom found himself regretting the imminence of a return home.

Lorna had been a daily visitor to his bedside and their relationship had picked up almost where it had left off a those years previously. During her visits they had both ensured that their conversations carefully avoided that area of contention that had been the hallmark of their previous disagreements. Much of the time was spent in detailing the minutia of what they had done, where they had been and what each of them had achieved, and any communication about their feelings was left only as an implication. Quite deliberately however, Lorna did not mention her recent illness. In her view, those sicknesses of the mind bearing on sanity were still stigmatized, inevitably creating doubts about personality defect. By contrast, she did everything in her power to reassure Tom that she was exactly the same person he had known before and she justified this to herself by arguing that his recovery would depend as much on stability and security as it might on medical care.

Seeing Tom again had tweaked Lorna's conscience. She knew that the break-up had been caused more by her mood swings than by anything he might have done. On the one hand however, the renewed emotional contact was one she would not have chosen for herself. She had accommodated the fact of them going their separate ways, boxed her feelings in a leak-proof mental compartment and worked, making her alternative life as attractive as she could. Closing the shutters on any window of unpleasantness was a well developed ability she had practised for years. On the other hand, she could not deny the depth of her response. In the first instance his reappearance had left her quite literally breathless.

The confusion of this paradox was beyond her understanding. Her new life was carefully ordered—as it should be. Any unknown factors were able to be anticipated and thereby prioritised and the scheme of her progress was therefore well within her control. Control being the operative word for the whole of her new life-style. During the silence of her long bed-side wait, she listened to the case she brought against herself. The advocate for the prosecution claimed that, given her commitment to her job, there was no room for emotional ties, no space for dependency or dependents and certainly no time to be wasted on regrets. The defence could only refer the jury to the strength of her physical and emotional reaction and to the depth of her need (now admitted for the first time). The impact of seeing him, followed so quickly by seeing him shot down in front of her, had ripped a tear in her security covering. The mental body armour she had taken so long to weld together was shattered by the same bullet that struck him down. But as far as the possible consequences were concerned—the jury was still out.

For a while she even considered trying to cause another rift with Tom, as though to find good reason to break away again. She half planned that this time it would be made to appear his fault, exonerating her and thereby clearing away her guilt. Yet she still found herself making the journey every day to his bedside and the voice in her head warning of the danger of further involvement was ignored despite her concerns.

Echoing her state of mind, her nights again became disturbed by tortuous dreams. It was the first time since her illness that she was aware of her nightmares. And, although she was never a very sound sleeper, the difference now left her feeling exhausted. The old night devils returned with a vengeance: Jimmy and his sweating palms her fury at the little girl she once was, all the fear and isolation the vulnerability and the guilt, the tenable guilt. It was almost too much. And if this was as a consequence of meeting Tom again, she argued with herself, then was it worth while. The answer she found was not one bred from her application of logic but one that was instinctive. Her reservations and doubts were acknowledged and she discussed them with herself continuously. She weighed the consequences with almost every waking moment—but she still made that bus trip. She still sat alongside Tom and she still struggled not to spoil whatever it was that made the contact with him so satisfying.

Initially, her visit to Ulster had been intended only to facilitate the return her late mother's body to the land of her beginnings. A burial in a place she had loved and to satisfy her dying wishes. In the process however, it had allowed her to renew old friendships, to look again at her old home and to revisit her memories of childhood. She had planned a short stay but one without an actual definition of time spent. After all it was now the summer holidays and, unlike the rest of the school year, for six weeks she could make up her own mind about where she might go and what she would do. She might spend a week there or she might even spend the whole six weeks. In the event, the decision was made for her by Tom's injury. He was shot only days after she had arrived for the funeral and two weeks later she followed him back to the Mainland.

Three months later, against all the odds, she agreed to marry him.

CHAPTER NINETEEN

1981

News: January 16th

Ex-Ulster MP shot by Loyalist gunmen: Three men smashed their way into a remote farmhouse today and fired seven shots into Mrs. Bernadette McAliskey the former Westminster MP Bernadette Devlin. Mrs. McAliskey who was dressing her two children at the time is critically ill in a Belfast hospital tonight. Her husband Michael who was also shot is said to be stable.

Diary: At aged nearly twenty-five I should know my mind by now. Why then this feeling of making a terrible mistake. Tom is as patient as ever—a nice man and I love him dearly—but marriage? God help me haven't I made enough mistakes for a lifetime already. It was hard for me to tell Tom about myself—the abortion, the inability to conceive, the abuse and the breakdowns—but I managed in the end. He just smiled and quoted the last lines from one of his favourite movies, saying, "No one's perfect!" (Joe E. Brown from 'Some like it hot'.) Thank God he retains a human perspective and a sense of humour—he may need it.

* * *

It was a cold afternoon in February when Tom and Lorna appeared together at the church doors as man and wife. A small knot of friends and relatives gathered together in the porch to cheer their calls of congratulations but the sound of their celebration was lost against the whine of an icy north wind. Confetti had been banned within the church confines but the car waiting at the kerb had been festooned with flowers and messages of good-will and even a string of tin cans, tied to the back bumper.

Nevertheless, in so far as she had wanted a traditional service, Lorna had been sadly disappointed. Tom had been raised in the religion of the English Methodists and as a consequence, the Catholic priest had refused to allow organ music, still less the celebration of a Nuptial Mass. He had also insisted that Tom should attend six lessons, designed to inform him of his responsibilities in marrying a Roman Catholic. The instructions culminated in Tom having to sign a declaration, promising not to interfere with the religious upbringing of any children that may be born to them. Privately the couple had laughed in regard to this last issue; the priest was unaware that Lorna was no longer able to have children. The small-mindedness typical of his calling had been justified by Father O'Reilly's reference to the strict traditions of the church when dealing with what he called 'mixed marriages'. His was a clear demonstration of a preference for the traditional prejudice, rather than for anything approaching the emergent ecumenical movement.

Significantly, Lorna thought, the fabric and atmosphere of his church was equally mean. It was a modern structure built from crude 'council house' orange brick and fitted with Pine furniture that was sparse and cheap. In her view, an ethos implying impermanence and more like a fast-food outlet than a house of God. Due to the fact that both her parents were deceased, Tom's Colonel kindly agreed to take her arm in place of a male relative. For reasons best known to himself, Peter had refused to play any formal part in the ritual and Patrick was still as yet waiting for his release from prison. Peter was in fact the only real relative to attend the ceremony, little had been heard from Theresa in recent months and she had not even replied to the invitation. Consequently, the guest list consisted of only a distant Aunt on Tom's side, Peter, six friends from Tom's regiment and two members of Lorna's staff from her London school. And whilst it was therefore, only a modest affair the quality of happy couple's commitment belied the lack of those there to witness it.

Tom was almost fully fit again. The only sign of his injury was an occasional shortness of breath and a tendency to tire easily, little enough under the circumstances. His doctors were delighted with progress and had termed the speed of his recovery, nothing sort of miraculous. He wore his dress uniform for the occasion and, in Lorna's eyes, looked every bit the military hero—albeit one from the British side. She finally settled for a smart dark blue suit complimented by a corsage made from immaculate white lilies.

The wedding breakfast was held in a small reception room on the first floor of a hotel in the High street. It was kept simple: a buffet, supplemented by sufficient drinks to relax the guests but, as Tom said, not enough to encourage rowdy behaviour from the other soldiers present. His Best Man was Brian Cocker, a Second Lieutenant and close friend who acquitted the needs of the office with a fair mix of style and good humour. Conscious as he was of Lorna's recent loss and having been advised of her somewhat delicate mental health, his speech was carefully constructed so as to avoid the standard 'mother-in-law' jokes often seen as the core of such occasions.

He was nevertheless able to reduce the small assembly to tears of laughter especially when he compared Tom's new status with his first efforts in the military training programme. Given the obvious constraints, the affair went well and everyone appeared to enjoy themselves. Lorna was only sad that the representatives of her close family were not more numerous and that her 'baby' brother Peter chose such to play such a limited role. It was not until she and her new husband were about to leave that Peter came to offer his congratulations. He caught them in the foyer, sheepishly shaking Tom's hand and whispering a few words in his sister's ear as he kissed her cheek . . .

"You're a real beauty Lonny," he said hugging her, "and Mum and Dad would have been proud of you. Be happy."

As he pulled back she was surprised to see his eyes had filled with tears but before she could enquire or comfort him, the crowd of well-wishers engulfed her. Peter hurried away and the last she saw of him was when he paused briefly at the door to glance back: dark eyes beneath even darker brows. It was a look that was strangely, unaccountably furtive turning his departure into a retreat. Ever since he was a child, given the circumstance, Peter would flounce dramatically out of rooms, his jacket flaring and his hair tossed. It was an affected demonstration that eventually became a genuine characteristic. On this, the occasion of her wedding however, he quitted the company anonymously leaving an impression of disillusionment and defeat. The image stayed with Lorna throughout the rest of the day adding to the litany of concerns she felt, prompted by the absence of her family.

A little later husband and wife sat together holding hands in the back of a taxi. Thankful to be alone, they left the small crowd of guests on the pavement outside the hotel and headed for the railway station. The same night, after a tortuously slow journey on a local train, they arrived at The Alexandria Hotel in Whitby forty minutes after the dining room had closed. Tom's romantic plans for a champagne dinner, served in their double room were of necessity therefore delayed for the next twenty-four hours. Instead they changed into jeans, sweaters and waterproofs and, braving the weather, went out for a walk along the harbour front.

This was a coast they both enjoyed. Beyond the outer harbour, Spartan and dangerous, the crashing tide crumbled over sharpening rocks, the wind swept down across the foam all the way from the Russian Steppes. The ice chilled air stung and quickened circulation in any areas of skin left exposed. It was a tonic better suited to their needs than any that might have been provided by the most exclusive of health clubs or champagne dinners. They laughed together as gusts of wind tore at their clothing and tangled Lorna's hair. They ran defying the force of the elements, stopping only to cling together to face the spray from the angry sea.

By far the most dramatic location on that coast-line, Whitby was nevertheless still a working port boasting a lively, if depleted, fishing fleet. A place where the flat of the North Yorkshire moor finally succumbs to the jagged shore-line, to tumble down over sandstone cliffs that create a natural haven from the storms that frequent this most unpredictable stretch of water. In summer months the tiny town was suffused with visitors however, it remained all but deserted for most of the rest of the year and that was how Tom and Lorna found it on the night of their honeymoon.

In Lorna's mind there was an equation between fresh winds, clean air and new beginnings. She knew that in some real sense they were both still in the early stages of convalescence, she from her breakdown and he from the gunshot wound. What better time, she thought to experience the promise of expiation, a much needed catharsis bringing new hope.

They stood for a while on the swing bridge that separated the two harbours, watching the boats rock at their cold moorings and the lights from cottage windows staggering up the hill-side. It was a panorama entirely in keeping with the noise of the sea at their backs, completing an external world of movement that contrasted with the still quiet of their very private warmth.

She gripped Tom's hand more firmly, stealing a glance at his profile. He was smiling and she loved him all the more for it. However, she could not help but recall her doubts when he had first proposed marriage in Chorley. For a long time after that, she had convinced herself that she would remain single. Her experience of family life had twisted her perceptions—which would dare chance such a close association, she'd asked herself; who would want to bear children in such a distorted world. And for some years, in respect of motherhood and marriage, doubt had been her constant companion. She looked again at her partner and confirmed her decision that if there was any man alive who could dispel her fears, any man she could trust in love, it was Tom.

"Are you hungry yet?" he asked, still smiling stupidly.

She replied, "Starving."

Knowing full well his question was prompted by his own appetite.

"Fish and chips?" he asked.

She laughed, "Fish and chips and champagne—of course."

He leaned over and kissed her cold nose, "Fish and chips tonight—champagne tomorrow night. I promise."

They linked arms and hurried to the south side of the harbour.

The town was famed throughout the region for the quality of its fish and chip suppers but in the winter, many of the cafes that served the visitors closed, waiting for the tourist invasion to begin again later in the year. Tom led her to a particular shop, one he appeared to know. The fact was confirmed when, as soon as they entered, he was greeted like a long lost friend.

A big woman stood behind the glowing glass of a display unit. Her face was round and rosy and when she lifted her arms in welcome, arms that were thicker than Lorna's waist, the flesh hung down in dimpled folds.

"Tom—Tom you devil—comes here," her voice echoed a regional twang as she bustled round the serving counter. "Come 'ere and let Auntie Molly get a look at you."

Close to, her size made her presence all the more dominating. She stood over six feet tall and Lorna guessed she must weight more than twenty-five stone. She grabbed Tom and lifted him off his feet; thrusting her face into his and kissing him loudly full on his lips.

"Oh Molly for goodness sake put me down." He yelled but he was as helpless as a baby in her arms.

"Now y 'know what y 'gets if you struggle." She said kissing him again.

The only other customer in the shop, an older man with a weather beaten face, stood grinning as he watched the performance and did not seem to care that his own supper parcel was getting cold. Obviously he enjoyed watching Molly perform and as she started kissing her victim all over again, he turned to Lorna and commented, "She's a lively lass is our Molly. She could even suffocate you're your young man if he struggles too much."

Fortunately at that moment Tom was released.

"And why haven't you been to t 'see your Auntie Molly you devil. It's been ages." Molly asked.

Tom stood dwarfed before his assailant, trying to catch his breath and regain his composure.

"Molly," he said finally, "we could have done with you in Belfast."

The big woman laughed a big laugh, a sound like demolition site and it was whist she was laughing that apparently she became aware of Lorna for the first time.

"And what have we here Thomas?"

Lorna stuck out her hand and smiled, "Hello. I'm Lorna—Tom's new wife."

"A—New wife—like he might have had an old one eh—eh Tom?"

Tom grinned and put an arm round Lorna's shoulders. "This one's enough for me Molly." He paused, clearly for effect and then added, "We were married today."

"So a fish and chip supper would be very acceptable as a wedding present." Lorna added.

The wisecrack brought on Molly big laugh again and when she stopped, she pulled Lorna close.

"Let's have a look at you Pet." She said. For a moment Lorna imagined that she was to be subjected to the same crushing routine Tom had suffered but the big woman simply studied her face. After a moment, much to Lorna's

Surprise, she leaned down and kissed her delicately on the forehead. It was a sensitive act, delivered with care and a complete contrast to the girl's first impressions of her.

"Welcome to the family . . . You are exactly as I imagine you'd be Lorna" she said, "or do you prefer Lonny?"

The question shocked Lorna. Lonny was a pet name that had only ever been used by close friends and family, an unusual diminutive given her as a baby by her father more importantly, not one that could easily have been deduced through any logical means.

Molly smiled at her surprise, "There now I've shocked you," she said, "but when you gets to know me better little Lonny, you'll understand I have a sense for some things—a special sense."

Tom confirmed the claim saying that his aunt did indeed have a surprising intuition.

"S' not just an intuition Thomas," Molly objected, "I has a gift for looking into people's lives." She still stared at Lorna as she spoke and she added much more seriously, "And I can tell you something else Thomas—you need to look after this young woman. She's had plenty to trouble her and she'll need lots of love and care. So you keep her close." Then she laughed breaking the spell saying, "Else you'll have your Auntie Molly to deal with."

The man who had witnessed their meeting turned to leave at that point, making tutting noises of disapproval as he went. As the door swung shut behind him Molly shook her head at his back, "Silly old buggar." She muttered, "Couldn't tell his arse from his haddock."

Their fish and chip supper was eventually served to them in the tiny kitchen behind the shop, a space that was entirely out of proportion with its owner. Conversely, it was completely in character with regard to both the quality of its pristine fittings and the general efficiency of its arrangement. Molly was highly organised especially with regard to her cooking. The Haddock they were served was fresh from the sea and coated in the most deliciously light crust of batter; the accompanying chips a delight of outer brown crispness covering a well cooked interior.

As they dined, Tom explained that Molly had been a friend of his family for years and, although there were no blood ties, the courtesy title of Aunt had been adopted out of respect for her closeness.

He told Lorna that Molly's family had been gypsies, travelling each year to pick fruit and hops in the relevant seasons. "Her Mother was a fortune teller—in a tent and wearing a headscarf. I never met the old woman myself but my Mum used to say she was the genuine article—whatever that is."

"And did you know she had this shop?" Lorna asked.

"Yes. She's been here for twenty years or more—settled down with a Whitby fisherman—much to her own family's disgust. He was lost at sea maybe seven or eight years back. She was always a great cook—and although I haven't seen her since college days, she hasn't changed a bit."

"How about the fortune-telling thing—can she really do it?"

He grinned, "You tell me. She certainly made you jump when she called you Lonny"

"Would she do a proper reading if you asked her?"

Now he laughed, "I wondered how long it would take you to ask. Let's ask her when she comes back."

Molly closed the shop early that night and joined them just as Tom was pouring a second cup of tea.

"Tea for you Molly?" he asked holding the pot over a fresh cup.

"Aye there's a good lad. Can't refuse a cup tea." She sat next to Lorna and asked her if the supper was up to expectations.

"The best fish and chips I've had since leaving Ireland. God knows why they can't do them like that in London. First class Molly—really."

The approval clearly pleased their host and she smile in appreciation as she sipped her tea.

"So, "she said a moment later still smiling, "I suppose this is your wedding night then. Not that I imagine there's anything new in that for the pair of you. You youngsters don't wait anymore—not like in my day."

Tom smiled back and shook his head, "As you say, we don't wait anymore. But—if we're getting personal—how about doing a reading for us?"

The big face opposite split into a huge grin," I thought you'd never ask—mind—how does Lonny feel about fortune telling, her being a Catholic and all?"

Lorna smiled at the new disclosure, "Possibly more true to say ex-catholic after today. To tell you the truth Molly, after you calling me Lonny I'm intrigued. I'd love to have you tell us our fortunes."

Molly cleared away the pots briskly, leaving only the cup Lorna had used on the table. She wiped the table with a cloth and then laid a fine cotton cover over it. From a drawer in an adjacent cabinet she produced a set of Tarot cards, they were wrapped in a heavily patterned silk scarf and this she lay to one side. Leaving the pack in the centre of the table.

"That was my Mother's scarf. She always used it when she did a reading. Now then . . ." She cut the cards several times and handed them to Tom.

"Thomas, shuffle the cards—give 'em a good mix-up, then cut them twice with your left hand and as you do so, ask the question in your mind that you want answering."

Tom followed her instructions and handed the cards back to her. Immediately she began to lay them out, one at a time in a huge circle. She explained that different segments of the circle represented different periods of Tom's life. She said it was important to look at back the past as it affected the interpretation of the future. A moment or two later she studied the cards and began.

Her first comments referred to Tom's recent gunshot wound and she was able to go into a surprising degree of detail about both the location of the injury and the place where it had been sustained.

"And if you hadn't had your head turned by a woman, then you mayn't have been shot at all." she said. As she spoke she looked up at Lorna suddenly—a look of recognition.

"But what little Lonny might have been doing in a war zone is anybody's guess. It was you—wasn't it Pet?"

Lorna nodded. Her scepticism about fortune-tellers was taking a beating and she was increasingly impressed by what she heard.

Another card turned and Molly exclaimed, "Ah the Wish Card. This is the strongest card in the pack and even though it's situated on the cusp—between the present and the future, its influence is paramount . . . depending on what we find next."

The next card was the Lightening Struck Tower, making Molly scowl, "Now there's a sod of a card—it means change, sometimes enforced change."

Tom immediately quipped, "Well getting married is a change," then he laughed, "but it wasn't enforced honestly."

After that, according to Molly, his future with Lorna looked bright. Molly guessed correctly that his question had referred to his marriage—but, Lorna thought, that was an assumption anyone may have made under the circumstances. However, her predictions for him were generally quite good except for something she called a 'trial'. She said it wasn't clear what that trial might consist of, only that it would take all his patience and perseverance to overcome it.

"You're a lucky lad really Thomas, so it's only fair that you should have a little problem every now and then. How you cope will determine how it affects you—and that's all I can say."

Lorna had watched the 'telling' with mixed feelings. Typically, she'd had the usual curiosity about her own future—about living a long and healthy life and about her career and her future happiness, but now she began to wonder if she wanted to know. Also, by comparison to Tom's question, hers were selfish concerns and she felt a twinge of guilt accordingly. Perhaps, she thought, her doubts were a consequence or a hang-over from her religion. Certainly the Catholic Church was adamant in rejecting the services of fortune tellers. The Church hierarchy would claim it was an unholy act, verging on the sacrilegious and, whilst she did not attend Mass any more still less receive the sacraments, she continued to pray regularly. An indication perhaps, that she still wore the remnants of that belief as a secret coat—albeit one that was almost threadbare.

Molly turned to her, "Pass me your tea-cup Lonny if you please." She said pointing to the solitary piece of crockery. Lorna leaned over and picked up the cup and saucer. "Tea-leaves?" she asked.

She must have communicated her doubt by the tone of her question because Molly took some time to justify the choice.

"Some of us believe that if an in-depth reading is called for, then very personal access is needed. I think you need some guidance my love—perhaps deeper than the cards can give you. And if I begin to feel any limitation, then I'll look at your palms. Okay?" Her smile broke the atmosphere of seriousness that had developed.

"Anyway I'm happier looking into the cup for you."

She paused again and then added, "There's nothing to worry about—you're a real worrier aren't you. Trust me my love and then we'll see."

As ritual demanded, Lorna turned the cup upside down and then twisted it round and round several times before handing it to Molly. The tiny container was promptly lost in the landscape of the large hands that held it. More like a doll's teacup, Lorna thought. Molly studied the leaves for some time before she made any comment.

"Show me your left palm Lonny." She said finally.

Lorna stretched out her hand face up and Molly gripped her wrist. "Ah," she said, "just as I suspected—you poor thing . . ." The reaction was instantaneous; Lorna snatched back her hand, pressing it tightly against its partner.

"I don't think I want to hear any more." She said, "I really don't believe much in all this mumbo jumbo and . . ." Molly finished the sentence in her stead, " . . . And it wasn't your idea." After a moment her voice softened,"

"You've had some serious pain to deal with Lonny but you need to listen to me—if only to gather your strength for what is still to come."

The statement galvanised an objection from Tom, "What the hell do you mean Molly?"

"I mean that your lovely wife has secrets, private matters that she holds close. Secrets that trouble her mind—and if she doesn't learn to address them—they could destroy her."

Molly's voice was low, almost a whisper and the tone was absolutely sincere. Clearly she believed every word she said but before Tom could register a response Lorna was on her feet. Her face was white save for unusual pink patches on her cheeks.

"Tom—take me back to the hotel please." She said.

Molly reached again for her hand but she pulled it out of reach.

"Let me help Lonny."

"Thank you—but no thank you." was the reply.

By the time Tom had got to his feet Lorna was halfway to the door. He had time only to give his aunt a look of apology before dashing after her.

Seconds later he was alongside his wife, his arm around her shoulders and a large white pocket handkerchief held to stem her tears.

They hardly spoke during the walk back to the hotel but Lorna eventually regained control over her emotions and Tom was the more content when she did. Typically sensitive to his wife's condition, he asked no questions and no explanation was offered. Privately, Lorna's feelings were very confused. Molly had been so kind and had meant to help, there was guilt therefore, but the reaction had been uncontrollable. She was convinced that the friendly fortune-teller had been about to expose all her secret fears and such a prospect had created an ungovernable panic. The room had become claustrophobic, breathing restricted and Lorna had had to leave as quickly as possible. She told herself that it was all due to stress and allowed herself the convenience of believing the trauma of the day had been the cause. After all, she thought, who wouldn't be extra emotional on her wedding day.

When they arrived at their room, she found it was filled almost to capacity with flowers. The sight lifted her spirits. The romantic arrangement had been made at Tom's request and it was one that still further confirmed her feelings about her new husband. She cried again, this time however, through joy.

The incident at Molly's shop was not referred to again until a couple of days later. Lorna broached the subject herself, telling Tom how badly she felt and how she must return to make her apologies. Tom was clearly pleased.

"We could call round there before we leave—maybe take a little gift and make our peace. What do you say?"

It was a good idea and she agreed without hesitation.

Much of their time in Whitby was spent walking. They explored the cliffs in both directions and made the climb to the ruined Abbey; they strolled through the maze of narrow streets, across cobblestones window shopping and delighted in discovering many of the tiny craft shops in the older part of the town. Whitby was famous for its use of Jet, a black semi-precious stone peculiar to that region and used extensively in the manufacture of jewellery. Tom bought her a delicately carved pendant as a memento of their visit. As well as walking, each day they tried to find somewhere new to eat. They were pleasantly surprised to find quite so many small restaurants, pubs and hotels that were prepared to serve those meals despite the season. One morning they hired a car and drove out across the North Yorkshire moor where they discovered the Cross Keys, a secluded and distant Inn boasting an exceptional menu. After their meal, they left the car and explored the nearby countryside, wandering through the moorland heather and enjoying the wildness of the local landscape.

It proved to be a wonderfully relaxing holiday, its most significant effect in the restoration of their relationship. During and after Tom's hospitalization, they had fallen in love all over again however; the full flavour of their earlier courtship had eluded them, until their stay in Whitby. Consequently, in that context more than any other, the honeymoon was successfully memorable. However, by day five they both felt that they had explored the limits of the little coastal town and its environs. They were both used to very active lives, she in the metropolitan setting of one of the busiest cities in Europe and in a profession with huge demands on her time and intellectual energy and he, as a soldier, often in life threatening situations, responsible for other men's lives. Not surprising therefore that, whatever the interest they had found there, the peace and tranquillity of the north east coast soon became boring. Accordingly, on the same day that they decided to revisit Molly, they also agreed to cut short their stay in Whitby and return to Lorna's little flat in London.

Lorna had no clear idea how she might be received by Molly but, in the event, their return went better than she could have ever imagined. As soon as she put her face round the door of the little shop, Molly had her in a bear hug. This time it was her turn to get the full treatment and although a more sober reception may well have been more acceptable, certainly less embarrassing in front of a half dozen customers, Lorna was nevertheless delighted that Tom's aunt bore no hard feelings. Tom delivered their gift—a bottle of single malt whisky called Dalwhinney—a favourite drink Molly enjoyed and received a big sloppy kiss in return. In no time at all the line of Molly's customers were acquainted with the detail of the young couple's recent marriage and the enthusiasm of their congratulations left Lorna to believe it could easily turn into a street party.

As before, they sat drinking tea in the tiny kitchen until Molly finished serving in the shop. Again she presented them with a fish supper but this time she joined them herself. Lorna was able to witness first hand, the enormity of the big woman's appetite and saw her eat three times as much as they did.

During the meal Molly regaled them with tales from her own background, stories about the lives of travelling folk and their work at country fairs and in the fruit fields of Kent. Many of the anecdotes were self depreciating but despite that, they were very funny. Even those with sad endings were framed in such a way as to emphasise their humour rather than the melancholy. And each time the atmosphere became saddened, Molly would render them helpless with laughter by adding some detail or comment that changed the mood entirely. Slowly it became obvious to Lorna that the stories and the jokes were the woman's way of bridging the gap between the two of them.

She knew that in the oral tradition of the Romany people, an exchange of historical data was a sign of friendship, a peek into the family history that implied a mutual trust. Thankfully, there was no mention of their previous visit or of her behaviour on that occasion. No explanation was called for and no apology was therefore deemed necessary. In some sense this was a measure of the big woman. Much later that night actually when they were on the point of leaving, Molly asked them to wait whilst she retrieved something from her flat upstairs. She said she had a present for Lorna. In Molly's absence Tom claimed he had no knowledge of what his aunt intended but when she reappeared she clutched a square parcel wrapped in brown paper.

"Now this isn't much my dears, just a little memento from your old friend Molly." At this point she paused, almost as though she was reluctant to part with the gift, but eventually, she handed it to Lorna, "Now I don't want you to open this until you're home."

As Lorna took the package, Molly held a hand over it for a second before releasing it. "And," she added, "You must promise me that you will polish it yourself Lonny—every day. Promise me."

It was a strange request but Lorna agreed despite her hesitancy. They thanked Molly, kissed her again and then left.

Back at the hotel, they packed their cases, paid their bill and ordered a taxi. The mystery parcel was consigned to Lorna's shoulder bag but inside the cab Lorna asked Tom to take charge of it, "I don't know what she's put in there but it weighs a ton." She told him. He took the bag and laid it on his knee as the taxi pulled away. After a moment he whispered mischievously, "Should we cheat?"

"You mean—open it now?"

"Yeah—let's have a look at what's inside. Here you open it."

Lorna struggled with the brown paper cube, but when she had removed the paper she found a wooden box. A beautifully crafted rectangle in walnut, the outside of which had been hand painted with symbols of the constellations. It was old, if not antique and although the lid was tight fitting and the joins all but seamless, it showed signs of wear.

"Oh Tom—it's beautiful." Lorna exclaimed.

"It's certainly a nice piece. See if you can open it."

It was a struggle to release the lid but she finally managed to do so. Inside she found a crystal ball wrapped in the same silk scarf Molly had told them had belonged to her mother. For a moment they sat there staring at the brilliant object.

"I'd like to bet the crystal belonged to her Mum as well." Tom said quietly.

Lorna was still engrossed by the smooth surface of the sphere in her hands and made no reply. She knew how important such objects were to gypsy communities. They were artefacts revered like religious icons might be—family heirlooms to be handed down through generations but—never ever to be given to people outside the family.

"It's a most thoughtful gift Tom," she said at last, "and some testimony to her feelings for you."

"Actually I think you mean her feelings for both of us—and an indication of her acceptance of you as part of the immediate family."

He took hold of the crystal ball and studied it. After a while he said, "Crystal is also said to have healing powers. It was used by some primitive societies to ward off evil influences and to protect against illness."

Lorna gripped his arm and rested her head against his shoulder. In the warmth of their mutual comfort, the need for healing seemed like the last thing she might require. Secretly however, she suspected it may be exactly what she might need.

CHAPTER TWENTY

1982

News: July 20th.

IRA Bombs explode in Royal Park.

Horror has come to London on a sunny summer's day. As a detachment of Blues and Royals trotted South Carriage Road in Hyde Park today, on their way to the colourful guard-changing at Horse guards' Parade a car bomb exploded a few yards away. Two guardsmen were killed and seventeen spectators injured. Seven army horses were either killed by the blast or had to be destroyed . . . . The IRA has admitted responsibility.

Diary: God knows where they expect me to find the time. There is never enough time to do all the planning for the curriculum changes, let alone all that I need to do for lessons. A good night's sleep might help—fat chance. Tom is now fully recovered and—thank God—out of the Army. There was a presentation at the barracks, a ceremony full of English pomp and gold braid. He found it as difficult as me to accept his 'hero' status. One of the Army 'high-ups' has helped him gain a good job working for a national security firm. They have offices across the country so there is no bar on our plans to move to a house—one of these days.

    The dreams are back again. St. Jude doesn't seem to listen any more . . . maybe I'm being punished.

* * *

As far as the rest of the teaching staff was concerned, the most significant outward sign of Lorna's status was her publication of the timetable. Once each year, just after Easter, the timetable—her carefully constructed timetable—was pinned to the staff room notice board. It was her answer to the annual conundrum concerning the length and number of lessons in each subject in each year group; the allocation of staff and the time of the day and week when lessons would be taught. It was a work of solitary dedication. And it was that time of year again. The display of cool authority which Loma was able to demonstrate in the face of such a task, left most staff imagining her to be a very special person indeed—much more special in fact than she thought herself. In her own eyes, her capability was one that relied simply on good organisation. She believed it was the one area of her professional life about which she was obsessive. Some of Lorna's colleagues however whispered that she had designed the ninth Beatitude to read 'The well-organised will control the earth.'

To many teaching staff, the production of the timetable was as mystifying a process as was the translation of the Dead Sea Scrolls. Most had no idea how anyone could make sense, let alone a disciplined system, from the complex and changing requirements of the curriculum and the disparate constraints placed on it by staff, government agencies and the local Authority. Consequently their response varied. Some were content in their ignorance, and others, envious; some boasted a degree of understanding and others simply complained—whatever the outcome. At one end of the spectrum there were those, the cynics, who thought her aptitude was a matter of luck. They treated her with open admiration tinged with envy, as one might have for a successful gambler. At the opposite extreme, others demonstrated a stereotypical 'Mothercare' attitude—that was sometimes shown for example to expectant fathers. In this category, by implication, the observers admitted their ignorance but to cloak the truth they pretended a different agenda. The 'You know better than me—but . . . 'syndrome. They talked in hushed tones, inevitably in private conclaves near the tea urn about the progress of the new delivery. Their faces would wear expressions of concerned pain, an anxious anticipation most often found otherwise in Emergency Ward delivery rooms.

The full range of the staff's response therefore, started with the cynics and ended with the sycophants. Sceptical older staff representing one extreme were always keen to estimate the chance of failure. They would make such comments as, "Bet you can't block the practical subjects again this year eh?" or "Wouldn't give you odds on Setting English in Year Ten." and so on.

In this respect it was transparent that such comments that were made, at least in part, to boast a familiarity with the process employed as much as with the terms used—a boast however, that was seldom able to stand the scrutiny of closer investigation. By comparison the 'Mothercare' crowd would restrict their observations to those expressing vague concern 'How's it doing?" they would ask sympathetically, or, "The end in sight—is it?"

And, unlike the cynics, they never made any attempt to discuss the minutia nor involve themselves with the terminology. They did not seem to mind if their ignorance was a fact of public knowledge.

Consequently it pleased Lorna to be able to demonstrate her skill. Her fast-lane promotion had continued and now she was a Deputy Head at the tender age of twenty-six—something of a record. There were over one thousand children in her school and, if one included the programme for the two cohorts comprising the Lower and Upper Sixth Forms, twenty-four different subjects were taught by seventy-five staff. Each individual pupil needed to access a fully comprehensive, academic diet, sufficient to satisfy the statutory requirements of Government, the pupil's potential, as well as the aspirations of their parents on their behalf. No mean feat given the variety of other constraints. It seemed to Lorna also, that, as there were relatively few women given the opportunity to tackle this management role, her achievement was all the greater.

As usual that morning, in anticipation of her arrival, the staff room was in a state of heightened expectation. The Heads of Department stood near the notice-board clutching cups of coffee, apparently chatting generally. Their positioning however was strategic. As each piece of A4 paper took its place in the jig saw, they were the first to be able to study the implications.

"Harry won't like that." was the first comment, leaving the Head of Mathematics shaking his head. The click of the staple-gun nevertheless continued undaunted.

"Upper school lessons in the afternoon again? "The Head of English muttered, "I thought we agreed about that?"

Lorna made no comment.

The impetus provided by middle management's complaints drew other staff to the notice-board and in no time at all there were a dozen or more teachers craning their necks to view the information. Lorna finally completed her task and turned to face them.

"I have individual timetables printed out for all of you," she said in an even voice," and I will put them in your pigeon-holes today. Please save any comments or complaints until the staff meeting this evening when you will all have the opportunity to express your views. The plaintive sounds of resistance continued nevertheless.

"Oh not that lot again. I've had them every year."

"Didn't we agree that I'd get my free periods on a Monday?"

"Upper school Science needs a morning slot Lorna—we discussed that . . ."

The ritual was necessary, as much to convince less experienced staff that their Heads of Department knew their stuff, as to register serious objections and Lorna made no attempt to argue the points they raised. That evening there would be a staff meeting to discuss the new timetable and that would be the place to answer questions.

Bob Hurst, the Head of Mathematics was, as usual, the most vociferous. No doubt conscious that two of his teachers stood close by, he adopted a businesslike attitude with just a hint of the 'disappointed school-boy'.

"We need to talk Lorna. When can we meet?" He asked in almost reverential tones. They had already consulted on several occasions before but now he wanted to impress his departmental staff.

"Tomorrow would be best Bob," she replied, fixing the last sheet with a loud click." "Fine," he said, as if resigning from the human race, "what sort of time do you suggest?"

"How about eight Am.?"

It was common knowledge that Bob seldom appeared in school before eight forty-five. One of the last to arrive and certainly one of the least talented teachers, he inevitably made a song and dance each year about some detail of the provision for Mathematics. It was his way of appearing more professional than the actuality of his performance indicated.

There was a moment's silence, during which one or two of the other teachers smiled secretly in appreciation of Lorna's tack.

"Couldn't we make it at break-time?' he offered. "My morning's already rather busy."

She smiled brightly and agreed.

Jim Burns, a Science teacher spoke up from the back of the crowd. The Head had always seen Jim as something of an agitator but Lorna knew better. She identified his public observations as being caused by an over developed sense of humour, rather than anything actually subversive.

"And this meeting . . ." he said, "is it a consultation in the proper sense or is it simply a lip service? I mean—is there any chance of change, or is it the usual faites accomplis?"

'Nothing is cast in tablets of stone Jim,' she replied with a grin,"—as well you know. However," she added maliciously, "after so many meetings with departments over the last few weeks, I shouldn't think there is need to change very much. Nearly all that you see here has been agreed already with Heads of Department."

Her statement caused a few heads to turn and she smiled as she left the room. In the corridor she met Mike Thomas the Head. His perpetual frown was even deeper than usual.

"Ah Lorna, just the person." he said.

As he spoke he took her arm and shepherded her along with him in the direction of his office . . .

"Give me a minute will you. You may be able to help."

Mike Thomas liked to believe he was a man of principle, a Head that commanded respect. In actual fact however, Lorna had found him indecisive, sometimes to the point of professional weakness. He surrounded himself with new technology in an attempt to create an impression of efficiency and in the same vein, his sole contribution and only perennial interest appeared to be in attending meetings. He was a member of innumerable committees and working parties and liked noting better than making statements to the press or expressing opinions on TV. Not surprisingly his staff found him remote and elusive and had grown to recognise that most day to day decisions were therefore, left to Lorna.

His office, far from being that of a typical Head teacher, had more in common with the type of communications centre one might find in the aviation industry. However, the two computers, the plain paper Fax, the two telephones and the racks of floppy discs only left his staff suspicious that he spent a disproportionate share of the budget on himself.

"Have a seat Loma." he said, slipping out of his jacket and sitting behind his outsize desk. He liked to impress visitors as a 'hands-on' manager and after a recent seminar had taken to working in his shirt-sleeves to make his intention explicit. Lorna found it embarrassing.

"Do you know a Mr. Blakey—son Nigel in Year Ten?" he asked.

"I take Nigel for English—a top group. Quiet lad, quite bright but lazy. Why do you ask?"

"His Father is coming in this morning—complaints about bullying. Could you deal with him for me?"

Lorna felt herself flush. This was increasingly a standard procedure designed to help Mike avoid confrontations with parents and she did not like it.

"Did he ask to see me? "She asked.

"No he wanted to have a word with me but I'm afraid I have to go out in a minute. Meeting with the Director down at the Civic Centre.'

"Do we know the details? 1 mean—is there any truth in the claim? Has anyone asked his classmates or his friends, his Tutor or anyone else?"

There was a moment's silence. Mike Thomas knew all about their policy for dealing with such accusations. He knew that before a parent was interviewed, an inquiry should be held into the claims and evidence collected. To sit in front of parents without the facts was a recipe for discontent leaving everyone involved dissatisfied.

"I had a word with his Tutor, Henry Bishop, said he didn't know anything about any bullying—said he would mention it to his group . . ."

"And?" Lorna asked.

"And—well that was only an hour ago—and the boys Father is due in . . ." he looked at his watch, "in about ten minutes."

Lorna took a moment to control her temper.

"It's not good enough Mike. It really isn't good enough. I suggest you phone Mr. Blakey and tell him make another appointment—at least give us a chance to find out if there is any truth in what he says. Anyway, I'm teaching all morning so I wouldn't be able to see him at such short notice."

Her Boss gave a sly grin and shook his head as though disappointed.

"If you're ever going to get your own school Lorna, you'll need to be able to think on your feet. Not everything falls into neat compliance with policy now—does it?"

He stood up and smiled down at her as he spoke.

"You must know how much I depend on you already Loma. You're my strong right arm and I wouldn't have anyone else deal with parents on the warpath other than you."

He came round the desk and stood close to her chair.

"Look, I know this is a bind and I know we don't operate like this ideally—but . . . ." now he leaned over her wearing his most disgusting grin, "but—as a special favour me—for your favourite Head teacher—do it for me—just this once eh ?"

His gradually approaching physical presence caused Lorna considerable discomfort. Not only did he suffer from a severe form of halitosis, but his aftershave was never able to disguise an equally objectionable body odour. She realised abruptly however, that it was the fact of his maleness that upset her the most, his maleness in close proximity An unquantifiable gender characteristic of which she had unexpectedly become aware. For a moment she panicked. She imagined he was about to make a pass at her and involuntarily she shrank back in the chair. Suddenly she wanted to be out of the office and illogically she found herself thinking she should kick his shins and make a run for it. She became light-headed.

"B-but my class.?' she heard herself say," what about my class?"

Now she could smell his breath. His face was close enough for her to see the tufts he had missed when he shaved that morning.

"Don't worry about the class." he said quietly," I've asked Tim to look after them—well he's in the next room isn't he and it won't take you long to get shot of Mr. Blakey."

The panic increased, making her face flushed and at that moment Lorna would have agreed to anything just to be able to get away from him.

"Okay," she said finally," okay. Now—you must excuse me."

She stood up brushing past him as she did so and having to move her chair back in the process just to avoid even closer contact.

She bolted back to her own office and closed the door firmly behind her. It was her intention to ring the boy's Tutor and try and glean some further information but she had no sooner sat at her desk when the phone rang. Mr. Blakey was in the foyer already. In fact the school secretary said she had just sent him round to the office accompanied by a Sixth Former and sure enough, there was a knock at the door that very moment.

Lorna took a deep breath, smoothed her skirt and called "Come in."

Mr. Blakey was a big man, standing well over six feet and his mop of slicked back hair was as black as his frown. They shook hands and he took a seat opposite her desk . . . His body language left an impression of contained anger even before he spoke. He sat with his hands clasped over a kneecap in a posture of anticipation, almost as though he was ready to fight. Lorna greeted him and told him she was there to help. It was a standard strategy to reassure complainants that all she wanted was a fair result. The impression intended was one of firmness but one willing to listen. Despite herself this time however, she noted that her presentation was slightly weaker. She found herself emphasising the co-operation on offer rather more than the need to find the actual truth. That day her visitor didn't even let her finish.

"That's all very well Miss Donnelly," the man's deep voice told her, "and nothing more than I should be able to expect—but my son is being bullied and all I want to know is—what the hell are you going to do about it?"

Lorna felt her colour rising. She worked to control her breathing.

"First of all Mr. Blakey you should know that, as soon as you made your complaint, an investigation was started and . . ." Again, she was not allowed to finish.

"An investigation, as you like to call it, isn't needed." Now he was leaning forward in the chair. "I'm telling you what the problem is. All you have to do is to sort out the little bastards who are doing the bullying" "and" she continued, "As I was saying, as soon as we have evidence that . . . ."

Again he interrupted," All the evidence you want is right here and . . ."

This time it was Lorna's turn. She raised her voice just sufficient to stop him.

"Mr. Blakey."

His expression was one of disbelief but she continued regardless," We cannot continue like this. I am quite willing to listen to what you have to say—but please, do me the courtesy of listening to my replies. Otherwise we're wasting our time."

He studied her face for a moment and then stood up. He put his clenched fists on the desk and leaned forward, towering over her.

"The last thing I want to do young woman is waste your valuable time." The sarcasm was undisguised. She started to object, saying that wasn't what she had said but he talked over her again.

"But you seem to be ignoring everything I'm telling you. Now—listen carefully and I'll say it just once more . . ."

Now he was a deliberately invading her space, an intentional move made to intimidate her—and although one part of her conscious mind realised what was happening, it worked. Despite the quiet voice deep in her subconscious, her panic rose and she heard a sound coming from her throat, a plaintive noise like that of a defeated animal. Suddenly, she was on her feet, tears streaming down her cheeks. All she could think was that this male wanted to punish her and that she must placate him. Feverishly, she began loosening the buttons of her blouse now weeping uncontrollably.

She was almost naked before he reacted.

* * *

During the previous year Peter had moved to London. Although the strikes of the previous winter were over and the city had begun to get back to semblance of order, the steel strike in March put blight on the new government's hopes for industrial peace and for the expectation of better employment figures. Good paramedics were hard to come by however, and the hospital administrative centre, sited in Hammersmith Hospital was only too pleased to find a fully trained recruit with excellent references seeking work. He found himself a temporary room near Ladbroke Grove tube station and quickly settled in to a new life in the big city. He worked long hours but loved the job. The sense of being needed and the state of almost continuous emergency in his day to day activity helped him accommodate his feeling of ineptitude and, as time passed, he grew to accept himself on more equal terms.

Life in London suited him. There was no one to interfere, no one to direct his private life, to criticise or pass judgement. When he wished to dress in women's clothes he did so but that did not stop him from making female friends. He knew his condition would be seen to be perverse in the eyes of most people but he had no doubt whatsoever about his sexuality. Cross-dressing, as it was popularly known, was no guarantee of homosexuality, indeed sexual preference had nothing at all to do with it. Moreover, he did not need to justify his behaviour to anyone least of all himself. For the first time in his life he was entirely responsible for and to himself.

He nevertheless sometimes examined his conscience with regard to his cross-dressing and wondered if it may derive from the treatment he suffered as a child at the abusive hands of his Step Father, Jimmy Ungerside. In some respect he regarded himself as fortunate, in that being so young at the time, the memory was weak. However, partly through working amongst medical practitioners he knew also that childhood traumas of that sort inevitably left a scar but the effect that such a scar might have was as much dependent on inherent personality characteristics peculiar to the victim, as it was on the depth of the depravity suffered. He liked to believe that Jimmy was as much a victim as he had made of his step-children and that his abusiveness was the effect of the abuse he had probably suffered himself. Consequently, if Peter's penchant for women's clothing was directly related to Jimmy's behaviour, it was little enough to pay.

It was through Peter's involvement with the hospital social club that he met Clare and Jimmy, the couple with whom eventually he was to share a flat. It was also through Clare and Jimmy that he was first introduced to the Brighton Club in Soho.

According to one or two of the longest established members, the Brighton Club had been started some ten or more years before. The brainchild of a couple of Gay musicians, they had initially imagined it might be exclusively a Gay club. At that time, around the end of the 1960s despite the draconian laws, the public ethos was one of greater toleration for what had been seen previously as, seriously deviant practices. Nevertheless, to find support for a commercial venture of such dimensions was to prove difficult even during the so-called 'Swinging Sixties'. Undaunted the musicians found a site—albeit in need of serious renovation—and began to sell shares in what they hoped would be a member's only club. It was not until a well known figure from the world of Pop music gave his backing however, that the club finally took shape and it was at his insistence that the membership rule was relaxed to enable access by any number of minority interest groups . . .

When Peter became a member, a large contingent of cross-dressers had already made it their favourite place to meet and this included Jimmy and Clare. It quickly became a focus for Peter's social world. He spent as much time there as his work schedule would allow and, in the process, made lasting friendships with a wide range of the club's other patrons. In some real sense, the life Peter enjoyed through the Brighton Club filled the gap left by what was effectively, the loss of his family.

He often thought about Lorna. He thought also about Patrick and Tessa but Lorna was the one he missed most of all. She had been the anchor that kept him tied securely to the family. And it was for that reason more than any other that he had made the decision to attend her wedding the following year. He thought initially that he might have had an opportunity to talk to her after the ceremony but that wasn't to be. Instead he had satisfied himself watching her happiness from a distance. She deserved her happiness and her man Tom, looked like the kind of person to ensure it on her behalf. It was nevertheless with a degree of sadness that Peter waved her goodbye that day. With such differences in their respective life-ethos it was unlikely that they would meet again. Afterwards he was pleased that he had not burdened her by trying to justify his life style, she had enough to think about and had already devoted too much time in trying to help her siblings. Better a clean break.

It was a year or so later that the subject of a reunion with his older sister was again raised. In what he took in the beginning as a chance meeting, he met one of her husband's relatives one night in the Club. On that occasion he was sitting at the bar, the first one of his group to arrive when he was approached by a very large woman. She came deliberately to sit next to him and, he remembered she had trouble mounting the high stool.

She caught his eye, "They're not made for larger ladies are they?" she said with a relieved grin when she had at last succeeded in her task. Her accent was from somewhere in the North, a pleasant sound that struck a chord in his memory.

"I often have trouble myself," he replied generously, "maybe they should lower the bar and make the stools shorter."

The big woman laughed and as she did so she scrutinised his dress, "I like the outfit Peter. Very fashionable." she said.

The use of his real name shocked him. He was certain he had not met her before and yet she used his name without hesitation or embarrassment.

"Sorry—have we met?"

"Not face to face luvvie, but I know a little about you—through your sister."

"Theresa?"

"No. Lorna—Lonny she's a lovely girl. She married my nephew Tom—lovely couple they are. I saw you briefly at the wedding."

Now his pulse raced. He had been thinking about Lorna that very morning and now, suddenly here was someone with a direct link to her. It was too much of a coincidence. He bought the woman a large scotch and began to ask her questions about Lorna but it was only after they had talked for some time that he thought to ask how she had come to visit the Club.

"Oh—I came to find you dear." She told him, "You see, I think Lorna needs to re-establish contact with her close family. She's had her troubles and she needs the security of knowing you all again."

She told him she was Tom's Aunt Molly and that she owned a fish and chip shop in Whitby and if that wasn't a sufficient peculiarity, she went on to say that she was a psychic.

"I took to your Lorna immediately, she's a lovely girl, and I made a secret promise to Tom that I'd look out for her . . . ."

"But how on earth did you find me—here?"

She laughed again, "That wasn't at all difficult you silly boy. As I told you I'm a bit of a seer. I'm often in London and your vibrations are very strong so I thought I'd drop in and pay you a visit to try and persuade you to make contact again."

Molly's statement made Peter feel a tingle down his back. She made it all sound so normal. He tried to explain that his absence was one he had forced on himself due to the embarrassment he felt certain his sister would feel if she knew about his cross-dressing. Molly thought this was a huge joke.

"Where do you men get such ideas from," she said, "it's like you don't remember your sister at all. When was she ever judgmental, when did she ever criticise you? Wasn't she the one to preach tolerance, to defend you, the one you could always rely on?" she paused, "Truth is Peter she'd love to see you and what's more important is she needs to see you."

Long after Molly had left the Club that night Peter's head was filled with what she had told him. If he could honestly believe that Lorna would not be shocked then he'd love to see her again. Molly had promised to persuade her to come to Soho. She'd said that as soon as Lorna knew where he was, nothing would prevent her from visiting him, all he had to do was want it to happen.

CHAPTER TWENTY-ONE

1982

News: IRA bomb suspect Gerard Tuite who escaped from Brixton prison is rearrested. A car bomb explodes in Hyde Park killing seven horses. Two guardsmen died and seventeen members of the public were injured.

* * *

Her voice tailed off. The memory was vague, like trying to look through frosted glass and each time the scene beyond was glimpsed—the pain.

"Go on,' Doctor Morton said encouraging her in his quiet way, "and then what?"

At first she had been shocked to discover that she had been a patient at the clinic for seven weeks and, even when a recovery was obviously imminent, the time scale in her conscious memory remained warped. She could recall Mr. Blakey standing over her desk and she could remember her feeling of fear but after that, the rest was only thin, half developed images, a seven week gap with jagged parts of the jig-saw, like the pills and the couch, left to tantalize her.

"You were telling me about your meeting with Mr. Blakey. Can you finish that off and then I'll make us a nice cup of tea." Doctor Morton asked quietly.

She remembered Mr. Blakey well.

"He was rather frightening really with a very deep voice and dark hooded eyes with thick brows. When I saw from the file that he was a lorry-driver, I imagined stupidly, arrogantly that he may not be able to express himself very well. I prepared myself to meet a less than average person—but he was far from average. Bombastic, powerful, very strong character . . . , he was frightening,"

She paused for a moment, "He was a big man—I mean very big—maybe six foot four. He made me feel miniscule, almost childlike." She paused again deep in the memory, "I don't think I like big men."

"Is Tom big?"

"Just big enough."

"Was Jimmy a big man?' Morton asked.

"Big? Jimmy? Not really. He was big round the middle. He was big and fat but not really, really big."

"Not like your Dad was?"

"Not at all, Dad was a big man alright", she paused thinking about the connection and then added hastily," but I liked him. I loved him in fact. He was the best father anyone could have ever have." She paused again, this time to ask, "What am I doing here Doctor?"

He smiled and put down his pad before he answered.

"You had what we like to call, an episode, and a kind of mini-breakdown, so we brought you here for a rest."

"A rest?'She asked.

"Yes—yes I think it's fair to call it a rest. You'd been playing too many different roles teacher, manager, mother confessor, wife and concerned sister each with their own areas of responsibility; splitting yourself too many ways—working too hard, staying up all night doing a timetable for your school—remember? You needed a rest."

She nodded slowly. The frosted glass began to clear.

"A parent, your Mister Blakey came to see you and you—well you had a bad turn."

"What did I do exactly?"

His soft voice was the only lubrication that enabled the mechanism of her mind to work again. A liquid food to satisfy her mental starvation. Early on he had told her that she would grow to accommodate her problem, in the mean time, he said, she must continue taking the tiny white pills and to start with she took six each day. The effect was soporific, removing her from the day to day reality that caused her fears. However, after the passage of time—how much time she was not certain—she found herself fighting against their influence.

That means you are improving," he'd tell her, "but slowly, slowly catchee monkee." he would always add—annoyingly.

"And?' he asked again.

She opened her eyes. For the first time in what seemed an age she felt absolutely normal again. She was laid back on his couch, seeing only the ornate ceiling rose. She rolled onto her side and looked at him.

"Why the smile?" he asked, peering at her over his half glasses. "I think I'm better." she answered," Can I sit up?"

"Whichever makes you comfortable." he said.

She swung her legs over the velour cover and stretched her neck and shoulders "This is a nice room.' she observed.

"It is a nice room Lorna—and you have been in here many times before."

"I know," she said," but—well—I think I've just noticed it."

He laughed. She could not remember having heard him laugh before and she felt pleased that she had caused it. It made her feel part of things again.

Lorna improved quickly after that session. The tablets were reduced to only two per day and the schedule of her day was relaxed. She could watch some television and she could choose her own food; she was allowed access to the library and permitted to walk in the grounds. But, best of all, the interviews with Doctor Morton became like visiting a friend for afternoon tea. She still saw him daily but now when she called, they simply sat at a small table in his conservatory and chatted. Given that she was and always had been such a private person, she surprised herself to find that she could talk openly with the doctor. She even answered his questions about Tom and talked without embarrassment about their sex life.

On the day she left, Lorna met with Doctor Morton for the last time and on this occasion in the morning. He had invited her for breakfast and although he offered the version holiday hotels like to call 'full English', she opted for toast and coffee with fruit-juice.

"That's something I should have talked to you about," he said between mouthfuls of bacon and egg, "—food." She frowned but he continued, "Simply—you need to build yourself up and you won't do it on toast and coffee."

She laughed and her laugh made him smile.

"That's really an Irish breakfast Doctor. For years my parents tried to get me to start the day with the frying pan—so did Tom—but without success. I like simple food."

"You like everything simple don't you Lorna?" he said," perhaps that's half the problem."

"No more problems." she replied emphasising the negative. "From here on, everything is going to be straight down the line."

Doctor Morton stopped eating and looked at her wearing a blank face. It had always been difficult for her to read him. "As long as there's nothing still bothering you?" he said.

There is one other matter," she said tentatively, "you never explained my reaction the business of my—well—why I began to undress?"

"Well, I think you had a kind of panic attack. You screamed a lot and tore your dress . . . ." He did not describe her behaviour in any more detail. Until she was ready to remember it herself, all he could do was to provide the contextual clues—then it was up to her. They talked for about an hour that day. Much longer than usual and Lorna started to appreciate the complexity of her condition. Doctor Morton explained that what had happened had been bound to happen eventually. Indeed he said he was surprised it hadn't happened before. He told her that he suspected that somewhere back in her past she had been faced with a threatening situation involving a man. Lorna filled in the gaps for herself. She could not count how many times she had had the nightmare.

"That kind of trauma often stays with us through to adulthood," Doctor Morton said, "and, if we don't come to terms with it, it can often cause feelings of severe anxiety. If it's left to fester anything might happen—at the very least such an occurrence could even distort the personality."

Apparently, as Doctor Morton saw it, the occasion of her 'episode' had coincided with a number of other concerns, some personal and others professional. In particular the completion of an important piece of work and the added tension prompted an undeniable stress situation. The appearance and behaviour of big Mr. Blakey, following so close behind that of her manipulating Head teacher had only served to increase the feeling of threat. It all sounded so simple, so straight-forward. But if that were the case, she thought, then why the trauma?

She told him she could recall thinking of Mike, her Head Teacher, at the same time Mr. Blakey was in her office.

"I wondered if you would remember that," he said slowly," I have a theory—but, for the time being, I'd rather not say what it is. You'll reach your own conclusion eventually but, if you're still uncertain by the time of our next meeting, we'll discuss it then—Okay?"

She nodded.

"There's only one other thing," he said. From his inside jacket pocket he removed a letter and studied it. The envelope had been opened. "This letter came for you last week. Naturally we have to open all mail addressed to patients for obvious reasons. I'm sorry we had to open this one though."

He handed it over to her and she pulled out the familiar pale blue paper and read it. It was from her sister Theresa. It told her that after the latest hearing, Patrick was due to be released from prison. It was a cold letter written without emotional commitment, without those bits of gossip she might have expected from a sister and Lorna realised that the gulf between them had not grown any the less through time.

Tom called to collect her and although he was as sweet and considerate as ever, she did not feel inclined to share her feelings with him. Another part of her mind seemed to watch her performance disapprovingly but it had no effect. She shut him out, as she had during his weekly visits, answering his inquiries briefly and deliberately as informatively as she could. He accepted her attitude without complaint and allowed her the silence and space she required.

Later that day, in the car taking her back to London, Lorna found herself feeling pleased. Patrick's freedom was like the final punctuation mark in her recent illness. As if God in his wisdom had removed the grit that had for so long caused her such irritation. She would write to him directly she decided, suddenly then she realised she didn't know where he would go.

CHAPTER TWENTY-TWO

1983

News: Evidence by a 'supergrass' led to sentences of more than 4000 years on 22 members of an IRA cell today. The cell's leader Kevin Mulgrew, aged 27 years was sentenced to 963 years for conspiracy to murder, attempted murder and other crimes—all in addition to a life sentence which he is already serving. The key witness, Christopher Black, is a self-confessed bully, perjurer, failed assassin and robber, the court was told.

Diary: I cannot decide whether I should celebrate or allow myself to fall back into a depression. I finally handed in my resignation today at school and opted to work only part-time and then only occasionally. I worked long and hard for my promotions and invested a huge amount of time and effort in making a success of the job—so it is hard to give it up. Harder still as secretly, I still enjoy the challenge. Nevertheless after my latest episode and sojourn at the clinic, it seems that my constitution cannot stand the extra strain. It has taken me a long time to decide that my health is more important than the job! And I keep asking myself if this is actually true? I've been married to Tom now for only a short time but I gather he will be relieved when I stop teaching. He is wonderful; he tolerates my behaviour—the memory loss, the tantrums and the occasional drinking bouts with the patience of a saint. I know however, that this last occasion put him under a terrible strain—and I couldn't bear to lose him. He is the main focus of my life. I polish the damned crystal ball daily for what good it does me and when I can recall the words, I also continue to pray to Saint Jude. What now I wonder!

* * *

Lorna was surprised to find that it had been the Head of Mathematics who had organised her leaving party. More so still that he had also insisted on doing a collection for a present. The information caused her to re-examine her conscience in his regard. She had always imagined him to be the leader of the opposition, the person most likely to criticise and the one who would undoubtedly start the malicious gossip. Not so it seemed. She remembered then, that when the news of her departure had been announced, it was members of the Mathematics department who had come forward first to say how much they would miss her. And more than any other sector of the school, they had also tried to make her last term as easy as possible.

Of course it had been Doctor Morton who had instigated the move. In his roundabout way he had planted the idea—the doubt, in her mind and then gently pushed her in that direction.

"What you need," he'd told her on a number of occasions, "is an opportunity to take stock. To rest up and regroup your forces."

He often used military metaphors, giving rise to her suspicion that he had once served in the Armed Forces himself. She had argued, of course, that she was still only twenty seven and as such, a youngster in the profession and that the job was getting easier every year, especially as she was now 'on top of it'. But he would not let it pass. He read the papers and listened to the all the new legislation concerning schools and knew therefore, that rather than becoming easier, school management teams were having a host of new responsibilities foisted upon them. Then he recruited her husband Tom to his team—the heavy artillery—and the fight was all but won. However, Tom was, as always, scrupulously honest. He did not apply any underhand tactics, neither subterfuge nor blackmail, neither however, did he soften the impact of his argument. He simply told her that her job was making her life worse than it need be—making their life together worse and damaging her health—that proved enough. The outcome was agreed—but only after, what was for her, a very difficult process of self-evaluation. They had a long painful evening of tears, an evening designed originally as a quiet romantic dinner at home before the fire; an evening that consequently stretched into the early hours of the next day as a result of the intensity of their discussion and the pain that it caused. It was significant that, on the subject of her health, Tom was prepared to express his feelings in such depth. Normally her husband was more reticent, less inclined to be critical.

"I worry about you all the time love," he stated unemotionally, "I never know if you'll be home for dinner, or if I'll get a call saying you're in the hospital again."

It was a telling summary and one she was determined should not be become an epitaph. She knew that the last time she had been in the clinic had been particularly difficult for him, at least in part due to her refusal to let him visit as frequently as he wished—and she could not excuse it because she still did not know why.

Once the decision that she should resign had been agreed that night, a capricious feeling of relief overwhelmed her and she became strangely euphoric. It was if she had wanted to be convinced; that she had wanted someone else to make the final decision, to take matters out of her hands and persuade her to leave the job—despite all her protestations. And once it had happened, once the corner was turned a vista of a new life suddenly appeared within her grasp.

Together they began to plan their future life—her new life, things she could now find time to do. She could write once more, visit friends and indulge her interest in exotic house plants. All being well, there might even be time to consider trying despite the odds to have a baby.

When the last day finally arrived, the end of term just before the summer break, her teaching colleagues presented Lorna with a crystal decanter and a bottle of Irish whiskey. Leaving presents, they said, might provide her with both short-term and long-term enjoyment. The reference to her drinking problem was meant kindly and she felt no animosity to the humour. In his speech however, the Head teacher was overly effusive, providing a eulogy, infinitely more appropriate for Mother Theresa than for Lorna and it was all she could do to resist a cynical response.

The staff room, the usual place where such occasions were celebrated, had been decorated with children's work, paintings and pieces of writing, each with her as the subject matter. A nice touch, organised by someone who recognised the emphasis she had always placed on her relationship with her pupils. The children had also made a collection on her behalf and had elected Tracy Wiggins, one of Lorna's Lower Sixth Form English group to present it to her. She did so just after the last bell sounded but not before a crowd of well-wishers had collected in the classroom. They gave her a book token, saying they knew how she liked a good read and an already tear-stained Tracy Wiggins added that one day they hoped to see one of her novels on the bookshop shelf. It was an emotional moment, oddly reminiscent of another departure she'd made, when she said goodbye to Ireland. Consequently, as she thanked them for their kindness, her own 'floodgates' opened and she added to the tears already more than abundant amongst most of the girls present.

By contrast this was far from the case on the occasion of the Staff presentation later in the day. Lorna had never been able to form the same quality of relationship with her teaching colleagues as she had done with her pupils. In this regard she knew all too well that, although the impediment had been largely of her own making, it was none the less real. For much of the time she had worked in a culture of mutual distrust, they apparently keen to query her professional ability, as she was equally to question their integrity. A situation that had inevitably degenerated still further each time she had suffered one of her episodes.

Doctor Morton had pointed out to her that the intensity of the effort she made to compensate, had contributed to the frequency of the episodes she had experienced. He explained that she needed—in her own eyes—to excel at her job. An aim she had created in order to maintain the respect of her colleagues even despite the fact that, according to her perception, the more she excelled, the greater the apparent animosity. He described this as an ambiguity, designed by her to promote feelings of failure and insecurity. A self-fulfilling contradiction that ensured maximum stress and minimum satisfaction.

By the time Tom called to collect her from school that evening, Lorna had discovered that the 'said' animosity was mostly in her imagination. The Staff were unanimous in their gratitude for her work and as one, wished her well for the future. Their reactions made a profound impression on her thinking and she tried to explain as much to Tom in the car on the way home. She stopped only when she found herself becoming morbidly regretful.

Privately she concluded that yet another section of her near past felt like a failure. She had allowed her imagination to distort the truth and that made her fearful all over again.

CHAPTER TWENTY-THREE

1987

News: November 8th

Ulster Bomb Blast on Remembrance Day. As marchers assembled for the annual Remembrance Day parade in the town of Enniskillen County Fermanagh, an IRA bomb exploded in a disused school, killing 11 people including three married couples. Sixty-three people were injured, some critically.

Diary: Tessa wrote to me—after all these years. I'd come to the conclusion that my little sister would never speak to me again and—now this letter. Apparently she lives in Liverpool—been there since Ma died. A succession of 'men friends' have treated her badly—almost like she sought out the nasty ones—and I fear for her health (mental and physical). I must try and see her, whatever the baggage we might still carry. Time to lay all our ghosts to rest.

* * *

Through a teacher's eye she noted that the laws of punctuation had been ignored—the length of some sentences would have exceeded the patience of Solomon—and the spelling was poor: another reason for sorrow. At home, the emphasis placed on acquiring a good education had been paramount and it was as though her sister had regressed in her application of basic skills. Critically, she concluded that letter's style and structure were more in keeping with the efforts of a fourteen year old pupil rather than those of a mature woman. Nevertheless the letter quickly reduced her to tears. It was an unexpected missive, closely written and covering three sides of A4 paper and, despite its attempt at humour, it communicated a climate of depression—one with which Lorna was uncomfortably familiar. It evoked a mood of tragedy as if the writer was unable to affect the empty hopelessness that filled her soul. Implicitly, it was also a plea for help.

Lorna read the letter several times and each time she read it, she cried. The tears were from pity and out of sympathy; from feelings of remorse and regret and also through frustration. She cried as much from her own feeling of helplessness as she did for, what she saw as, the waste—the terrible waste that had so far been her sister's life. The letter had come from Liverpool where Theresa now lived. In the opening paragraph she admitted that she was surprised to find herself writing to Lorna but she had allowed the impulse, only because there was no one else to turn to. Typically the kind of back-handed compliment for which she had become famed, even as a child. Presumably, in order to fill the gap of the time since their Mother's death, Tessa described a shorthand version of her life since then. It was a desultory tale of repeated betrayals, of abandonment and finally of an attempted suicide.

Apparently, shortly after her Mother died, Tessa agreed to travel to Merseyside with Jake—described as a friend. Jake however, was a sometime businessman, old enough to have been the girl's father and clearly a 'chancer' in terms of his dubious business ventures. Despite his big car and flashy suits, it transpired that Jake was not quite the success he claimed to be. For much of the time he was a salesman in the catering industry, not surprisingly frequenting a large number of hotels and restaurants. The veneer of his life style and its apparent affluence was therefore only a reflection of the environment in which he worked. In fact he lived almost entirely on credit and the affair had ended when he left Tessa early one morning in an unpaid for hotel room. In what seemed like an attempt to increase his status, Tessa blamed the October, Black Monday Stock Market crash for sealing Jake's fate, an inconsistency in time and sequence that was confirmed when she later admitted he had also lost his job. The so called 'crash' hadn't actually occurred that year—an error Lorna decided that was symptomatic of her sister's confused state.

There followed a series of four other similar liaisons, all in the Liverpool area and each resulting in a similar fiasco. Significantly, Lorna noted that in every case Tessa's 'friends' were all men much older then herself. Often they were men who had recently left their wives or who claimed to be in the process of leaving their wives; middle-aged men who, by all accounts, were suffering the first onslaught of mortality fear—a male menopause. Typically they were all men who felt they had failed to achieve the professional success which they inevitably claimed was theirs by right of effort. The only exception to this pattern it seemed was when Tessa met Gerry.

Gerry was a part-time lecturer at the local Art College and, after the last in a long-line of disappointments with older men; Tessa had enrolled at the college as an extra-mural student. On the occasion of their first meeting, Gerry was responsible for the Life Drawing class that operated on two evening per week. Like others before him he had claimed that his real talent laid in the painting of portraits and urban landscapes however, he had been unable to distinguish himself in either sphere, his work proving unsalable.

Consequently on Tuesday and Thursday evenings he taught drawing to nine or ten students, providing an opportunity to study the naked form of Lesley, a typist and part-time model originally from Balham. According to Tessa, most of the class had a serious, if amateur interest, in improving their drawing technique. That small group of voyeurs inevitable in such circumstances, who came simply to ogle bare flesh, soon became bored and left after the first two weeks.

Perhaps through Tessa's innate talent for drawing—she had always been gifted in that way—Gerry lavished a lot of attention on her and her work. They struck up a friendship and before too long the girl moved to live with him in his flat. It was clear to Lorna that, even at that stage, Tessa's need for affection far outstripped Gerry's actual affection for her. Within a month he had her posing for the class, a convenience that allowed him to pocket the fees that Lesley had been paid and a first sign of his selfishness.

Tessa wrote, 'His manner in bed is primitive—he demands total obedience and sometimes enjoys beating me—for fun, he says. To be honest, as long as it isn't too severe, I don't mind too much, sometimes it 'turns me on'. However, occasionally it isn't funny. One Friday evening he had his mates round for drinks and he asked me to do it with one of them. He said they all fancied me and it would be a new 'kick'. They all watched.'

And predictably, the Friday night option became a regular practice. It was weeks before she discovered that Gerry had been charging his friends for the privilege.

'The bastard made me into a 'prossie' Lonny—and all the time I just thought I was doing it for his enjoyment.'

The letter ended abruptly if not unexpectedly, by asking if she could borrow some money, 'to make a new start.

* * *

Lorna sat before the French window looking out onto her little patch of garden. She sat there for a long time thinking about Tessa and comparing their lives. The tears left her throat feeling dry and her skin extra sensitive and now she had a headache. Of course she would send money. There was the Building Society account, the fund they'd put by for home improvements and that could be tapped. She and Tom had moved into the flat in Nottinghill as soon they returned to London. Described by the agent as a garden flat, in fact it was a half basement in Elgin crescent. There were two bedrooms, a kitchen and a living room—just enough for their purposes and as Tom had negotiated a successful transition from the Army to a managerial job with a security firm, they could afford to save for the first time.

She had given up her full-time teaching position after her repeated illnesses and had chosen instead to work only periodically, on what was known as a supply basis. The agency would telephone her each week offering odd days employment at schools across the Capital and she could accept or not as she wished. Her experience as a Deputy Head teacher clearly gave her a status that many local schools admired and she generally had first option on covering for their absent staff. Freed from the strict discipline of her previous administrative responsibilities, Lorna had begun to enjoy teaching all over again. It was not always possible to guarantee teaching her subject exclusively, one day she might be taking twelve year old pupils for French and on another it could be Geography or even PE. Happily there were some situations that did call for her specialist expertise and two schools nearby regularly used her for Sixth Form studies in Advanced Level English. Generally the lessons were prepared for in advance but she was nevertheless able to make a personal contribution, extending the content, suggesting alternatives and expanding the information. Most importantly, the pressure of a full-time career had been removed. She knew also however, that if at some time in the future, she might wish to return on a full-time basis, due to her senior management experience, she was likely to find employment easily.

She made herself a cup of tea and read the letter again at the kitchen table. This time she scrutinised it even more carefully, looking for hidden nuance which she may have missed. Superficially it was casual—offhand even—but knowing the writer so well, she could detect a note of panic, urgency in the tone and she determined that she should make the effort and journey north to see her sister. Tom arrived home just after six that evening but it was not until after their evening meal that she showed him the letter and expressed her concern. Without prompting he immediately suggested she should make the trip to Liverpool.

". . . and we can dip into the savings—can't we?" he asked," I mean—a couple of hundred could make a helluva difference to her and we won't miss it."

On account of his training as an officer, Tom was a careful man. He liked to have the detail of any project well worked out in advance, naturally a generous person; he nevertheless tended to be prudent with money. His response was therefore especially sympathetic. Lorna kissed him.

"You're an old 'sweetie'. Thank you."

He knew how much importance his wife attributed to her family and however limited the contact may have been between them in recent years, he knew also how much security she gleaned from them.

The rest of the evening was spent planning Lorna's trip.

Initially, Lorna thought she might telephone Tessa to tell her she was on her way, on reflection however, she concluded that her sister might say she did not want to meet with her. She could imagine a scenario in which Tessa would cheerfully accept any money offered but would not want to have her older sister's disapproval—face to face. She could foresee an argument developing and all manner of embarrassments for both of them. Instead she decided to make the trip unannounced and rely on the element of surprise to quell their disagreements. And if there was no room for her to stay at Tessa's home, then she would find a B&B and make do with that.

Having made up her mind Lorna was suddenly excited with the prospect of the journey. It had been some time since she'd travelled anywhere by herself and the idea of the long train journey provided a surprising degree of stimulation. She telephoned the railway booking office the next morning and reserved a seat for the next day.

* * *

Clearly, the street had once provided homes for the emergent middle-classes. Proud Edwardian houses with imposing stone steps leading to porticoes; heavily panelled doors framed by ornate mouldings and, in the front elevation at least, huge sash windows. Unfortunately, it was in a very poor state of repair. It was the sort of location where one was immediately struck by the difference that could be made by an injection of cash. The same was apparently true in respect of the latest inhabitants.

Tobias road in Liverpool was an urban eyesore. Paint peeled, rubbish collected in the streets, facades were cracked leaving detail damaged and the walls of many building looked to be under stress. Dustbins positioned at the kerb-side overflowed, allowing the detritus to litter the pavement—and whilst it may well have been the day for rubbish to be collected, in some curious way, the garbage did not look out of place.

Although it was almost mid-day, the road was all but deserted. Curtains at the windows she passed were still drawn and although there was evidence of life through the dim reflection of bare light bulbs behind the curtains, few people had as yet emerged. A thin young man, a teenaged perhaps, sat on the steps in front of one of the houses drinking milk from a carton. His jeans were torn and dirty and even though the morning was cold, he wore only a tee-shirt. His eyes followed Lorna's progress and as she drew close, she had the distinct impression that he was poised to leave hurriedly. Closer still she caught his eye and nodded, smiling as he finally drained the carton. His reaction was cautious, eyes fixed and blinking like a frightened deer.

Number Forty-seven was four doors further down the road and the panel of doorbells, inexpertly mounted alongside the front door confirmed the impression of a house converted into apartments and bed-sits. The fifth bell advertised the fact that this was the home of—Gerry Graham ATD. Artist. She pressed the button and heard the distant sound of the bell from somewhere above.

"Y 'lookin fer Gerry?"

She turned to find the thin young man staring up at her from the base of the steps.

"'Cos he'll still be in 'is pit."

Before she could respond, a window on the second floor screeched open and a head poked out. The face glowered down at her.

"An' what the fuck might I ask d 'you want at this hour?"

Even at that distance Lorna was able to identify the moustache and the long hair as those described to her by Tessa.

"Gerry—Gerry Graham?" she asked.

"'Oo wants t 'know?"

She took a deep breath, "I've come to see Tessa. Is she up there?"

Without answering the face disappeared.

"You've done it now Missus," the thin man said, "He'll be in one helluva mood. Probably t 'inks you're a Busy."

Lorna turned again, "I gather you know Gerry?" she asked.

"Oh yeah. Him an' his bit-o-stuff . . . You a friend of Tezza's den?"

"Yes . . . me . . ." she started to say, but he didn't let her finish.

"She's okay Tezza is. A bit of a looker . . . an' she does a turn . . ."

The big front door opened suddenly and Gerry stood there in his underpants, defiant and aggressive. As soon as the thin young man saw him, he grinned.

"Ah warned her Gerry—but she took no heed t 'me."

The response was immediate, "Fuck off Jimmy an' mind yer own business, else I'll give yer a slap."

Jimmy moved away grumbling to himself and then Gerry turned to Lorna, "And what the hell d 'you want with Tessa?"

The flat consisted of three rooms, a tiny kitchen, an even tinier store-room cum studio and a living room that doubled for a bedroom. The toilet and bathroom were off the landing, a facility shared with the occupants of the next flat. Once she had introduced herself, Gerry's attitude had changed completely. Suddenly she was the welcome guest. He asked her inside and bounded up the stairs ahead of her, shouting for Tessa to make herself respectable. He laughed all the while as if something hugely funny had just happened. When Lorna finally arrived on the second floor, Tessa was the door waiting for her. The younger sister wore only a blanket pulled round her held by her fist. Without a word Lorna put her arms round the girl and hugged her.

"Lonny—y 'should have told us you were coming."

The voice was weak and thin.

"D 'at's no way t 'greet yer lady sister," Gerry said, the sarcasm blatant. "She's come all d 'is way t 'save you from a life of misery . . ."

For Lorna there had always been something repellent about the Scouse accent. In her mind it was a distortion of the Irish Brogue, clipping the first words through a sound of nasal congestion—it irritated and annoyed her. However, the accent only emphasised the air of arrogance that appeared to be endemic amongst the people there—and Gerry was typical. Her Mother would have called him 'Bold'.

Tessa pulled back and turned to their tormentor, "Shouldn't you get some clothes on Gerry. You look disgusting like that." She snarled at him.

Lorna tried to ignore the man, "You've lost weight Love, and you're thin as a stick."

Gerry spoke again this time from across the room as he pulled on some canvas trousers," She's fat az a pig, stuffs 'er face all the time an she's got a spare 'Dunlop' round her middle."

The sisters ignore him completely and sat together on the side of the bed. It was obvious to Lorna that her sister was under some serious degree of strain. She had lost a considerable amount of weight and when she spoke, a tic twitched in her left cheek; her pupils were enlarged and she was a little unsteady on her feet. Lorna deliberately made no comment but worried that all this may be the effect of drugs. She was not there to pass any kind of judgement. Her sister's lifestyle was a million miles away from that which she enjoyed herself and criticism would only cause enmity.

It was obvious that Tessa and Gerry were short of money. There wasn't even a bottle of milk in the fridge with which to make a cup of tea and the place was shabby in the extreme. The wallpaper was streaked with dust, peeling back from patches of damp plaster and the much cracked and mottled ceiling carried only a bare light bulb. A lorry passed by outside and the windows rattled, their frames honeycombed with wet rot, leaving the glass panes dangerously insecure.

"Ah'll go an' get some milk eh?" Gerry intoned nasally, "'Cos if you want a drink we're gonna need some."

Tessa grunted an affirmative from beneath the folds of a very heavy and very dirty man's sweater which she was pulling over her head at the time.

"You gorrany money 'den?" he asked.

The answer was a foregone conclusion and Lorna pulled out her purse even before her sister answered no.

"I have some change here." She said flatly. The two one pound coins were swept from her hand without thanks and a moment later the sisters were left alone, listening to the heavy footsteps echo down the bare stairs. After the front door slammed, they held hands sitting side by side on the bed.

"So, "Lorna whispered, "how can I help?"

Tessa's eyes clouded and the slow tears made channels down both cheeks. She opened her mouth to answer but her words aborted in a strangled sob. A moment later she was in her sister's arms but it was several minutes before she could speak coherently. In fact the situation was so obviously apparent, there was little she needed to add but, once she started, Tessa talked quickly, the volume of her unhappiness venting without caution or hindrance. As she spoke her voice rose uniformly, sentence upon sentence until at last, it screeched in Lorna's ear. Now the bravura of the letter was lost, the arrogance of the recent present dissipating in the face of a shared past. With all sign of confidence gone, the clock turned and Tessa reverted to the frightened little girl, still asking favours of her big sister.

There was no question in Lorna's mind about the options available and once Tessa had quieted, without any kind of consultation, she began to collect her sister's few belongings and put them into carrier bags. Acting on instinct, she gave no thought to the consequences; she knew only that she must take Tessa away from this place—from that man.

"You're coming home with me. Get your shoes on we're leaving now." The statement was defiant and Tessa made no objection. There was no discussion about the practical considerations and certainly no mention of Gerry. Within four or five minutes they were on the staircase and seconds later, Lorna was slamming the front door behind them.

At the corner they saw Gerry leaving the shop across the road. He was clutching a newspaper and a carton of milk. He recognised immediately what was happening and whilst he did not attempt to follow them, he shouted obscenities. Briefly his voice filled the cold street echoing from the buildings but unsurprisingly no one paid any attention to him least of all the two sisters.

CHAPTER TWENTY-FOUR

1988

News: March 7th: Three members of an IRA Service Unit were gunned down by British soldiers wearing civilian clothes in a Gibraltar street. The shootings—at point blank range in broad daylight—are believed to have been carried out by members of the SAS after security forces had feared the IRA were planning to set off a car bomb.

March 16th: A Loyalist gunman opened fire indiscriminately and hurled grenades into a crowd of mourners at an IRA funeral in Belfast today, killing three people and injuring fifty. The shooting occurred when the bodies of the three IRA members, killed by the SAS in Gibraltar ten days ago, were being lowered into their graves at Milltown cemetery.

August: Six British soldiers died when a land-mine exploded under their bus in Northern Ireland.

Diary: Tessa seems to have pulled through thank God. She is working hard and should at last find a career or herself soon. Like the song says: 'The only way is up now.' We are still negotiating for the house in Uxbridge; hopefully we should be in before Christmas. If the adoption goes through successfully—we should have a real family home at last. The future looks good—as long as I can keep myself on an even keel mentally. Whatever it is that troubles me appears to be in remission for the time being. Fingers crossed and thanks to Saint Jude.

* * *

Lorna had loved the flat in Nottinghill. It served as their first home together as well as an effective bolt-hole when her job became too much to bear. She had been happy there although, apart from Tom's presence, this was due more to the proximity of the Portobello market than the size or quality of the accommodation. The Uxbridge house however, was a joy from day one. A tall Edwardian semi.-detached house still boasting many of its original features, it boasted five bedrooms, a tiled kitchen sufficient to house a table with eight place-settings and, best of all, a conservatory. Uxbridge was the last stop at the western end of both the Metropolitan and the Piccadilly Lines, a life-line via the underground train service to central London—should she ever feel the need. She had grown to accept that the new location, situated just inside of the M25 boundary, implied that London's facilities would become distant improbabilities, but she but she did not mind. The exchange was well worth the cost. The icing on the cake of the move was the news that the authorities were prepared to permit the adoption to be finalised. Sean would become her son officially, it was the best Christmas present she could have ever asked for.

They had started the adoption process some eighteen months before. A decision that, whilst it did not initially preclude her having a natural child, paid testimony to the fact of their failure to do so far. Despite her previous history, the doctors now claimed there was no good reason why Lorna should not bear children but they could do little more than suggest various sympathetic therapies to prompt the situation, none of which had so far achieved the desired result. To complicate matters further Lorna started to experience a series of problems with her periods. Her own GP intimated that in the near future she may need to have a hysterectomy understandably such a prospect emphasised in her mind the importance of achieving a successful adoption.

They had been introduced to Sean a year ago and despite his age, he was then almost fourteen years old, and he quickly became their firm favourite. An intelligent, quietly spoken boy, Sean had lost his elderly parents in an air accident whilst he was still only a baby. There were very few relatives and none prepared to accept responsibility for him, consequently the vast majority of his life had been spent in children's homes. Surprisingly perhaps, he had resisted the worst aspects of becoming institutionalised, retiring instead to hide behind a book. Books were his passion. The adoption service manager had been keen to find a place for the boy but admitted that she had almost given up hope of ever doing so.

"Most couples are looking for babies or toddlers at least," she'd told Lorna, "they're afraid to admit a teenager into their homes for fear of how he might develop."

Ever the champion of the underdog, Lorna had immediately bonded with the boy. It was relationship that blossomed with each successive visit Sean made to the flat and thankfully one that was also echoed by Tom. Over the following months they had filled in the application forms, attended several interviews and apparently met the statutory requirements, all that remained was to take the final step. Their new son was as excited as his prospective parents and in the final stages, spent as much time as was permitted in the flat.

At the end of November, after several days of chaos spent packing, paying final bills for the utilities and instructing the removal firm, they finally moved to Uxbridge. There were two days when months of planning were made manifest; two days also in which the added value of having a teenage son was well proven. Sean was a massive help, not only was he big and strong but he was quick to find solutions to problems associated with the packing.

After the last box and the final stick of furniture had been delivered, Tom and Sean erected beds upstairs whilst Lorna unpacked foodstuffs and filled the fridge before beginning an evening meal. Naturally the whole house was in a state of disarray but there was a palpable air of satisfaction that was shared by all three of them. At some stage, Tom found himself down in the kitchen with Lorna when they heard Sean singing. The boy was fastening the last bed-frame together on the first floor when he broke into song. Tom and Lorna stopped to listen, grinning stupidly, "And that's what makes it all worthwhile." Tom said.

Lorna kissed him, "Couldn't agree more." She said.

Lorna could not remember ever being happier. During the three weeks leading up to Christmas, the two men in her life had achieved miracles in the house. The kitchen had been reorganised, carpets had been laid on the first two floors, the bedrooms were habitable and, after many options had been explored, the furniture had been arranged to her satisfaction. Due to the vast difference in scale between the house and the flat, their furniture seemed to be lost in the new spaces. The three piece suite that had so recently crowded their living room now appeared to have shrunk and the dining room table, even with both leaves extended still left the kitchen looking bare. There was a need for lots of new—or nearly new—furniture she decided and began to plan a visit to the local sale-rooms.

The only blot on the landscape was the first post they received at their new address: a letter from the hospital giving Lorna a date for what was now deemed to be the necessary operation. She was assured that it was a relatively simple procedure and that she would be out and about in just a few days she was nevertheless still nervous. She knew however that she needed to minimise her fears in case Tom realised her trepidation. As her self-proclaimed protector he was bound to react badly if he detected any degree of danger to her health and the last thing she wanted was to see him worrying.

Neither Tom nor Sean seemed to be unduly bothered by the lack of furniture, indeed they revelled in having so much space. Sean commented that the worst part of living in the home had been never having any really private space.

"There was nowhere I could close the door on—no place where I could guarantee to be on my own." He said.

It was a sentiment with which she could readily identify. In both her family homes, space had been at a premium and, until she had moved into her flat in Nottinghill, she had shared a similar frustration. Comparing the experiences with Sean however, inevitably brought them closer together.

Paradoxically, despite her satisfaction with the move, eight days after they arrived in their new home, Lorna experienced a panic attack. As usual it came at night, just on the point of her falling asleep. She had been thinking about her conversation with Sean and what he'd said about having his own space when suddenly she became afraid and, without just cause, she began to tremble. She put on her side-light and tried to read a novel but after a few minutes she had to get out of the bed. She was trying not to disturb Tom but just as she was putting on her dressing gown he turned, "Are you alright Love?" he asked.

"One of my funny turns," she replied, "—don't worry, I'll go down and make myself a cup of tea."

He sat up, suddenly alert to the possibilities, "Want me to join you—I don't mind?"

"No. I'm fine. You go back to sleep. I'll be okay."

She left the room with Tom still sitting up in the bed.

By the time she reached the kitchen however, she was anything but okay. The sweats had started, presaged by an indescribable feeling of foreboding. Suddenly the prospect of the operation was terrifying. Every corner, every shadow seemed to menace her, challenging the security of her sense of logic. She boiled a kettle and struggled to maintain control as she made the tea. Her hand began to dither and the anxiety surged again, making her breathless. She sat at the table and sipped the hot drink but her vision began to blur just as the voices started in her head. The too familiar feeling of unreality captured her and she felt herself slip into darkness.

* * *

The doctor arrived in the early hours of the morning, a Locum with more than his fair share of patients to visit. He talked quietly to Tom in the passageway outside the bedroom before giving Lorna an injection to make her sleep.

"This will help," he said kindly, "but, I've told your husband that you must contact your own doctor first thing in the morning."

On the way out he stopped again to have a whispered conversation with Tom, by then Lorna was already drifting off into a dreamless sleep.

CHAPTER TWENTY-FIVE

1990

News: The Prime Minister stated that he would initiate talks between the parties concerned to seek a solution to the troubles in Northern Ireland.

Diary: I have no wish to have this operation however; despite the time it has taken to schedule the hospital visit Doctor Thomas claims it is necessary. The delay caused by my 'episode' almost had me believe it would not happen. Well—I've had my share of hospitals. Also, to find myself subject to the surgeon's knife at my age is more than a little frightening, (especially in the hands of a male surgeon) I will be out before Christmas deo gratias. I only hope all goes well.

* * *

His face was gray like the distant hospital concrete, his knuckles tightly white on the steering wheel. He was more afraid, than she was herself.

Typical, Lorna thought, men had no stomach for the carefully studied violence of surgery. In her experience however stainless the steel, however merciful the intent, the acceptance of surgical incursion offended against male sensitivity, whereas a woman's body was used to trespassers. Faced with the prospect of institutionalized, public pain, men shared nothing of women's' proactive stoicism. Theirs was an aptitude only for retaliation, most usually in unlit places. A response timed in dark microseconds rather than hours under the heat of white lights. Not surprisingly therefore, a hospital environment of cool corridors, uniformed nurses, crisply starched bedding and sanitized, orderly cleanliness was anathema to them. Men's' understanding of violence was confined to bar rooms, on street corners, against hard pavement slabs and in back streets. Sometimes, for some of them, it was also a characteristic of the bedroom. And, as with that brand of sexual encounter preferred by some, it was inevitably accompanied by large applications of turmoil and agitation. Most significantly in either case, whatever the degree of orchestration they claimed, their effort was often characterized by a lack of order and minimal control. A curious anomaly, she thought, considering men's self-proclaimed addiction to logic and organization.

To be fair the traffic that morning was bad. The M4 was second only to the frustrating M25 when it came to traffic jams. Tom drove carefully, like he had done when she was pregnant (and she'd still lost the baby). Fear proving a better speed regulator than any imaginable traffic cop or speed camera. By contrast, she was easily able to keep her own panic in check, and to hold the images of what she knew was to come in a calculated suspension of reality. It was convenient for Tom to argue that this proved she lacked imagination. She saw it as strength of purpose and let's face it, in that regard, she had had plenty of experience.

On the journey to the hospital she tried to lighten the mood in the car by talking about their plans for the coming Christmas. Her efforts were met with little more than stony silence. As usual they were to have a house full of friends, a crowd that would undoubtedly wreak havoc in what was normally a quiet home. But it was a time she savoured. Unfortunately her efforts to distract her husband went unrewarded and she was left to read the depth of his silence as testimony to his level of stress. His answers to her questions were monosyllabic, as though to distance him from what was to follow and, on those occasions when he did find words, they were most often only words of abuse for other drivers.

The hospital monolith, a 1960's monstrosity of pre-caste concrete units, reared up to domineer a major road junction, making access to the sprawl of its satellite car-parks possible, only from one direction via a boundary road. To make matters worse the boundary road was punctuated by an endless succession of traffic humps, a procession of sleeping policemen that formed a debilitating honour guard for new arrivals. In her case a final hurdle in her reluctant steeple—chase to the operating theatre.

They joined a procession of cars trundling slowly round the grounds seeking somewhere to park but, fifteen minutes later mid-way through their second trip round the perimeter, a parking place still continued to elude them.

"And thank you too." Tom snarled at some equally confused and obviously disorientated female driver. Her appearance from one of the minor side roads had been without warning, causing him to break sharply. The sort of mistake anyone might have made—even a man—but had such an opinion been voiced, it would have only aggravated her driver's frustration all the more.

"There's no rush love." Lorna said quietly.

"Indeed." he replied voluminously, at the same time scowling at the woman driver's apologetic smile.

"Well there isn't."

His smile tightened. "Nevertheless," he muttered, "along with legions of other brain-dead-Sunday-lady-drivers she would be well-advised to stick to supermarket trolleys."

Lorna prickled, "And that's . . ." she was about to say sexist when she saw the parking space, "there's a place—over there."

The discovery of a place to park was like a win on the Football Pools, bringing a smile to her husband's face for the first time that morning and, as they unpacked her small case, she sighed with secret relief. Perhaps now he would relax. Unfortunately, the smile lasted only minutes. They were caught in a sudden rain-storm and his grin liquidised. The unexpected downpour took them by surprise. Obviously, by his reckoning, it had lain in wait until they were on foot and only half way to the reception area. A unique circumstance—this rain—never before experienced in the British Isles.

"This isn't funny," she heard her husband mutter; "you're a sick bastard sometimes."

Lorna shook her head," Tom people will think you're a bit odd if you talk to yourself."

"Actually I was telling God what I thought." he snapped back.

Tom was one of life's great complainers and if ever he lacked an audience or a target for his complaints, he would refer the matter to a higher authority. Although not normally a religious man, he had long since developed the practice of irreverent conversations with the Almighty, many of which became one-sided slanging matches. But, as he also did the same with his late Uncle Joe and with his long since departed Father, she was not surprised to hear him employ the same tactic to the Supreme Being.

Often it caused her to wonder about the mutual tolerances evident in their relationship. How, for example she wondered, might he have fared with another, less understanding partner?

They entered the foyer at last, dripping from all extremities.

Used to dealing with the management of professional people Lorna took charge of the situation with an easy confidence. She talked to the administrative staff and later to the Charge Nurse in the ward, quickly and efficiently sorting the detail of her admission and the programme for the operation. It was a level of competence that had been hard won. Founded partly in her professional life, it had prospered as she matured, leaving her more than equal to the task of being Deputy Head of a large comprehensive school. Conversely, she liked to think that her competence had also resulted from the regular no-holds-barred verbal combat with a husband and a teenage son.

As a child at home in Ireland, she had grown to accept the confrontations endemic in a family that thrived on debate. But it was later, through the many late night discussions and debates with a husband who would never surrender his point of view that her skills in defending her opinions had finally developed to maturity.

"Your husband can stay for a while if he wants to." the nurse said, breaking the spell.

Lorna smiled. It was a statement that at one stroke, successfully placed Tom in, what was for him, an unfamiliarly minor role. Nevertheless, to give him his due for once he did not respond with a verbal attack but gave the young woman a weakly, discrete smile and nodded gratefully. And it was not until the nurse had left the room some minutes later that Lorna began to understand the significance of the change in him. She was arranging her toiletries on the bedside cabinet when he put a hand on her shoulder. She turned to find his face strained and his eyes staring.

"You . . . . you don't have to go through with this you know," he said, "Not if you really don't want to."

"Well, obviously I'm not looking forward to it—but it's necessary."

"Yeah, I know that—but—I mean, if you're afraid then . . ."

Now his concern was unashamed, his cheek twitched making it look as though, like a small boy, he might burst into tears at any moment.

"There's nothing to worry about Tom. Hundreds of women go through this . . . . it's only a hysterectomy."

"Yeah—but you're not hundreds of women."

She slipped her arms round him and pressed her face to his. The suddenness of his anxiety came as a shock. She had misunderstood his mood. She hugged him and whispered reassurances but he gripped her tightly and kissed her, almost as though saying goodbye. Unexpectedly his fear became infectious.

CHAPTER TWENTY-SIX

1990

Six o'clock News:

The Prime Minister Mr. John Major today called on all sides representing the electorate in Northern Ireland to seek a peaceful solution. He nevertheless remained adamant that Sinn Fein would not be able to attend talks held to find a solution, unless the IRA gave up its weapons."

Diary: I hate it when people talk about you as if you weren't there or could not possibly understand—like you were in another room. I drift in and out of consciousness but I nevertheless understand all that they say. I'd like to scream my objection but that would prove too painful. Please God Tom comes and takes me home soon.

* * *

She could hear that someone was having difficulty breathing. It was a sound that reminded her of the time when she had had pneumonia as a child: a rasping airless noises, punctuated by hasty swallowings. It was a horrible memory; the inability to catch enough breath and the gasping emptiness of the vacuum. She empathised to such an extent that she felt herself break into a cold sweat. It was just as if a weight had been laid on her chest—a heavy body laid on top of her, crushing all the air out of her lungs. Panic gripped her and unaccountably she thought of her Father.

She remembered the sounds he made, lying behind the plastic sheets of the oxygen tent all those years ago. An echo of night time noises from another life.

The doctors at the hospital had called it a sterile environment and, although she did not fully understand at the time, the words were etched in her memory. Little details came back to confirm the sense of horror; her mother's tear-stained face and tight lips; Peter's questions—asking why they couldn't see their Dad and Patrick's sullen silence. At her side, her sister had gripped her arm so violently that the arm had been left bruised—the fingerprints of bereavement.

The thought of the bruising made her realise it was a daytime dreaming nightmare the kind she had suffered all her life but still she could not wake herself. The flashbacks continued:

Arms bruised purple and yellow; arms hidden for the shame of the bruises and her scratching; darkness; alone and isolated; fear of being found out and the crushing weight of guilt.

Awareness was finally restored when a cool flannel was laid across her forehead and a distant voice asked, "Are you alright love?"—Tom's voice.

With the new reality came the certain knowledge that she was the one struggling to breathe and then the pain began in earnest.

Tom's face hovered. One of several heads floating in the gray of the ceiling but another faraway voice was the first to speak.

"She looks much better today."

"Well she could hardly look worse."—Tom's voice this time—and with more than a touch of irony. He was annoyed. She knew the tone He was struggling to keep his temper under control. She closed her eyes.

"You had her notes—God knows how the hell you could ignore the fact of her asthma. It smacks of incompetence to me."

Clearly he had lost the battle for self-control.

Usually his outbursts caused her to complain. She would often as not adopt an injured tone and cover the embarrassment she felt by demanding he behave himself, threatening to leave the party, the shop, the company or wherever the location of the disagreement happened to be, if he did not conform. It had been root of innumerable arguments prompting the slamming of many doors and her stomping out of a variety of situations. Surprisingly, this time she felt no concern at all. The protestations of the doctors were matched by her husband's accusations, voices were raised and threatened recriminations were exchanged. As usual Tom had the high ground and in the face of his evidence, despite the aggressive manner of its presentation, the medics began a tactical retreat.

"You must appreciate that we are very short staffed at this hospital." one voice said. "And I can assure you that your wife is receiving the very best attention possible . . . ." an older voice echoed.

" . . . . under the circumstances—you mean." Tom added. This time his reply was loaded with sarcasm.

"Gentlemen, you should know, I have already written a letter to the Health Authority representative who deals with serious complaints and I've named the pair of you. If my wife doesn't show immediate signs of improvement—say within twenty-four hours—then I will have no hesitation in sending the letter."

The moments silence stretched like a slow yawn until Tom concluded, "Now—if you don't mind, I'd like a little time alone with her."

As the shuffling footsteps receded Lorna realised the import of what they had been saying. Quietly, she began to panic just before sleep came again.

* * *

The days seemed to merge but the animosity between Tom and the doctors continued unabated. By day four it was painfully obvious that she would not be going home on day five as had been the original prediction. She was still too weak to leave the bed unaided and most of the tubes she had acquired were still in place. She ate little of the hospital food provided and consequently had no strength. Now the pain from the operation was bearable—just, but her breathing continued to cause concern. Asthma was endemic in her family and, increasingly as she had grown older, she had suffered its limiting effect. Despite all this however, it was Tom that she worried about most.

He visited her every day, often sitting for hours at the bedside, even when she slept. Much like the bull of his birth sign he stood guard, aggressively prohibiting any but the most essential disturbance to the quiet of her room. Several times she had heard him take the doctors and nurses to task, complaining at the noise they made and the slowness of their response. She knew also, from occasional comments by her regular nurse, that he had had a knock-down drag-out row with the Consultant in full view of the main ward. He had said nothing to her about the subject of his complaint but she knew his temperament well enough to realise that he had the capacity to cause more bother than the hospital had ever seen before. He was not one to suffer fools gladly and, the obvious depth of his concern for her apparent lack of progress would inevitably increase the likelihood of a major incident. She had often seen him create a public scene in shops and restaurants when poor service, rudeness on the part of staff or the lack of reasonable quality in their purchases was the stimulus. She had sometimes accused him of enjoying confrontations but she also knew that, as on this occasion, the vehemence of his response was just his way of looking out for her best interests.

She smiled when she imagined him in action. Once moved, he could be awkward beyond the point of reason, occasionally awkward even to the point of physical violence. A performance that was usually made more the telling by his capacity for language. His vocabulary and the manner of its application covered a spectrum from that used by the most erudite, to that one might expect to find in a back-street brothel. And he would apply this talent unashamedly in whatever degree he thought necessary.

Although his family had been lower-middle class people, he had still experienced a struggle to get his qualifications. His parents had run a pub and could see little practical sense in any kind of academic study. Consequently, nothing had been easy for him. Well hidden beneath the surface of his aggressive protection however, she knew him to be a kind man and a husband of exceptional sensitivity. Not surprisingly therefore she felt secure in the safety of his care.

That day for the first time her head was clear. The previous night was the first since the operation that she had not needed morphine to help her sleep. It was a great pain-killer but she had found one of its side-effects was it tended to leave her disoriented during the following day. The difference was so spectacular that she had made a mental note to try thereafter, to avoid the use of the drug as much as possible. That morning, she had even eaten the dreaded breakfast porridge and drunk the dark sepia coloured tea.

She heard voices outside and a moment later Staff Nurse Jones entered behind young Doctor Malcolm. They exchanged the usual pleasantries before he told her that they needed to change her transfusion needle. Due to a lower than usual blood count, a transfusion of four units had been necessary and this was administered via a fine tube to the back of her left hand. Unfortunately the needle had clogged and the supply had thereby become much reduced.

"Don't worry; we'll just plonk it in another vein, no problem." Doctor Malcolm told her.

Fifteen minutes and six attempts later, Loma was beginning to feel like a pin cushion. After the first four attempts, the back of her left hand had proved such a painful site that he had transferred his attentions to the right hand—not however, with any greater degree of success. Twice, Nurse Jones had offered to take over the procedure and twice he had refused her help, by this time, his patient was clearly getting close to hysteria.

"I'm terribly sorry about all this," the Doctor muttered trying again as blood dripped, "you see the problem is that your veins are very thin . . . ."

"About as thin as your professional skills." Tom said from the doorway.

His arrival had gone unnoticed but Lorna knew immediately that his presence was about to be felt.

* * *

At first she imagined the complaints were aimed at some junior member of the hospital staff. Perhaps some innocent young nurse, tired at the end of a long shift. The sarcasm was bitter and the atmosphere of threat explicit.

" . . . and if this is what you call organisation, you need your head examining. I've had it with you—from now on—you can fuck off for me."

The language was too much but, it was only after she opened her eyes and found Tom sitting there by himself that she realised he was addressing his private dose of vitriol to his Maker.

He saw her smile and his grip on her hand tightened.

"Look whose awake then," he muttered, "and how is my Pandora this morning?"

The rebuke she had intended was stillborn and she found herself grinning at the reference. He had embarrassed her in front of Jenny and Jake weeks ago by declaring that her operation would be like the opening of Pandora's 'box'.

"Like I've been under a tractor wheel all night—but I'm okay—honest."

He kissed her fingers, still held tightly in his fist, studying her reactions in disbelief as she spoke.

"That nurse said they'd take out the drain this morning." he offered.

His news was meant to make her feel better but the thought made her squirm. The idea of anyone starting to mess about with her again turned her stomach. The item to which he referred was a half inch tube that protruded from a hole in her side and its purpose was to allow excess blood still seeping from the internal wound to drain away. For the first time she imagined the scars she would carry. As well as the hole for the tube she had been sliced across ten or twelve inches of her lower stomach and although the doctor had told her the scar would be hidden by any bikini bottom, she was unconvinced. So much for the beach, she thought. There had been a time when the stretch marks, the unforeseen bonus of childbirth, had been her main concern. Now she would have scars more like Frankenstein's daughter.

"After all this, I'm going to look like Frankenstein's monster." she said, giving voice to her fears.

He grinned back, "So that's how you see me is it?"

She tried to enjoy his humour and make a smile but suddenly, she felt close to tears. Whatever he said, how could he ever fancy physical contact with her again? Something was over—ended, and momentarily, the regret she felt almost overwhelmed her. A solitary tear trickled down the edge of her cheek.

"Hey," he whispered, sensing her mood, "there's no need for that Love. We've been though worse than this, haven't we? Like you used to tell me—you just concentrate on getting better and leave the bastards to me."

She had told him exactly that all those years ago when he lay close to death. But that was another life-time—a period of nightmare and loss. The memories flooded back, vivid and colourful: Tom gasping for air; blood pumping from bullet wounds in his torso and in her soul—total panic.

Thank God at least it means I can go home she thought and the time frame shifted.

The feeling of anticipation almost generated a sense of excitement, the kind of thrill she used to experience as a child on Christmas morning, like waiting at the altar rail for her first holy Communion or in expectation of Tom's touch after they were first wed. The cloud was lifting at last and she was convinced that it was only a matter of time—a short time before her trauma—whatever it was—was revealed. However, the more she focused on it, the more the excitement turned to doubt.

Having excused himself early from work, he was at the hospital for nine that morning. It had been the worst ten days of his life and he could hardly wait to end the trauma. Lorna was coming home—at last. In the car on the way there he had carefully scrutinised the detail of his complaints. A list, long enough to satisfy any ombudsman and sufficient to cause any newspaperman to have an orgasm of self-righteous delight.

"Well the bastards won't get away with it this time." he told himself.

He was determined that whatever else might happen, he would pursue the hospital authorities, if necessary, as far as the courts. The level of, what he saw as unprofessional conduct, verged on criminal negligence and he was determined to publish the facts at the first opportunity.

The car park as usual tested his patience almost to breaking point but after so many visits, his ratio of success in finding a parking place had improved. Now he knew the quieter corners, he knew where the deliveries were made, where he might leave the car for a short spell, even if it was in bays reserved for doctors. He locked the doors and carried the small case containing Lorna's change of clothing to the side entrance. He had been told the previous day that his wife was very likely to be allowed to go home. It was not one hundred percent certain—just very likely. The nurse had told him that when the drain from Lorna's side showed a daily discharge of less than 80 milligrams they could remove it and allow her to leave. Not before time he thought. He was convinced that his ministrations in their home, however amateur, would be more attentive and certainly more caring than those she had received in the hospital.

The ward was quiet when he arrived. The breakfast rush was almost over and patients were finishing their cups of morning tea. There were no other visitors and he went unchallenged to the small private room where Loma had been situated. Behind the double doors he found her sitting on the side of the bed.

"Hey," he said," what's all this. Do they know you're up and about?"

She smiled. "No problem Doctor Tom. Nurse Ferguson helped me up first thing. All the tubes are out and, other than a cannon-ball wound in my side, I'm fit and well," she paused, "—and ready to go home."

He took her hand and kissed her on the cheek.

"And this is one husband who'll be delighted to get his wife back." he whispered. He gave her the suitcase and she went into the bathroom to change.

Whilst he waited he strolled over to the big window to watch the traffic below. The view was terrific from the seventh floor and with the almost total absence of noise, disjointed and surreal. After a moment or two he turned back and scanned the room. Lorna's medical record book was laid on the bedside table. He picked it up and idly thumbed through the detail of her operation and the drug care she had received afterwards. On the back page he found a record of the wound discharge. With such a loss of blood no wonder she had been so weak he thought, then he registered the final readings. They had been recorded that morning at seven o'clock': discharge—one hundred and twenty milligrams.' His hands went clammy and he felt himself flush.

"You okay in there?" he called out to the bathroom door.

"Fine—won't be a minute." came the answer.

She emerged a few minutes later looking pale and tired "There," she said, "all ready and waiting."

He tossed the book back onto the table.

"I suppose the doctor was here—I mean when they took your drain out?" he asked.

"Oh Tom don't start again. Yes the doctor was here—and he signed the forms to discharge me. Look in the book. It's all there."

He forced a smile.

"Okay—just asking. Come on then love, let's get you home."

Unbeknown to Lorna, Tom had made up a bed downstairs. He anticipated that the climb up thirteen steps might cause her a problem. He should have known better. When she got home from the hospital, Lorna would have none of precautionary measures . . .

"They discharged me Tom, "she said loudly,"—so as far as the doctors are concerned I'm fit enough to be home and to behave normally." His sigh of resignation caused her to relent, if only a little "Anyway, its ten nights since we slept in the same bed and I've been looking forward to a long cuddle."

As usual, her scheming worked, and Tom laughed.

"I'd almost forgotten what a shameless hussy you are. Okay, but whilst you're down here you must keep your feet up and rest—promise?"

She promised and she did as he suggested—more or less. It was hard for her. She was not a good patient and felt that she was imposing on him also; she actually wanted to do things for herself. However, he would not allow her even to make a cup of tea. He sat her in the drawing room with her gardening magazines close to hand, the remote control for the television on the arm of the chair and a large jig-saw puzzle—one of her favourite therapies—on a table nearby.

"I don't want anything to go wrong," he told her," so stay where you are and I'll look after your every need."

And he did.

One of the less pleasant tasks he took on board was to change the dressing on her wound. This needed to be renewed at least once every day and some days twice. He said nothing about it to her but the whole area across her lower stomach was badly bruised and increasingly it concerned him. The deep blue and purple marked a swathe across her belly, surrounding the place where the drain had been inserted. It was as if she had been beaten. She made no comment about it herself and seemed to accept the fact of it without question.

During the evening of her third day at home she went to the bathroom on the first floor to take a shower. He had offered to help but had been told she was still capable of washing herself—"Thank you very much." She had only been up there a couple of minutes when he heard her call out for him. He ran to the stairs and took them two at a time. The bathroom door was open and the shower was left running. He found her sitting on the side of the bath a towel clutched to her side. She was pale and gasping, looking as though she was about to faint.

There was blood everywhere. The carpet was spattered, the sink porcelain and the bath were streaked and the towel she held to her stomach was soaked.

"Tom," she said in a forced whisper," Tom love—something isn't right.

* * *

The doctor was less than helpful and he left Lorna more confused than ever. On the one hand he claimed that the operation had been a success whereas on the other he expressed concern about her blood loss. He was loathed to admit it but seemed to lay responsibility, if not blame, on the after-care at the hospital. For once, Lorna was only too pleased to leave Tom to explore the doctor's tortuous line of reasoning, a cross-examination that would undoubtedly leave both of them exhausted. Instead of allowing her to become embroiled, she laid back on the couch and let them all get on with it.

They had arrived at the medical centre when it was already quite late and the evening surgery had finished. Initially therefore, Sister Thomas was adamant about it being too late to see the doctor. She proved to be the archetypal bodyguard, a nurse of the old school, making it painfully clear that doctors were the most hard-working people on the planet as we as being the least respected. She muttered words like ingratitude into her Arcadian stiff white collar and it was only after irresistible pressure from Tom that she finally agreed to examine Lorna's wound herself.

The wads of gauze and cotton wool were removed and, as if her body understood the need for another rehearsal, on cue the blood pumped out. Sister Thomas responded quickly. She grabbed fresh dressings from a nearby table, tore off the paper covers and pressed them to the source of the bleeding.

"Hold that there," she ordered Tom," not too hard—just enough—Yes, like that.

They hear her sensible shoes clip clopping down the stairs and a moment later the doctor's voice. They returned together. He scrutinised her belly for, what seemed like an age, then he shook his head.

"She'll have to go back to the hospital," he declared," she may need to be drained again." Lorna's heart almost stopped and the panic returned.

"Is that really necessary?" she asked, knowing already what the answer would be. Doctor Braithwaite gave his response to Tom, as if it had been his question. More evidence that she was again just a slab of female meat. When he finished talking to Tom, he turned to look her in the face for the first time, smiling, like she was brain dead.

"I'll make an appointment for you first thing in the morning; meanwhile you can only staunch the bleeding with dressings. Do you understand?"

She prickled. Enough was enough she thought.

"It's the belly that's wounded Doctor not my mind. Now then, I'd be obliged if you could please tell me exactly what the problem is?"

There was a moment's silence. He studied her as if for the first time, his face showing a mix of feelings from surprise to hurt. Like, 'Did the 'meat' actually ask a sensible question?' Sister Thomas tutted quietly and put a fresh dressing on the wound.

"It's a problem of drainage," Braithwaite said finally, this time addressing himself to the patient.' All that bruising on your tummy indicates that blood from the operation has collected there. In some respect, it's just as well that it found a way out. It could so easily become infected."

"Thank you Doctor." Lorna replied—and she meant it.

She left Tom to explore the allocation of blame and she lay back as he tried to get Doctor Braithwaite to quantify the precise nature of the risk—to measure the immeasurable. On the way home in the car Lone cried quietly to herself in the dark. The last thing she wanted was to return to that hospital. She was sick of being messed about with, fed up with tubes and injections, tired of all the physical abuse.

CHAPTER TWENTY-SEVEN

1992

News: January: Ulster—The IRA has made its worst attack in Northern Ireland since 1988: seven Protestant construction workers were killed instantly and seven others injured when a bomb destroyed a van transporting them from a work-site at a British barracks near the village of Omagh.

July: Police found mutilated remains of two men who were tortured by the IRA as informers.

Dec: Ira brought central London to a halt through two small bombs which injured four people. There was chaos amongst Christmas shoppers as the warnings given were inaccurate.

Dec.23: IRA announces a 3 day cease-fire for Christmas.

Diary: This is the year I have been dreading the most. If all goes well Sean will get his place at university and move on to the next stage of his education. The house will be empty when he goes and the ally I have nurtured since 1988 will find other causes to champion—perhaps. Maybe I should have resisted the school's advice and had him wait, instead of allowing him to take his exams early. I did the same myself and where did it get me? We have had him for so short a time.

* * *

Sean was studying in his room, not an unusual event given his dedication and the urgency of his quest to find a university place. He had proved to be all that Tom and Lorna might have hoped for in a son, adapting to life with them without sign of any of the traumas common in such situations. They had been warned well in advance that when the adopted child suffered such traumas, the effects could easily disrupt the adoptive parent's relationship and lead ultimately to a rejection of the new child. However, from his first arrival Sean had proven to be sensitive to the ethos of his new home. He had been considerate of their feelings, careful in his behaviour and well worthy of the praise they lavished on him for his achievements at school. To Tom's delight he was able to demonstrate an aptitude for sport without dissipating the energy necessary for his academic studies. He always made the first team both in Cricket and football and his PE teacher reckoned he was a natural athlete. Equally, from Lorna's point of view, Sean had become her confidante. Their shared interest in literature prompted many discussions and debates and through him, for the first time in years, her desire to write had been rekindled.

He would sit his 'A' Levels that year and the predictions from his teachers were good. If they were met, he could expect to achieve four passes at 'A' Grade—one of those being in French. Consequently, he was expected to gain a place at his first choice university which was Warwick. His Head of English at school had tried to persuade him to take the Oxbridge entry examinations but the boy resisted. Having done his own research, he argued that Warwick was 'the' place for English studies and could boast a staff of lecturers who would understand his background and his ambitions to be a writer, without prejudice. Tom had been hard to convince. He believed that a degree from one of the premier places of advanced study would open doors for his son that Warwick would not but Sean's mind was made up. His resolve in this matter had impressed Lorna and she saw the contrast with her own beginnings where the opportunity was snatched only in order that she could leave home.

Sean came down from his room about three in the afternoon and found his mother reading the newspaper at the kitchen table.

"Tea?" he asked and she nodded, grinning with pleasure at his attentions.

Sean enjoyed his afternoon tea almost as much as she did herself and, especially at week-ends, it had become one of their rituals. Tom was often out at that time of day and the occasion provided an opportunity for mother and son to engage in one of their usual far-ranging discussions.

He filled the kettle as she watched. There was no doubt that he was a handsome boy, dark-haired and dark-eyed and already standing as tall as his father, she concluded that one day he would break female hearts with ease. He moved easily and with a grace uncommon in boys and it came as something of a shock when she suddenly realised he was already a man.

"So what's new then?" he asked as he placed the cups and the teapot on the table.

"New?"

"In the newspaper?"

"They're trying to guess the date of the election—if that's new. Most of the pundits reckon April—it seems."

"Then it'll be goodbye to Mister Major," he quipped laughing, "and good riddance as far as I'm concerned."

"And—after we suffered all those years of Thatcher." She replied meditatively.

The kettle boiled and Sean turned. He faced her with a cynical grin, "On the other hand," he said, and "your friend Mister Kinnock better pull his socks up. Some of his proposals sound as daft as Maggie's."

Lorna was quick to reply, "You're as big a cynic as your Dad. Politicians are just people like the rest . . ."

But he didn't let her finish, "People must be the last word to describe them—any of them. And I'll give you a forecast—most of my generation won't even bother to vote. We've seen them—all of them—make such a mess of things, we think none of them are to be trusted."

This was a favourite bone of contention between them and Lorna responded on cue.

"Everyone should be obliged to vote—like they are in Australia. It's not a privilege, it's a responsibility. How else can you expect to exercise your democratic right?"

Sean brought the freshly filled teapot to the table along with the biscuit tin. He was smiling again and shaking his head. A deliberate performance of condescension, "Mum, "he said, pouring the tea, "really—exercise our democratic right! You get five minutes of democracy every five years or so—and if that isn't bad enough—now there is hardly any choice on offer between the parties. Our politicians are only in it for what they can get out of it for themselves. The thick-skin they acquire once in office is designed only to hide their greedy ambition."

Lorna poured the milk. Now it was her turn to smile. Her son was as fiercely political as she had hoped he might be, questioning, criticising and finding fault. It was a treat to listen to him—however faulted his argument.

"So how would you rate someone like Tony Benn?" she asked mischievously, knowing full well this was one of her son's hero's.

"For every Benn there are ten Nixon's," he snapped back, "twenty Thatcher's and hundreds of Heaths—need I mention Profumo or any of the others of that ilk. And then of course there's the Ulster travesty."

The fact that Sean had seen fit to mention Ireland was a sure sign his cage had been rattled. It was a subject on which she claimed the most personal expertise, "Ah," she said, rising to the bait again, "so I suppose you're now going to argue the Republican cause?"

The implied reproach was accepted and her son dropped his eyes as he sipped the hot tea, "Of course not—at least not in favour of terrorism. The modern IRA is mad—they must be."

"The Irish have often been described as mad," she replied quietly, "but those who claim it are usually just retaliating. The Irish have been a burr under the English saddle for generations."

After dinner that evening the same conversation was resumed. However this time Tom took part. The evening news had just announced that a bomb had ripped apart a van carrying construction workers, in which seven people had been killed. Sean, his appetite whetted through his discussion that afternoon, began a harangue about the ineptitude of the security forces and the government who sent them.

"Now they can't even protect innocent building workers," he declared, "what hope is there for the rest."

"It's much more complex than you might imagine Sean," Tom replied, "it's not like fighting a pitched battle—with terrorists you never know just where they'll come from."

His son sat forward in his chair clearly dissatisfied with his father's comment, "So, you mean we have to accept atrocities like this—is that what you're saying?" Sensing a potential confrontation, Lorna tried to quell it before it was established, "He didn't say anything like that Sean—and you know he didn't."

Her intervention made Tom smile; he understood her concern, just as he understood that his son was baiting him. Accordingly, he deliberately kept a level voice when he replied, "Let's get our terms of reference agreed before we start an argument eh. Like you, I have little time for politicians, but to understand the problems over in Ireland, you need to do more than just read a history book. Originally, the Republican movement was honourable—I believe. They simply wanted the English to leave their country. Given the same situation we'd do the same. Unfortunately their cause has been sidelined. Now, the movement is populated by gangsters, criminals largely who don't give a fig for a united Ireland and whilst they plant bombs and rob banks, the others foist a moral obligation on the community that is outdated. And it proves to be a value system from which they conveniently exclude themselves."

As soon as Tom paused for breath Sean resumed his point, "But all you're saying is that they have learned a lesson from the gangsters that govern our parliament—so now they're politicians in the true sense."

The argument went on until well after the table was cleared and washing-up dried. Lorna eventually grew bored with it and went into the other room to watch television. The arguments rehearsed in her kitchen were those that she had witnessed many times before. Tom—the peacemaker—the one prepared to tolerate and even to compromise, against Sean the typically volatile young lion. The young man was tired of compromise, of stale old solutions and desperately wanted change. She left the room as Tom was in the process of pulling rank, referring to his first-hand experience, his age and his hard earned knowledge.

In the sitting room she sat on the big settee, put her feet up and watched the evening newscast. There was a degree of comfort in hearing Sean defend his views against his Dad, especially as she knew that however heated their argument, the respect they had for one another inevitably blunted the edge of their aggression. Sean had a good mind that he could use to good effect but he also had a sensitive nature—one that sometimes reminded Lorna of her younger brother, Peter. She often wondered about her little brother—in fact both her brothers. It was strange that out of the whole brood, she should be the one closest to her sister Tessa. Fortunately, since her flight from Liverpool and the disgusting relationship with Gerry, Tessa had made a new life for herself. She had spent some time living with Lorna and Tom and it seemed that the support and security she gleaned from them was enough to prompt a change in her. The speed of the transformation had been remarkable and now, after a period of training, she had a position of responsibility with the potential for a career in social work. It was perhaps the one profession in which her previous experience proved an asset.

Relaxing contentedly in the warmth of her happy reminiscences, Lorna must have fallen asleep. She had learned to live with her nightly disturbances, the bad dreams and the occasional nightmares and, as a consequence, often took the opportunity to enjoy an after dinner nap. Some time later she awoke to the sound of Tom answering the telephone. His voice was animated and she deduced he must be talking to an old friend. A few minutes later he crept into the room and, imagining she was still asleep, crouched next to her.

"Lonny," he whispered, "Lonny you'll never guess who I've just been talking to—it was Molly."

For a moment Lorna thought he might mean her neighbour Molly from Ireland—but then she realised who he meant, "You mean—your Aunt Molly from Whitby?"

"The very same—and she's in London. I invited her round. You don't mind do you?"

The memories were suddenly live. The crisp northern air, the sea, the rugged coast—and the fish-shop. Most of all the warmth of the big woman's welcome, "Of course not—is she going to stay over with us?"

Tom grinned, "I hoped you might say that. I didn't offer but—I'm sure we can persuade her. It's been ages . . ."

"Eleven years to be precise," Lorna said, "the length of our marriage."

"She's dying to meet Sean and—I think you'd better polish up the crystal ball before she arrives—she's bound to ask about it."

Suddenly they were interrupted by a voice from the doorway, "Who is dying to meet Sean?" Sean asked.

* * *

The big woman's presence commanded the room. Her size however,—even greater than Lorna remembered it—was dwarfed by the force of her personality. Everything about Molly was excessive from her hair, a lion's mane that was now pristine white, to the volume of her voice—a rich baritone. Beyond the confines of her northern home she seemed to have grown in stature—now she was truly a giant and those that she hugged her welcome to, stayed hugged and she hugged everyone.

Sean liked her immediately. He was intrigued by her individuality, he marvelled at her confidence and was left dumfounded at the range of her perspicacity. He whispered to his father that she knew things about him that she could not possibly have known—logically. There was also a marked difference in the manner she adopted in debate—and debated everything with Sean almost on sight He found that whilst in discussions at home, however heated they became; he was used to a reasoned logic, the opportunity to put his view and the assurance of a kindly audience. By comparison, Molly was bombastic. Often she refused to listen—without a fight and she presented her arguments as though they were cast in tablets of stone.

After Sean had finally gone to bed that first night, Molly sat with Tom and Lorna before the sitting room fire talking. She admitted to them that much of her performance with Sean had been specially designed for the occasion and for his benefit.

"These young 'uns need to find that not everyone is as willing to listen or to compromise as their parents are, else they'll have nothing to fight about. I like to fuel their fires a bit—let's them exercise their thinking. And your lad has a good head on him."

It was an original view, typically idiosyncratic and entirely in keeping with Molly's nature. However, she could not understand why Tom and Lorna found it quite so amusing.

In anticipation of her visit and remembering her preference, Tom had called at the off-license and bought two bottles of fine single-malt whisky. Molly drank it like water and before long her demeanour was affected accordingly. And although her hosts did not consume anything like the same quantity, both Tom and Lorna were also affected. It was probably as a result of the alcohol that Lorna brought up the subject of the crystal ball. She even went to the sideboard and retrieved it from the cupboard.

Molly unpacked it carefully and set it down on the coffee table.

"And have you looked into it Lonny?" she asked.

"Occasionally," Lorna admitted reluctantly, "but without any kind of success. All I see is glass . . ."

Molly looked for a moment then smiled, "Then I'll look into it on your behalf—if you'll allow a silly old woman her oddities."

She removed the silk scarf and ran her hands over the surface of the sphere, all the while staring intently at its interior.

"Ah Lonny," she said after a while, "you've certainly had your troubles—but your little sister is fine now and so is your big brother—at last. All you need to concern yourself with now is your own health and well being."

Lorna's temperature suddenly seemed to drop. The alcoholic fuzz that had clouded her vision cleared, replaced by a feeling of trepidation. Despite all the evidence, she had still doubted Molly's claims but the declarations just made frightened her all over again.

"My health is fine Molly." She lied.

"And the nightmares?"

"Not half so bad as they used to be."

Molly's warm hand enclosed Lorna's fingers and their eyes met, "You must learn to share your problems Lovie," she whispered, "and to ask the right questions of the right people—else your nightmares will become real."

Whether through the drink or by virtue of Molly's wise perceptions, it was not clear but that night Lorna slept soundly. The reading with the crystal ball had struck chords that resonated with her experience, disturbing the self—assurance she regularly awarded herself. Inevitably, the truth was self-evident no matter how sincerely she tried to deny it. Doctor Morton had once told her that if all else failed, he could increase her awareness of her troubled past through hypnotism. She had refused his offer repeatedly, fearing that whatever the nature of her hidden trauma, it may prove too painful to stand the scrutiny. Now, for the first time, she felt a new confidence in that respect and decided to call the doctor and seek his further help.

Having had such a good night's rest, she awoke at seven in the morning and was showered and dressed before Tom was out of bed. It was her intention to cook a traditional 'full English' breakfast for their guest that morning, a small thank you for Molly's kind attentions to their appetites when they were in Whitby. However, when she arrived in the kitchen she found Molly was already at the cooker. More surprisingly still, Sean was at the table tucking in to eggs and bacon.

She stood at the door, "Good grief—was there a fire?"

Sean grinned sheepishly and told her that he had woken early, "No point in just laying there—so I came down to cook breakfast for everyone—but Molly beat me to the stove."

Skillet in hand Molly grinned, "And how did you sleep Lovie?" she asked, "Well—I trust?"

"Very well," Lorna replied, "best night I've had for ages."

"That's good then—means you've reached a decision—as long as you don't change your mind."

The big woman hummed as she fried the eggs apparently content to serve up meals even when she was on holiday. She stayed with Lorna and Tom until mid-afternoon but after a light lunch, insisted she had to be on her way. They tried to persuade her to stay longer but she claimed there were 'things' she had to do back home. Lorna drove her to the railway station to avoid the rain. London could be confusing unless one was used to the crowds so, before she allowed the big woman to go, she made certain that she knew the times of the trains and the various platforms she would need to go to. Molly laughed at her concern and hugged her before she left the car, "Tom did well for himself when he found you little lady, but remember what I've told you. It's time to start looking after yourself now—before it's too late." She paused and then added, "However young Peter might benefit from a bit of sisterly advice—when you have a minute."

Lorna was surprised, "I didn't know you knew Peter. I lost touch with him after he moved from Thornaby. Have you seen him?"

"Met him briefly a little while ago last time I came up to London."

"Where?"

Molly smiled, "There you go again—everyone else gets priority. I met Peter in London in a night-club. I was taken there by a friend. Now you must understand I have a wide variety of friends and some of them—well—they're a little different. You'll find Peter at the Brighton Club, most Saturday nights—but don't you go there trying to do too much for him. All he needs is to know his family still care. Remember Lorna your energy is precious—conserve it."

Molly was out of the car and on her way to the ticket office before Lorna could press for more information. Typically she left the mystery of how she'd met Peter, how she'd identified him and why she thought he might need help unanswered. Nevertheless, the fact that he might need help and that he was living in the same city as his older sister were all that Lorna needed to know. She made a date in her mental calendar as she drove home.

* * *

Soho's narrow back streets were never the most accommodating places for the casual visitors, most especially if such visitors were unaccompanied females. Beyond the bright, Saturday night lights of the tourist infested main thoroughfare, the atmosphere degenerated quickly. The ethos there was more in keeping with some previous century than with the modern present. It was dark and it felt dangerous. And long before she located the Brighton club, Lorna began to question her wisdom in making the search by herself.

In the first instance Lorna had looked for the club's address through the London Telephone directory, later she'd scrutinised the small advertisements in several of the 'What's on in London' type publications—all without success. At that stage she was tempted to believe that the club was a figment of Molly's imagination. The big woman from Whitby maintained an agenda well beyond the understanding of most normal people and it would not have surprised Lorna to discover that her claims were a fiction designed for some ulterior motive. She decided finally however, that the only way to be absolutely certain would be to visit Soho and see for herself.

It had been a long time since Lorna had visited that part of London. Other than an occasional trip to Liberty's department store, she had not been in that area since she was a schoolgirl during the latter days of Carnaby Street. A school trip, ostensibly designed as a visit to the National Gallery had culminated in an unplanned sight-seeing tour, conducted by her friend Helen Bonar. Their quest was to search for the 'swinging London' of the popular magazine stories and they had sneaked off from their main party group to make their way to what Helen liked to describe as the 'real' London. The knee-trembling excitement they experienced in their anticipation of what they might find had proved well worth the trouble they accrued when they finally returned to the coach. On close examination however, Lorna had had to admit that the famous street and its surrounding coterie of clubs and shops were really nothing more than a tourist trap—accordingly a disappointment.

Since then, either the place had changed considerably, or the schoolgirl visit during daylight hours had not given a true impression. The 'silly young woman' that had been the Soho of the '60s, '70s and even the '80s, had not worn well. Now she was a careworn, middle-aged hag—mutton dressed up as lamb and what had been the excitement in those streets was now suffused with a feeling of threat. Most of the friendly little shops had disappeared in favour of sex emporiums, nightclubs and glitzy bars. By the same token the people were also different. She was left with the impression that the men she passed were obviously there, either for a boy's night out, or working as pimps cum nightclub doormen.

After walking round for more than an hour, Lorna screwed up the courage to ask a strip-club doorman if he knew where the Brighton club might be found. He was heavily built person dressed in a smart three piece suit and sporting a boxer's face. The suit was filled to capacity and, Lorna observed, little if any of it was fat. After she'd asked her question he looked down at her with almost total disinterest, "First left then second right," he said eventually, "but y 'don't want to be hanging around places like that darling. Bleedin place is full of freaks."

She thanked him and quickly crossed over to take the side street he had indicated.

The club was sited in a basement beneath a boarded-up shop front. A small sign flickered in red at the top of a flight of stone steps, an access leading to the entrance, hardly wide enough for one person to pass without brushing the damp walls. Beyond the front door, a tall blond woman sat behind a reception desk. She was smoking a cigar.

"Membership?" she asked in a deep voice when she saw Lorna.

"Actually I'm not a member but . . ." Lorna started to say. Before she could finish the blond told her it would be twenty-five pounds admission, "And," she added, "We'll need to get a member to sign you in Pet. You'll have to apply for membership as well—it's the Law."

Lorna agreed, albeit reluctantly parting with the money.

Ten minutes later she found herself sitting in a tiny booth, one of a dozen or more that described the perimeter of a small dance floor. A bar was situated behind her and most of the early evening clientele stood there drinking and chatting. At the far end of the dance floor a pianist rippled the keys to produce an accomplished rendition of a Scott Joplin tune.

"And what would Madam like tonight?" A voice asked.

She looked up to find a waitress standing over her table. A woman of indeterminate age who should not have been wearing the mini-skirt that exposed her legs to such disadvantage.

"A white wine—a dry white wine please." She replied.

"One dry white wine—shan't be a minute."

Moments later as the wine was delivered, Lorna asked the waitress if she might know Peter, "His name is Peter Donnelly—tall and thin—a nice person . . . ."

The waitress paused as if to consider the request and as she did so Lorna studied her for the first time closely. It was then she noticed that the waitress needed a shave—it was a man in drag. It dawned on her then what type of club it was.

"And you say this Peter—is your brother?"

"Yes."

"Then you'd know where he came from—would you?"

Lorna smiled; at least this was progress, "Most recently from Thornaby-on-Tees—before that from Ulster."

The creature in the short skirt grinned, "Right on both counts Love. I'll just see if he's free to talk." He minced away towards the crush at the bar.

By now several couples had taken to the dance floor and were shuffling about clutching one another. In the dim light it was difficult to tell what such combinations consisted of: boy/girl, boy/boy or girl/girl. The openness of the pairings impressed Lorna; it took courage to put one's sexual bias on public display. She had not known many people who were Gay but those she had met, always made her feel comfortable in their company. A number of female colleagues had expressed a similar view and she began to wonder if it was only heterosexual men who felt challenged by those with different social morays. As she sipped her wine, the waitress returned with two men. The portly middle-aged man in the business suit spoke first, "I hear you want to speak to Peter Donnelly?" he asked.

"Yes," she said, "I'm his sister."

"And why do you want to talk to him now?"

His aggression surprised Lorna and she snapped back immediately, "Why I might want to talk to my brother is nothing to do with you—now or at any other time. If he happens to be here I'd be obliged if you could tell him that Lonny wants a word with him. If he isn't here—then I'll leave now."

The portly man looked a little shame-faced but his companion, a thin faced brunette in a silk evening dress spoke up, "We're only concerned for Peter—he doesn't have too many happy memories of his home and family and—we wouldn't want to see him upset."

It was a concession but Lorna still smarted from the interference.

"Well whilst I appreciate your concern, the matter is between my brother and me. If he doesn't want to see me that'll be fine, I'll just go." She started to get out of her seat as she spoke but the brunette suddenly leaned over the table to stare in her face, "Just as tetchy as ever Lonny," she said, "I knew you'd flare up and lose your rag."

Lorna looked up into the woman's face, the dark brown eyes and the laughter lines—and suddenly she knew she had found her brother.

Lorna sat talking to her brother for the next two hours. During that time the club filled with a variety of members, none of which she found it easy to identify in terms of gender. As Peter pointed out however, the significance of cross-dressing was often misunderstood. The inclination to wear the clothing of the opposite sex did not automatically mean the participant was homosexual. And whilst he freely admitted that some of his friends were Gay, he told her that, "Cross-dressing is simply an inclination—a preference—if you like." Surprisingly, Lorna did not find it hard to accommodate the fact that her brother sat talking to her wearing a silk dress. She found it harder to understand that so many people, especially men, were prepared to demonstrate their 'preference' in one place at the same time and harder still to comprehend why Peter should need to associate with such a community.

Peter however, worked hard to convince her that he was happy, that he felt he had found a niche amongst friends and that he wouldn't have had it any other way. She thought she detected an underlying brittleness in his protestations and almost began to question him—thankfully for all concerned; she resisted and let him have his say uninterrupted.

He told that he had arrived in London before he recognised his bias and without any conscious intention of joining the Gay community. He had worked at a number of different jobs, mainly office work involving clerical or administrative duties, before eventually finding a position as a window-dresser for a department store in Oxford Street. And, he said, it was through his association with other 'dressers' that at last he came to understand himself.

"The trouble was Lonny, once I'd committed to this life, I didn't know if I'd be welcome amongst the family." He paused and she felt him watching her closely, "Anyway," he added, "at that time, Patrick was in prison, you were in hospital and Tessa had gone off to Liverpool with some old man—I was on my own."

She put her hand over his and gave him a reassuring smile, "Well—you're never going to feel like that again. Take it from me that you'll always be welcome at my house. And you should know that you have a nephew now—Sean. A big strapping lad, just as argumentative as the rest of us but hopefully much cleverer. He will be going to university shortly and I'm sure he's love to meet my little brother."

"And Tessa?"

"Tessa has come to her senses and also lives in London—she's a Social Worker would you believe, and doing very well at it. She left the old man and a host of other nightmares back in Liverpool thank God. Also I'm told that Patrick is no longer a guest of Her Majesty's prison service—and I'm fit and well—sort of."

Peter looked up at the mention of Patrick's name, a troubled look and, detecting the problem she added, "And as far as Patrick is concerned, your gender preference and all that might go with it, is your business. If he ever shows up and has objections we'll re-educate him."

Lorna had told Tom about her intention to search for Peter but she had failed to mention she would be searching in Soho. She knew he would be worried about her so she rang him from the club at ten-thirty, just to put his mind at rest. Typically, he listened to her tale without complaint and, patiently as ever, agreed to collect her from the tube station around twelve-thirty.

By then Peter's friends had been introduced to Lorna, Sheila (previously known as John) Bowden was the waitress; Cissie (previously known as

Anthony) Hammond was one of the crowd at the bar and the portly man was Brian (previously known as Mary) Allen. Peter's chosen name was Rita—after his mother. They were a friendly, gregarious crowd and proved to be good company without any sign of embarrassment or any of the usual social pretensions (other than the obvious). They kept Lorna entertained and refused to allow her ever to buy a drink.

When the time came for Lorna to leave, Peter/Rita walked her to the door where her taxi was waiting. She had overstayed her time limit and missed the train so she had telephoned Tom yet again, this time to tell him she would take a taxi home. At the club entrance near the top of the steps, Peter kissed her and gave her a hug. A couple passing by made disapproving noises and it wasn't until they had gone that Lorna realised what they must have imagined.

Peter's response was casual. He said, "I don't take any notice of people like that anymore." and she had to agree with him.

Lorna had enjoyed herself however, she realised that it was unlikely that Peter would ever visit her home. She had tried to obtain a promise from him with regard to a visit but the best she could get, was an assurance he would telephone her regularly.

On the journey back to Uxbridge Lorna had an opportunity to take stock of her evening and she concluded that perhaps the last part had been the best. The disapproval of the passing couple, however mistaken their view, had made her feel like one of the conspirators. And, no matter what the cause, there was no doubt in her mind that the Brighton club hosted just such subversion. The members there represented a counter-culture, a separation from mainstream society, to some extent forced on them by the narrow-minded reactions of a homophobic community. It was a pity

CHAPTER TWENTY-EIGHT

1996

News: London: Seven IRA bombs go off in the Capital's West End

Diary: I do not know how Tom is able to put up with me. He tolerates behaviour above and beyond anything any husband should have to, from his wife. But I cannot help myself. I am becoming convinced that my problems are physiological rather than mental. I worry that I have the human form of BSE something they are calling Creutsfeldt Jacob disease (CJD). Doctor Morton is a tower of strength as usual however I suspect that he has probably had enough of me too. Recently he resorts simply to prescriptions for new drugs—pills to calm me down and pills to send me to sleep. If only there was a pill to make normal.

* * *

Lorna was tired but a state of restful sleep was still impossible to achieve. So much to think about—so much to worry over. Another disturbed night dragged on into the very early hours. The kitchen drew her downstairs, a solitary visit to the oasis in the darkness of her sleepless wilderness, yesterday's newspaper and weak tea proving a substitute for rest. The cat rubbed itself against her bare legs and made plaintive sounds asking for food. 'Cupboard love' she thought, 'a typical male'. Immediately she chastised herself for expressing the cliché, the males in her life—certainly her later life—were far better then she deserved. As she often did on such occasions, she began to think about Sean, their adopted son. He was currently enjoying his final year at Warwick University reading English but despite all the maternal advice offered, he continued to resist the idea of doing a Post Graduate Teaching qualification. No doubt he could appreciate her concerns about his employment prospects but refused to take the easy 'insurance' option. During his last visit home they had almost fallen out on this account she remembered.

"At least you could get some Supply work in schools, even if you didn't work full-time." She'd told him. "And that would help keep you solvent."

But he would not listen; "I want to write." Was his standard answer. He claimed he could get trapped into the humdrum world of nine-to-five and his talent would be bled from him. And his Father had not helped matters. He thought of his son as a brave soul, sticking out for what he wanted, refusing to settle for second best. "He has to make up his own mind." He argued blindly.

Writing indeed. She knew about writers, scribblers of all sorts and none of them save a chosen few ever made a decent living. None of them had any kind of security—not even the journalists. To imagine he might be the one in ten thousand . . . . She caught herself and stopped. Was this really Lorna Donnelly, the same Lorna Donnelly who had once dreamed the same dream of literary success all those years ago? The one everyone described as talented; the one who had won the essay prize year on year and the teacher who had encouraged so many of her pupils to write. Guiltily she remembered the half finished novels; the short stories shelved after a second refusal; the searching autobiography she had started and found too painful to finish.

She sipped the tepid tea.

This was her thirty-ninth year, one off the big four-O and suddenly she began to see herself as being old. Was this really all that there was in her life, all that there was ever going to be? She tried to itemise all that she had reason to be thankful for; the help and assistance she had received and continued to receive; the husband and son; a successful if somewhat truncated career—but it did not help. All at once she was overtaken by a deluge of self-pity.

The door-bell rang twice and the cat started in surprise. They were two short tentative rings, uncertain if they wanted to be heard. The clock on the cooker told her it was ten minutes past two, not surprising they were tentative. Who would call at this time in the morning?

As she rose from her chair she listed the possibilities in her mind: the Police, a next-door neighbour—a burglar! In any event it had to be bad news, an accident perhaps—the Police calling to say Sean had crashed his old car—or worse. But surely the Police would wait until morning proper—unless it was a fatality. And would a burglar be quite so hard-faced, testing to see if anyone was at home? At the kitchen door she hesitated. Should she call Tom? He would be furious if he found out she'd answered the door at this hour—but stubbornness prevailed. Nevertheless, she took her walking stick, the one Doctor Morton had loaned her when she was first recovering. It was a dubious weapon of defence given her delicate state of health but even so—a potential weapon.

She twisted the dead-lock and pulled the bolt back. It was an effort but she managed finally. The door swung back just wide enough for her to peer through the gap. There was a man on the doorstep, a big, heavily built man with a bag over his shoulder. He wore a cap and a long overcoat and her first thought was—'burglar'.

"Yes?" she asked, trying to adopt an aggressive tone but wishing she had called Tom after all.

The man stared down at her and his smile was just visible in the shadows.

"What do you want?"

The smile grew broader still, "Lonny?" he said quietly. The voice was vaguely familiar, "Lonny, it is you, isn't it?"

She opened the door wider, still uncertain but with the beginnings of a doubtful recognition.

"Yes—my name is Lonny . . ."

The man laughed quietly—a laugh from the past prompting half formed memories.

"Be God either you've shrunk or I've grown too big. Don't y'know me Lonny?"

Now she swung back the door fully so that the passage light fell on his face: a rugged unshaven face with pale blue, hooded eyes.

"Haven't you got a kiss for your big brother Lonny—it's Patrick."

He spoke softly and suddenly she felt faint.

* * *

"And you've just left him sitting in the kitchen—our kitchen?" Tom's question was everything she had expected it to be.

"Well where else do you think I might have left him?" She answered quickly trying hard not to get annoyed.

Tom rolled out of bed still clutching the morning cup of tea she'd brought up for him. He was upset.

"It's not as though he's on anybody's wanted list," she added, "and even if that were the case, even if he was still a member of the Republican Army, he's not going to plant a bomb in our kitchen—is he ?"

Tom just shook his head and dressed quickly

She knew that she had worried for years about her brother Patrick, more so still about him meeting up with her ex-soldier husband. The irresistible force of the British conquerors meeting head-on with the immovable object of Irish patriotism represented by the two most important men in her life. As time had passed without contact with her brother, she had imagined him lost; allowing herself the indulgence of believing the meeting might never take place. Now it was about to happen in her kitchen and she was afraid of the consequences.

To be fair to her husband, despite his personal involvement, he had always taken a liberal view of the Irish Troubles. He appreciated the dichotomy, he understood the history and sometimes, he even sympathised with the Irish 'cause'. However, that was a far cry from having a self-confessed IRA soldier in his house.

"And have you invited him to stay?"

Tom's question was muffled by the heavy sweater he was pulling over his head as he asked it.

"If he wants to stay—then he's welcome." Lorna paused hearing herself become more strident than she'd intended, "He is my brother after all Tom."

Her husband straightened his collar and smoothed his pants as he looked at his reflection in the wardrobe mirror. He did not respond immediately but instead, appeared to consider her outburst. He turned finally and faced her—suddenly he smiled, "And is your old man becoming a right-wing reactionary after all these years?" he laughed," I can read you like a book my love—the cogs turn with the enmity piling up in the works. Come here."

He reached out and took her in his arms, gently crushing her to him and pressing his face into her hair, "You must know—if you want him to stay here—then he's welcome to stay as long as he likes—and you'll get no arguments from this ex-soldier. I promise."

She was so relieved she could have cried. He kissed her—a long kiss that made the tensions fade, then he held her out at arm's length, "What am I going to do with you Lorna Donnelly? And are you going to introduce me to this man of mystery or what?"

She took his hand hurried him down the stairs where they found Patrick still sitting at the kitchen table where she had left him. As they entered the Irishman stood and held out a hand.

"You must be Tom," he said smiling," all she does is talk about this feller Tom." They shook hands, "And if you've made my Lonny as happy as she seems Tom, then I owe you a very big vote of thanks. She's still my little sister after all."

"That cuts two ways Patrick," Tom replied, "for more years than I care to remember, all I've heard about is her big brother Patrick—the best and most caring brother in the world apparently. Glad to meet the legend at last."

Lorna was so pleased she could hardly contain herself. From the first moment she had identified her brother on the doorstep all she had been able to think about was how he might—or might not be received by her husband. She had imagined a whole variety of confrontations, some with harsh words being said, some even ending in violence. Nothing could have made her happier than to see two of the most important men in her life meeting at last and apparently becoming friends.

Whilst the men talked Lorna cooked breakfast. She was unusually content to play a subservient role in order that she could listen to the development of the conversation between Tom and Patrick. Naturally enough, to begin with they were tentative with one another. They compared notes on their respective childhood memories and told one another anecdotes—sometimes humorous about their problems as teenagers. They found that they shared an interest in history, particularly modern history so it was not long before they began to discuss politics. To Lorna's surprise they were amazingly considerate of each other's views, especially when talking about Ireland Indeed; she concluded from the side-lines that they agreed on more aspects of the problems in Ireland than she might have ever guessed. She was sure that without consciously intending as much, they concentrated their discussions on their personal experiences.

Tom talked at length about his time in the Army and how he found it sometimes hard to carry out the orders given him by his superiors and Patrick talked about the IRA. Her brother admitted his membership of the organisation but, rather than focusing on the claims of the Movement vis a vis a united Ireland, he talked instead about his companions—especially those responsible for the decision making. It seemed that both men had experienced problems with authority figures and found equally that blind faith in orders from their superiors were often impossible to accept without explanations being given. Generally any criticisms made were of their own side and by the time the table was cleared again, they had apparently breached the divide between their respective national interests.

Tom had to go to work but when he had left, Lorna and her brother sat chatting together for the remainder of the morning. There was such a lot to catch up with and in order to amplify her story, Lorna produced a photograph album. She talked about Sean and described her career in teaching. Finally she talked about their Mother's funeral in Ireland.

There was much to tell, some of it sensitive but they soon fell back into the same well-tried routine they had perfected as children. Often, in the whispered dark at the top of the stairs, after the two younger children had gone to bed, it became their practice to exchange a truth for a truth. In a world then where lies were the currency both in the Press and through speeches by politicians, they devised a system in which, if one of them told a secret, the other was obliged to follow suit. And they would know it was an honest, truthful statement when it was prefixed by the expression, "On me Ma's grave . . ."

"You haven't changed a bit Lonny." Patrick said, giving her one of his lop-sided smiles. "You have though," she replied, "me old Patrick is still in there somewhere—but he's much harder to find." She stopped herself, realising suddenly that he might take offence.

Momentarily his pale blue eyes hardened, then he smiled," And how d 'you see the change little sister," he asked, "better or worse?"

"Have you been active?" she asked ignoring is question, "I mean in the Movement—did you carry a weapon?"

He paused and then replied, "Aye—and planted bombs—and if not meself, I made it possible for others to do so."

"But you didn't kill people did you Patrick?" He glanced away and sighed but she wouldn't let him avoid the answer, "Did you Patrick? On yer Ma's grave?"

The echo from so long ago made him smile again followed by a short brittle laugh, almost akin to an exclamation but, seeing how serious she was he stopped himself, "On me Ma's grave Lonny—I once shot a man—a secret agent. I'm not proud of it but it was justified."

"Justified, how can you say that? You know it's the worst sin imaginable—taking a man's life . . . There can't ever be a justification."

There were tears in her eyes ad she was so shocked, she almost shouted her accusations."

"Was it any different for those wearing the British uniform?" he said quietly, "and you call it the worst sin—well I can think of worse. Isn't it worse when a whole people are subjugated—denied decent housing or opportunity in education; isn't it worse when foreigners put their soldiers on your streets, when half a nation becomes murdering turncoats. Didn't our own Father pay the price?" He stopped for a second and then added, "It was justified Lonny because it was either him or me."

The arguments were not new, she had heard them recited many times as a child, but to listen to Patrick rehearse it now and claim it as his own, chilled her. No small wonder she detected a change in him.

"Oh Patrick." It was all she could say and he fell silent as a consequence.

To break the mood she took one of his cigarettes from a packet on the table and asked him for a light. Through the flame of the match he caught her eye and smiled, "Don't go back to bad habits just because of your brother."

She inhaled deeply, finding relief in the nicotine 'rush'.

"Okay," Patrick said, "that deals with me, now—how about little Lorna Donnelly?"

"Nothing to tell." But her answer was made too quickly and they both realised it at the same time.

"Aha." He exclaimed, "So now it's my turn—remember—darkest secrets please—on me Ma's grave?"

Forced into conscience corner, Lorna felt she had no option and she began to tell him about her psychological problems. Once she started, in some strange way, it was a relief. A relief to tell him especially. Tom was always a willing listener, but even with him she tended to hold back. She told Patrick about her breakdown at school, about the hospital and the therapy. She tried to explain the business with Tessa and even found herself saying that she had been in an unstable state when she married Tom. She talked about the honeymoon and meeting Molly at the fish and chip shop, about not having sex on their wedding night and finally she told him about her abortion.

The bile stored for so long had become venom and the more she talked about the little fat man, the butcher from Thornaby, the more the poison poured. She detailed the happenings when he used to abuse her, her terror, her disgust with herself and she described the ambiguity she felt towards their Mother—part love, part blame.

She told her brother about her nightmares and her uncontrollable mood swings, her drinking binges and her blackouts and, by the time she ran out of words, she was sobbing in spasms, the tears darkening her blouse front. By then her big brother was alongside her, his arm around her shoulders and his huge hand pressing her head into the rough wool of his sweater. Patrick was still the rock to which she could safely anchor—as he had always been.

CHAPTER TWENTY-NINE

1996

Diary: It's such a relief that Tom and Patrick have hit it of together. They are two of the most important men in my life. I was always afraid that when they finally met face to face, there would be hard words—a fall out with me as usual—piggy-in-the-middle. I was especially pleased with Tom; he was sympathetic and prepared to give ground—his sacred ground. And Patrick toned down his bias almost to a level of acceptability I never imagined he would tolerate. It was a huge relief. He tells me he will soon go back to Ireland—but what he will do there is anybody's guess. I pray that he will steer clear of his previous friends; their association can only make for more unhappiness. I told him I think he should settle in England—keep away from the temptations of Eire—like an alcoholic needs to keep clear of hard drink.

The very presence of the Republican cause is enough to restart his addiction to violent solutions. I had a letter today from Tessa—she seems to have found a real niche for herself at last. Who could believe she would be a social worker!

* * *

"I'd like to do something normal." He said mysteriously implying a pause at the end of his sentence, "Something—people do sort of everyday."

Lorna laughed. Her brother's naiveté had always surprised her and never more so than now. She could remember his concern as a child about the move to England. Shortly after the first discussion, they had been alone doing weekly chore of tidying their bedrooms when he turned to her and said, "If we do go across the water—when you grow up—promise me you won't have any babies Lonny." "And why not. Why shouldn't I have babies?" she'd asked defensively. In her imagination she thought he was about to confess to jealousy. "Well—I heard Molly from next door say that the English still eat their young."

The request for something 'normal' was almost as gauche.

"And what might you regard as 'normal'?" she asked, struggling not to smile.

He thought about it for a minute and then suggested he might accompany her that day when she went shopping. She was pleased to agree but it made her curiously sad. Here was her big brother, the ex-convict, ex-terrorist, the one who was so worldly wise, asking to join her in the most pedestrian of activities, the kind of everyday normality studiously avoided by most of his gender. Usually men—especially married men would do anything to avoid a shopping trip. He recognised the question in her face and added, "I know what you're thinking Lonny—but it's the normal things—like shopping, like cooking a dinner for the family even like doing the housework that I've missed. I've never done any of those things, "he paused, "come to think of it there's so much I've never done. I've never voted, I've never held a dinner party—I've never even been on a foreign holiday . . . ."

She took his hand, "Oh Patrick," she said, "I understand—even Batman doesn't spend all his time chasing criminals—so why shouldn't you help me at the shops."

This made both of them laugh.

Later that morning he pushed her trolley as she chose vegetables and cold meats, cleaning materials and frozen food in the supermarket. And, amid the piped musak doing the most normal things, she found a private opportunity to dwell on the feeling of alienation they shared. To different degrees, each in their own way, they had both engaged in practices that brought them to public notice and despite the high-profile scrutiny implied, they both remained outsiders—he through his affiliation to a terrorist movement and she by way of her continuous psychological problems.

In this last context however, her health had been a little better of late and, once she had recovered from the hysterectomy that her doctor insisted was necessary, she was confident things would improve. The nightmares were less frequent but their dominance had been overtaken by an intermittent migraine. She was still in touch with Doctor Morton, a kind perceptive man who had done more than most to restore her equilibrium, but now she seldom saw him. They spoke on the telephone and exchanged letters frequently. He had always told her that writing things down was good for her condition. He had encouraged her to maintain her habit of keeping a diary, "It's more than a record," he said, "it's a chart of your progress, designed by yourself."

It felt comfortable shopping with Patrick although, typically male, he insisted on re-organising her basket, stacking tins and jars according to size. She nevertheless decided he would make someone a good husband.

At the check-out, despite her protests, he paid the bill.

"Only fair," he said, "we all need to make a contribution."

In the car park he sorted the plastic bags into neat rows in the boot and then sat beside her whistling old tunes as she drove home. The rear access to the house solved an interminable problem of parking and enabled the unloading to take place without strain and with Patrick's help; the shopping was thereby transferred to the cupboards and the fridge-freezer much more quickly than usual. When the car had been emptied Lorna filled a kettle and began to make tea for them both, "You can come again," she said appreciatively, "it often takes twice as long as that to unpack the car—Tea?"

"Yes please—two sugars."

She warmed the pot and spooned in the dark leaves a she waited for the kettle to boil.

"What was that tune—the one you were whistling in the car?"

He grinned, "Once upon a time, singing that in England would have got me arrested. It's an old rebel song, goes like this.

'In a lonely Brixton prison, where an Irish rebel lay. Close beside a priest was standing, 'ere his soul should pass away' . . . ."

It was a sentimental tale of a young Irish patriot's death in a British prison. As such it had once been banned and the penalty for singing it was then imprisonment. Patrick sang it in his rich baritone and the obvious depth of feeling in his voice brought back memories of their father's singing. Lorna was not surprised to see that her brother's eyes were moist when the song ended.

"Always gets to me." He admitted wiping his eyes.

"You're just an old romantic," she said, kissing his cheek, "but I love you all the more for that."

They relaxed with their tea and biscuits in the sitting room. Patrick began to ask about Sean. Lorna had talked about their adopted son continuously but as yet Patrick had not met the boy.

"He doesn't always come home at week-ends," Lorna said, "but I'll ring him. I'm sure he'll be keen to meet his legendary uncle Patrick."

In fact that same Friday afternoon Sean appeared at the front door not more than an hour after his mother had tried to contact him at his college. She had presumed he had made other arrangements when she failed to reach him and, needless to say, she was delighted when he arrived home.

"Did you get my message then?" she asked.

"When did you telephone Ma?" he asked.

"About an hour ago." she replied.

He grinned, "You know it takes me about three hours to get here—how could I get your message?"

She ignored his sarcasm and hugged him. For her the separation, albeit for Sean's best interests, was a cross she bore unwillingly. She hated to see him go and each homecoming was a relief for her. After a moment he struggled free from her grip.

"You'd think I'd been to the Amazon Ma." He said extricating himself.

By now Patrick was on his feet watching the reunion with obvious pleasure and waiting to be introduced. Finally Lorna turned, "And this—this is your uncle—Patrick . . . Patrick meet Sean."

The two shook hands.

"Aha—It's the Irish terrorist himself." Sean quipped.

Without a flicker of surprise Patrick responded in kind immediately, "And this is the errant son—t 'is good t 'meet you at last Sean. Be God you're bigger than I expected. How old d 'you say you are?"

"As old as me tongue and a bit older than me teeth!" Sean replied—still grinning.

"My old Ma—your Grandma—used to say that." Patrick replied.

"I know—my Ma has told me at least a thousand times—but it's good to meet you too. I've looked forward to meeting you face to face for ages."

There was a joy for Lorna to witness this first meeting between her brother and Sean and she experienced a sense of achievement and resolution far greater than she had hoped might be possible. It was immediately made all the more satisfying when she saw how their humour meshed.

Another piece in her jig-saw was complete.

CHAPTER THIRTY

1996

Diary: Patrick fills me with a happiness I'd forgotten. I suspect there is closeness between siblings that can never be replaced—even by a loving husband. Memories shared that hark back to earliest recollections, before opinions were formed, whilst opinions were being formed and when they were first tested against brothers and sisters. I know I perhaps spend too much time thinking about the detail of my past and it surprises me sometimes to appreciate how I've lived so closely at the edge of the conflict in Ireland—almost without a real involvement. Looking back at the scribbles in my diaries, I see that little of what happened around me affected me at all. As both a child and an adult, all my concerns were those related to family and friends and I'm left to wonder if this is normal. There must be many victims on both sides of this 'trouble' whose only thoughts were, like mine, about their mundane day to day happenings, the mechanics of everyday life. Little good it did them. How lucky I've been.

* * *

With Tom away overnight at a conference and Sean out with friends, that evening Lorna cooked dinner only for Patrick and herself. She produced one of Patrick's favourite 'fillers', a corned-beef hash. As a little lad, if he was ever asked what he would like for dinner, his answer was always the same. It used to make his mother laugh.

"T 'think he's the son of a butcher, and all he wants is meat from a tin." She used to say.

Outside an autumn storm exercised the capacity of its strength, making the fixtures in the house rattle and the kitchen fire to occasionally belch clouds of smoke. The hot coals glowed in a fitting accompaniment to good simple food and after they had eaten, they sat before the blazing hearth with a glass of wine. Warm and secure, the situation reminded Lorna of her image of their life in Ireland as children. She loved her other brother and sister but Patrick had always had a special place in her heart. She used to think of them as a team, an exclusive duo, a Batman and Robin who shared their secrets as much as they shared their woes. It was only natural therefore that on such an occasion they should reminisce about that time in their lives when they existed as a family.

Their conversation however, highlighted significant differences in how they remembered their time at Denby road. And whereas in her mind, it was a time of loving comfort amongst family members who were content in one another's company, Patrick felt differently. He claimed to remember harsh words between their parents and occasions when their mother was tears; he said there were tensions that were never explained and regularly an atmosphere of stress. He told Lorna that he could recall when she was ill and the late-night meetings between their father and groups of strange men. Meetings where voices were raised in anger and of him being sent to bed early to be out of the way when such meetings took place.

Lorna was sure he was imagining things but she chose not to argue the point. She knew from her own experience how one's memory could play tricks and distort the past. Listening to her brother that night, she also felt a secret sense of satisfaction; his memory was just as faulted as hers had been on occasions.

"So—you and your man are happy together then?" Patrick asked, changing the subject.

"In clover," she replied smiling at the thought of Tom, "he's all that I ever wanted—don't you think he is?"

"He certainly seems to fit the bill. The first British soldier I've ever met with scruples."

"And you've met them all have you?" Her response was automatic. It was always her fashion to act as his conscience and never more so than if she felt he was being too obviously biased.

He laughed guiltily and tried to justify his comment, "I was only going to say that . . ." But she didn't let him finish, "Oh yes, I know what you were saying. But just think how you'd react if he said something like that about the Irish."

"Okay—okay then little sister, mea culpa, mea maxima culpa . . . I stand corrected and contrite."

His contrition made her smile, he hadn't changed a bit, she thought. He was still a little boy. She saw that he was watching her and she raised a questioning eyebrow. He leaned to her and took her hand, "God I've missed you Lonny." He said seriously, "There aren't enough folk like you."

"If anyone else tried to correct you Patrick Donnelly, you'd end up fighting them. I think one of me is just enough. Probably one too many if the truth be known."

Her smile turned brittle and he noticed immediately, "What now?" he asked.

She shrugged her shoulders and turned back to face the fire, "Nothing."

But he wouldn't let it pass, "Go on Lonny—what . . ."

"It's just that—well when I'm with you or Tom or even Sean, everything is fine. I feel needed and secure and I can keep my balance . . . ." Having started she heard herself begin to talk more quickly, "But otherwise . . . , often I don't like myself much. I know I'm unstable. I can't trust my reactions. My temper flares for no reason and I find myself saying and doing things that don't make a lot of sense.

Patrick still held her hand, now he raised it to his cheek, "Take it from your big brother, you're pure gold Lonny, probably the most balanced one in the family," A tear made its way down her cheek, "And given what we had to put up with as kids—is it surprising that we've had problems."

She dabbed her eyes, "There now look what you've made me do."

He passed her a big white handkerchief.

"It's all in the past Lonny—but know this—you were always the anchor we all clung to both times."

She looked up quickly. His last comment was an echo of something her mother had once said.

"Both times?"

"Both times." He repeated the phrase with emphasis.

"Mam said something like that the last time I spoke to her—but Patrick, you must remember—it happened a lot more than twice. Jimmy was a pig and he was always chasing me—always in my room at night for years. He was . . . ."

"I didn't mean that," he brother said stopping her, "I meant—the two of them."

It was as if a cold draught blew across Lorna's shoulders making her neck stiffen and chilling her body. For no good reason, suddenly she was deeply afraid. A fear that quickly turned to anxiety and it was several seconds before she could voice her next question, "Two men. Which two men Patrick. There was just Jimmy and . . . ."

"Jimmy—and Dad." Patrick said quietly.

Lorna dropped his hand as if it was a burning coal.

"Patrick," her voice raised half an octave, "how can you even say such a thing. Dad loved us all. He did everything for us. In case you've forgotten he even died for us. He . . ."

Her brother's face had paled at her outburst but he stared at her his curiosity blatant. He tried to touch her but she recoiled all the while staring at him.

"Lonny love, you've forgotten—or you've hidden it away. Dad abused us all—especially you—and Jimmy did again later." He stared at her now, willing her to remember. "And what's more, didn't he sell information to the British and that's why the patriots killed him. I thought you knew."

Someone was screaming and the noise filled Lorna's head. It was an exceptional sound like an animal in pain, rising and falling in a high pitched intensity. It was only after Patrick stood up and slapped her face that she realised she was the one making the noise.

Suddenly she was claustrophobic, the room closed in on her and the temperature seemed overpowering. The man—Patrick—towered over her, restricting her space, confining her breathing and disapproving of the noises she made. His approval was mandatory, his pleasure a requirement. She must demonstrate her willingness, prove her submission. The front of her blouse was loosened before he reacted, before he grabbed her stifling her struggles to undress. She tried to tell him, assure him she would be compliant but he didn't seem to want to hear. His tight grip hurt and although she was afraid, she knew she would allow him to do whatever he wanted to do.

After that the pool of darkness closed around her and this time it came more quickly than usual. A sensation of warm, safety. Daddy knew best and she mustn't tell her mother—it would only upset her. Daddy loved her best of all. Then the images played out on a distant screen—the images and the feelings. The crushing weight of him making almost impossible to breathe, the pain—the repeated pain, again and again, the stench of male sweat and the stickiness. After the stickiness it usually stopped and then she wanted to be alone, to be allowed to sleep. It was nice to be loved he'd said and she heard him again say how he loved her. The noise went on but she decided to ignore it.

The bed was warm and luxurious and the room was quiet—blessedly quiet. If only it could stay this quiet. She opened her eyes and saw that Tom sat next to the bed reading a book; she liked to watch him when he was unaware of her. He was so handsome—her Tom. Her arms felt bruised and she remembered that Patrick had held her tightly. A joke was a joke but he'd gone too far this time and she promised to tell him so. The bedside light hurt her eyes so she closed them and began to drift again. However, just before she slept, she remembered that Tom had not eaten. He would have to get his own supper that evening she thought—perhaps he might share it with Dad.

Dad always came home late from the shop and always had to have his dinner warmed up in the oven.

Now she was held tightly again and she didn't like it . . . There appeared to be straps holding her down on the bed—but the bed rocked from side to side. The motion was sickening and she wanted to complain to Tom. He'd put it right. He was still sitting next to her but his book had disappeared and now he just watched her. She smiled at him and he stroked her forehead. He spoke to her but the noise from the road outside made it hard to hear. He leaned forward and whispered, "Don't struggle lover," he said, "the straps will stop you falling off the stretcher."

What she was doing on a stretcher in the first place he didn't say. Another man appeared, this one wearing a white jacket. She watched him load a hypodermic syringe from a tiny bottle and then plunge it into her arm. It didn't hurt much but the effect was instantaneous. The faces swam and she slipped backwards into darkness.

CHAPTER THIRTY-ONE

1999

Diary

They are all talking about me, wondering if I'm okay and all I can do is think about my Dad—my real Dad. The images keep coming back in huge waves—great throbbing waves of fear and regret and wondering why he did what he did to me. The pictures are horrific. There's me—and then there are the bomb blast victims—hundreds of people killed and for what? For his pleasure? The horses in Hyde Park, the poor soldiers—Tom lying there with his life-blood pumping out of his wounds—saying good-bye. His Aunt Molly frowning and shaking her head when Jimmy creeps into my bed.

I hate these pictures. I hate the memory of the feeling. I hate myself for not fighting harder—for beginning to like it. Dad under the oxygen tent—breathless—muttering about treachery. His or mine? Those men who came to the house, hard-faced men making threats—I heard them threaten my Dad. Later he came upstairs to me making excuses. 'This isn't so bad.' He'd say. But what does he know about 'bad'. It's so bad it's killing me. And what happened to Saint Jude—my favourite saint. If I'm not a lost cause then what is? But he doesn't seem to listen anymore—maybe he knows about my guilt—the real me. Then there are the gunshots at night; running feet; dogs howling as their throats are cut by the Squaddies; children screaming; the crackling of fire—the rain falling; Dad in my office demanding to know why I'm not doing my job properly; everyone in the staff room watching my shame . . . . and Mam knew all the time.

* * *

Lorna laid in her hospital bed—immutable, a figure of stone, entirely resistant to the surrounding world. For more than twenty-four hours she had been on hold—her programme frozen, faulted. This was the seventh episode she'd experienced in the two years since finding out about her real father. Now the reasoning process was threatened as she tried to make sense of it in her head—a process like writing her diary.

It was hard to reconcile the years of medication with the root cause. All those nights when bad dreams had troubled her rest and later as an adult—the sexual aversion. Could it be so simple? Could life be so distorted? Was there time—even if there was opportunity for a new start? She imagined Tom—her lovely Tom. "But life isn't fair." He said again. And whilst there was an element of feeling freed—suddenly loosened from restriction, there was another that bound her still—as "We're all bound by our past"—Doctor Morton this time, calm as ever. So many lives affected, most of all her mother—always sad, always looking the other way to avoid the shame; her feeling of failure, her humiliation. Her penchant for butchers—butchers who shared a perverse attraction for children.

She tried to recall her father, the image had been incomplete for so long. His size—a domineering presence; his authority—and his touch. The blame she had laid at Jimmy's door was now redirected. Jimmy had been only the successor, an heir apparent to what was by then an institutionalised practice. His misbehaviour a memory on which to focus as a pubescent child; a convenient mental camouflage hiding the real culprit. The actions had been well hidden behind a forest of unmentionable shame, behind the rocks of reluctant admittance. The iniquity of indescribable childhood confusion.

So much was clearer now, so much more explained. Tessa's search for affection at any cost; Patrick's search for somewhere to lodge his loyalty and poor Peter with his feelings of ambiguity. Two greedy men had all but destroyed the lives of those they claimed to hold most dear. That they were misguided was certainly a fact but that were culpable was equally true. Better that they had been emasculated than subject their children to such abuse. Like the trick of a magician, it was all hard to believe and although the nerve had at last been exposed and the memory refreshed, it was still incredible.

She sat up in the bed and poured herself a glass of water. Her throat was dry and, through clenching them, her jaws ached. However, as she drank the cold fluid, her chest muscles relaxed, it seemed, for the first time in ages. Although it had proved impossible to staunch the flow of images from her childhood, the long hidden memories were almost too painful to tolerate. The process of accommodation would, of necessity, be slow—an absorption by small degrees.

"Lorna," a voice said and she turned to find the staff nurse standing close by, "how are you feeling today?"

She was feeling considerably better but the decision to reply was one she found impossible to command. The pause lengthened until the nurse smiled and took her pulse, "Don't worry—I understand. I think you look so much better but don't overdo it, you've had a very difficult episode . . ."

The word 'episode' triggered a memory of Doctor Morton. His favourite word to describe her situations—nevertheless a disturbing word, with implications of continuity meaning one of many—one of a set . . . . She wondered if she would ever be free of episodes.

The nurse put a cool hand on her forehead and looked satisfied when she took it away, "All you need is a good sound sleep. Why don't you lay back and I'll bring you a nice warm drink. A cup of tea?"

"Weak and sweet please." She heard herself say and the nurse left smiling.
Had she really spoken?

That night she slept well without any disorderly dreams and the next morning she felt better still. Physically it was as though she'd run a twenty mile marathon. She ached. But throughout the next day slowly, her strength returned. Better still, her mind cleared and her thinking became more regulated. Secretly she decided that this last 'episode' would be the turning point, from this point on her mental life would recover. She began to see her illness as a weakness and determined to muster her resources in order to combat it. She charted the necessary changes she would make and laid her plans accordingly. It was almost like doing a school timetable.

Forming her new resolutions and identifying new strategies with which to implement them provided her with renewed energy, making her experience a sudden surge of confidence. It was like some religious enthusiasts claimed in being 'reborn' and she could hardly wait to tell Tom and Sean about it.

* * *

Tom was asked to wait by the secretary but almost before he could settle in one of the armchairs that graced the outer office, Michael Delaware appeared at the door. They shook hands and he was ushered into the consultant's inner sanctum. They had become quite good friends over the last couple of years,

"She's very much better Tom," Delaware said, "fully conscious again and quite bright with it—but I'm afraid the news isn't all good."

They sat opposite one another across a glass topped coffee table and the file of Lorna's medical history lay between them.

"But she is better?" Tom asked optimistically.

He liked and respected Michael Delaware. The man was one of the most eminent people in his field—a clinical psychiatrist with an international reputation that belied his age. Consequently when he said the news was not all good, Tom realised there were serious problems.

Delaware chose his words carefully, "As I said—she is very much better—however, she believes that having identified the root of her problem, the problem will simply go away. I have to tell you that this is not the case."

Tom frowned, "But . . ."

Delaware interrupted, "Sorry Tom. I know what you've been told in the past—and I am not decrying the hard work done by other doctors—sadly life is seldom that easy. The best way I can describe it is by saying that the kind of traumas Lorna has experienced have themselves become an issue. If you like—another part of the cause. Once, they fed on the hidden memory, now they are self-sustaining."

Tom shook his head, "So what are you trying to tell me?"

"Being able to identify what caused the initial disturbances does help—but it would have helped all the more if she'd known it—say in her teens. Each episode of her various incidents have added weight to her instability. They have contributed to the cause—become part of it." He paused watching Tom's face. "Often trauma is held in our muscles, the very fibre of our body. Strong emotion and other hard-won knowledge are therefore bound up, if you like, entrenched in our bodies and will therefore have a perceptible impact on the ways we use our physical self."

Tom flushed, "And the prognosis?" he asked fearfully.

Delaware sat forward and opened the file, "Lorna will need to be on medication, probably for the rest of her life. She will continue to need help to combat her neurosis and her depression. No doubt she will have periods—perhaps long periods when she will appear perfectly normal and during these she will be able to acquit her professional and domestic responsibilities perfectly well . . . .But, the fact is I believe her problem is chronic. Does she still teach?"

Tom was white-faced, "No, "he said, "some time ago, after the last major collapse she resigned. There have been odd days when she's done some supply work but nothing with any pressure."

Delaware turned another page, "Good." he said, "I think she should avoid any kind of stress—and I mean any kind. The nature of her condition is such that should she continue to experience the same severity of incident as she did recently, she could experience a complete regression and become catatonic. In that case she would be beyond any guaranteed help we have available at present."

The two men sat in silence for several minutes. Tom could hardly believe what he had heard. It was almost a terminal sentence and he was unsure how he could deal with it.

"Does she know—I mean have you told her any of this?" he asked finally.

Delaware shook his head, "It wouldn't serve any useful purpose. I think all we need do is to alert her to the care she must take and to emphasise importance of her medication. Other than that—let her have her moment of triumph. You see—now that she can identify the root cause of her problem—and she has finally accommodated the fact of her father's abuse, she really believes she has been cured."

* * *

News: November 1999

The peace process in Northern Ireland remains in doubt. The Ulster Unionists appear to be split over the latest initiative by the Government in Whitehall. Some members maintain their concerns about the handing over of weapons by the IRA. However, Mr. Trimble appears to be ready to accept the promise by Sinn Fein and the IRA that this will happen after the devolvement of power to the Province.

Splinter groups including the Real IRA and the INLA insist they will not disarm and promise to continue, what they see as, their armed struggle. Meanwhile Mr. Blair's government in London has said that if the terrorist groups on all sides do not disarm, the new parliament in Northern Ireland could be stripped of its authority even after devolution.

The situation remains tense.

Diary:

I cannot recall exactly when I arrived at this place and that annoys me. I can't even remember precisely why I'm here just that I'd been ill, I think. The dreams are so vivid that it is increasingly difficult to separate them from actuality and, as reality is so elusive, I find myself wondering if this, 'now', is also part of a dream.

I was born a Catholic in a loyalist Northern Ireland enclave and was ever conscious therefore of the sectarian divide: a quality of being riven that matches precisely the pattern of my later life.

I know that I always liked to write things down, to make a record in an organised form usually in my diary. I remember I used to write a little each day and, whilst what happens to me currently may be of small importance to the world at large, the compulsion to record it remains strong. However, if I were to try and write this down in a complete form it would surely turn out to be only a confused series of snapshots—exactly the way that the episodes jam my memory. And whilst the night-time remembering is more explicit now, the body of the narrative remains indistinct. I often lay awake trying to hang onto the edge of some apparently seminal dream with the promise a greater clarity. Sometimes, even with the immediate expectation of consciousness, I squeeze my eyes shut tight knowing that a different reality is imminent but the concentration always slips away, evading the grasp of my will.

The worst effect of the drugs they prescribe is the way they fragment my memory producing a pot pourri of non-sequential snippets that often makes little sense. And if the point is to help me relax and to accommodate my life's small experiences, then the process is a paradox.

To think of my life as small makes me sound as if I am a humble person and I am certainly not that however often I may have been humbled. To some degree I still consider myself to have been lucky. I have loved and have been loved in return, I have enjoyed my family and I took the opportunities that were offered to use the modicum of talent and intellect that I was blessed with. What more can one expect?

I am a practical person, one that does things one that effects a change; a doer rather than an observer and therefore, to find the boundary between reality and imagination so tenuous is a major frustration. The difference between 'now' and 'then' fluctuates until sometimes I believe that 'then' is 'now'. And to make matters worse, apparently there have been a whole series of 'then' that frame my 'now' with varying degrees of importance. At this moment in time, I am convinced that this really is 'now': the conscious present. My reasoning suggests that this is so because I find myself returning again to this hospital bed, usually each time just before my drip is changed.

Also I note that the sequence of the memories here, no matter neither how real they seem nor how involved in them I find myself, are seldom experienced more than once.

I believe I can remember everything—almost—with only one exception. Maddeningly the exception eludes me. The omnibus of my childhood, my youth and the period of my maturity roll past, generated by a mental search engine specifically aimed at uncovering whatever it is, I can't recall. And I try to remember—I really try hard. Unfortunately, like now, the more I try, the more the trying upsets me. I haven't prayed seriously for many years but on these occasions, I find myself repeating the words of a prayer to St. Jude the Patron of lost causes. Each time however, I get only as far as the second sentence before the nurse appears to replace the drip and once the drug hits my system I'm off again.

'Blessed Apostle St. Jude, Patron of lost causes and matters despaired of, pray for us who are so miserable. Make use I implore you of that special privilege of bringing speedy help where help is most despaired of . . .'

* * *

Lorna saw him the moment he entered the ward. There were only four beds in there and two stood empty. He stopped at the door and grinned. He was still like a little boy she thought, his expression a mixture of shyness and bravado. She smiled back brightly and waved to him.

Even from that distance Tom could see—could believe—as far as anyone could see—she was well again.

December 1999

News: Yesterday the way was opened for a historic power-sharing government in Northern Ireland. After much tension, the Ulster Unionist Party endorsed David Trimble's proposals and agreed to enter government with Sinn Fein. Mr. Trimble was congratulated by Tony Blair and the Irish Government and said there was now no reason why decommissioning should not follow devolution.

End

Initially the context of the story is the conflict in Ireland and in some ways the troubles of Lorna and her family reflect that situation.

Lorna Donnelly is the eldest in a family of four children: Catholics living in a Loyalist region of Belfast. The story originates at the time of the first IRA ceasefire and culminates about the time of the Peace Accord some 37 years later. Mr. Donnelly is killed by the IRA and his wife decides to migrate with her children to England. She meets and marries Jimmy Ungerside a butcher. Jimmy is a serial child abuser and to varying degrees the whole family suffer at his hands, especially Lorna. The effect on the girl's development and later on her career is seen as an echo in tandem of the 'Troubles'. The same is also true of her sister and two brothers. Each chapter includes a contemporaneous news report and an excerpt from Lorna's diary each linked by some similar notion of abuse.

Lorna eventually marries but the episodes that torment her psychology continue despite concentrated periods of treatment. It is not until she is made aware of another significant cause that there is finally some hope of real recovery.

Lightning Source UK Ltd.
Milton Keynes UK
UKOW04f1210250913

217897UK00001B/95/P